The Blind Mirror

stories by Jan Beneš

The Blind Mirror

TRANSLATED FROM THE CZECH BY JAN HERZFELD

AN ORION PRESS BOOK

GROSSMAN PUBLISHERS, NEW YORK, 1971

Contents

Part One

Part Two

Contents

Part One

What Do You Know
of the Kaplan Turbine?

I live in college, and I'm eighteen. Most of the people I know are eighteen, or else they're seventeen or ninteen, one here and there may be as much as twenty, but most of them live in college. Somebody has said that it's a wonderful thing to be eighteen, and the warden who takes care of us at college in our out-of-school hours even says that it's a beautiful thing to live in college, and we're lucky, but you notice that all those people who say that sort of thing are past eighteen, and a good long time ago, too. I don't know what interest they can have in how old we are, or what this really signifies. It's a very queer thing, something like that cord with the white corks, stretched across the swimming pool. When a girl's eighteen, all she hears is that she has plenty, but PLENTY of time, or else it's: You'd better get a move on, girl, or you'll find you've missed the boat, and you won't even know how. Although a five-year-old human cork can swim beautifully where even a hundred-year-old nonswimmer would drown.

The worst thing about *all that* is that somehow one NEVER gets to know *why*, what it's good for or why it's necessary, apart from making children, and finding something for the abortion commissions to worry about. But they say it's nice. I'm in no position, really, to have any opinion about it at all. Not even whether it's a good thing or not. Only I should positively hate to think that I'd missed the boat, especially if I didn't even know how. I know all these older and very experienced people say that at eighteen one is understandably foolish, but nobody ever tells you how a foolish person is to recognize that she *is* foolish. And most of the people who don't live in college, and don't go to classes with me, and Daddy and Mom among the rest, seem to me as if they've NEVER been eighteen. Or else decidedly they don't know what it's like to live in college when you're eighteen, and when all the other girls can tell long stories about how ruined they are, and how it happened that they got themselves ruined, and what it's like when they still go on ruining themselves, and all the while this is going on they shove my head under the blankets, so that I won't hear what the grownups talk about. Being innocent, in a case like that, isn't at all a beautiful thing, even though our headmaster says we're the most ruined boarding school in the whole region. He used to be the director of a boarding school, and can't get used to saying "college."

But all this hasn't really anything to do with this business. What has to do with it is the Kaplan turbine, and Karel Major, who used to come after me three times a day in school to borrow an eraser or a pen, or some other necessity. Once he even borrowed a mirror, he said he had something in his eye. A girl knows at once, when a boy starts coming to her like that, whether he really needs what he's borrowing, or whether he's merely borrowing it in order to establish a connection with her, and have something to talk about. And Karel is a very good-looking boy, ALL the girls say so.

Once he borrowed my eraser, or rather he PRETENDED to borrow my eraser, and then he PRETENDED not to want to give it back to me, until at last we agreed that he'd give it to me the next day after school. He wanted it to be that same day, but it's better to keep a boy waiting a little, at least that's what all the girls say, so I told him I had to go to the tailor's, and hadn't time that day.

In the evening I got out my best skirt and cut two and a half inches off the hem, and then the whole room helped me to get it straight, so that I could wear it for my date and also go to class in it. With the lunch money my parents sent me I bought a sweater two sizes small for me, white, and coming right up to the neck, with red patterns on the sleeves and across the breast in front. In college we've only got a small mirror, but all the girls said it looked smashing, almost like Brigitte Bardot, or maybe even better. And I thought myself it wasn't so bad. Not that I was all that anxious to go to that rendezvous, somehow . . . but when one has already made such preparations, it hardly seems sensible not to go. And if one has a rendezvous at all, one has to look one's best. So that in the end I didn't even want to go to bed, so as not to have to take off that sweater and skirt.

In class it was all right as long as I was sitting at my desk. Karel and I had only given each other a look, just to show that everything was understood, and in the afternoon we would meet behind the building. That day he didn't even come to borrow anything. Then in came our mathematics teacher, Štětina, and right out of the blue he called me up to the blackboard. It was a bombshell, he very seldom picks out anyone to test. I made believe to be arranging my things neatly on my desk, and I was thinking to myself that THIS was the punishment for everything for which I'd been preparing, and all because of Karel I was going to get an "unsatisfactory," and if I did get it, and I didn't know of any reason why I shouldn't, then I NEVER wanted to see Karel again as long as I lived, and I wouldn't even THINK of going to that rendezvous. *Please, God, please don't let me get "unsatisfactory," don't let him give me a black mark, and I won't go to this meeting at all, but above all don't let me get that black mark, please don't!* And then, when there was no putting it off any more, I picked myself up and went to the blackboard.

Only Mr. Štětina, whom we have also for descriptive geometry and physics, didn't tell me what I was to do at the blackboard, or why he'd called me up there at all. He began to dictate some example, and before I even had time to get it written down, much less take a quick look to see whether Karel had noticed how

5

well that shortened skirt and the white sweater fitted me, and how well I looked in it, suddenly our mathematics teacher pulled out his eyeglass case from his pocket, and for a long time he went on cleaning his glasses and testing them and cleaning them again, staring at the window and sighing, and then polishing the lenses again, while I stood there with the chalk in my hand like a fool, until at last he put his glasses on, and straight out of the blue he began to lecture, not about this example or anything about quadratic equations, but about the Kaplan turbine, which he said had made us, small nation as we are, celebrated throughout the whole world, at a time when we were not even independent, when no one knew anything about us, and everywhere the term Bohemian was interpreted as simply meaning "Gypsy." And before we could get our bearings after having these turbines thrown at us, he was cleaning his glasses again and saying, ah, youth, youth, what a beautiful thing it is, and how he himself still felt young, very young. And then he cracked his knuckles in a way that always sends shivers down my spine, and stared out of the window, nodded his head, looked at the pattern on my sweater, and said: "Well, well, run along and sit down, Miss Ulrich, why are you still standing there? . . . Yes, run along!" And he rocked from his toes to his heels and went "Hmhmmhmmm!" Then he looked at his clock—he carries in his pocket a thing as big as an onion, like a weight from the curtains—saw that the bell would be ringing in a moment or two in any case, warned us not to make too much noise, picked up his things and left.

And I went to my rendezvous. For one thing, I hadn't got that "unsatisfactory" in math, although I'm terribly bad at it, and for another, Karel had asked me again if I would come, and I had said I would, so that really this was an absolutely new rendezvous, agreed upon after that conversation I had had with God. And we had our rendezvous in the cemetery. To meet in the cemetery is decidedly better than meeting in the street, at least in a town like ours, where there's always somebody passing by, or you have to keep moving on, and in the end you're as worn-out as the postman, with blisters on your heels and runs in your nylons. In the cemetery it's quiet, there are trees and benches, and it's easy to be a little bit afraid there. It makes a tremendous impression on boys, or so the girls say, when a girl is a little bit afraid. Of storms, perhaps, or traffic. Then the boys get immensely strong. A strong boy is a splendid thing, and if you have one everybody envies you.

We sat down on a bench by one of the graves, quite an old and deserted one right by the wall. As a matter of fact the whole cemetery was deserted, because it was the Jewish cemetery, and in our town since the war there aren't any Jews left, at least I don't know a single person who could be a Jew, and nobody ever came into this cemetery now, it was like a jungle there, all trees and shrubs, and graves with the stones rolled aside, where the Germans had moved them to steal gold teeth and rings from the dead. But I only know all that from hearsay, it's a terribly long time ago, I wasn't even born. But all the girls in college arranged the dates they cared most about in the Jewish cemetery. The gate had been taken away for scrap, and the wall alongside the road was almost completely demolished, because everybody is building something, and you can't get bricks anywhere.

As we sat down I pulled my skirt down AS THOUGH to cover my knees, but the skirt was too short to cover them really, only maybe he wouldn't even have noticed that if I hadn't pulled it down AS THOUGH to cover my knees. He just sat there beside me, and he kept on heaving in great breaths as though he wanted to say something, but then he swallowed and said: "Oh . . . nothing . . ." and waved his hand to show that it really was nothing. Although the girls in college always swore that first of all he would make AS THOUGH to take my hand, and at first I must pull it away from him. . . . And when he did so-and-so, they said, then I must say this . . . or do that.

But he didn't do anything. He just sat and looked at the rear side of the monuments, and at an overturned pedestal with a gilt inscription: FAMILIE LUSTIG, and the little path that used to be covered with gravel; and then he lit a cigarette, so that we should be just like grownups.

I thought of how the girls had spent ages at noon making up my face, and how I'd been half an hour in the school cloakroom painting my eyes before I came out, and I said: "Do you think the Americans or the Russians will be the first to fly to the moon?"

But Karel still didn't say anything, until at last he broke off a twig from one of the bushes behind our bench, and began to draw in the dust of the path under our feet; then he coughed, and said: "You know, today I went and looked up about those Kaplan turbines . . . that's a very interesting thing. Terribly interesting. You know? Here you have *this,* you see, like that . . . and here *so.* . . ." And then he began to scratch with his twig in the path under our feet, drawing a sort of jumbled picture. Turbines, or bits of turbine, or various different turbines, and all the time he was asking me: "You do understand, don't you?"

And I said: "Yes," and swallowed my tears, because it isn't a good thing to cry in front of a boy, and in any case it would have spoiled my mascara and the make-up on my face.

The longer it went on, the darker and darker it grew, and in a little while it was all the same what sort of eyes I had, and everything, and I could have burst into tears just from rage, and Karel was still bobbing about on his heels on the path, and striking matches so that he could see those turbines of his, and so that I could see them, too, and all the time he still kept asking: "You do understand all that, don't you?" and maybe by then he wouldn't even have noticed if I had burst into tears, and I didn't want to do it so loudly that he would *have* to notice. At last it was very dark, dark as night, because it was in October, and finally he ran out of matches, and I said that I must go home now, and in that narrow skirt I had to climb over the board fence that had been put there instead of the gate, because it was so dark that we couldn't find the hole in the wire netting that had been put up in place of the stolen wall. But even while I was climbing, Karel was still thinking for a moment in the dark, and then asking: "It didn't bore you, did it?"

"Of course not," I said. "Those turbines are terribly interesting things."

"And you did understand it?"

And I said again: "Of course I did."

"That's good," he said, and then we went on climbing, and the lady with the pole was just going by, the one who turns on the gas lanterns, and we had to hang there on those dirty boards for an age before she managed to put her pole together and get the hook into the wire loop, and the lamp finally came on.

Then Karel helped me down, and at least ten times more he asked whether I had understood clearly enough, and whether I had *really* understood, he said perhaps some other time he could explain to me something else that I hadn't quite understood. Only it was nearly nine o'clock by this time, and I had to go back to college, and what was more important, he had to go home, because he lived in private rooms, with his uncle, and had to be in by nine o'clock, or to be absolutely accurate sometimes he managed to get excused until later because of a Youth Union meeting or something of that kind, and came to college with the boys to sit on the front steps and smoke. So he went off, and at last I could burst into tears. Over all that wasted make-up, and the work I'd put in on my skirt, and my new sweater. And over my shoes, which I'd painted with nail polish to make them look decent, and got the stuff all over my hands in the process, and there wasn't a drop of polish remover anywhere in college. When you want to burst into tears half of these things would be enough cause, and they'd all happened to me.

So I did. I cried all along the street and then past the porter and all up the stairs, and whenever I wanted to stop I remembered about the nail polish or my shoes, or the work on my skirt, and it just went on and on. So that the girls in my room, who had been waiting for me on pins and needles, let out a shout of triumph when they saw me all smeared with crying . . . triumph, because now I was ruined, too, and it had made me cry, too, and they asked me: Yes? and I said: Yes, because I was so frightfully ashamed to be the only nonruined girl in the most ruined college in the region. And when they kept on asking really, and what was it like, and tell us all about it, I told them it was with Karel, and in the Jewish cemetery, because I'd heard all this told so many times in college, and the Jewish cemetery figured in at least half those stories, being the nearest and most suitable place for such events in the whole town. And living in college is something quite different from living at home, or even in a hotel. At home nobody borrows your dressing gown, and no hotel porter ever claims he's standing in the place of your mother. So in the end I gradually began to believe my own story, and it seemed to me that now I really was ruined, since all the others believed it, and since I'd heard so many of their tales about what went on in the Jewish cemetery. And when the warden came in that evening with a sheaf of questionnaires in connection with our work allocations after graduation, and there were all the usual bits to fill in about whether you belong to a propertied family, and about your revolutionary activities during the occupation, and all those stupid questions that the girls always make fun of, then the girls said to me: "Don't you give it a thought that you haven't got any revolutionary activities to put down, at least now you're ruined like the rest of us, and no longer a reproach to our college, which is the most ruined college in the whole region."

So that I began to cry all over again, to think what a frightfully deceitful, lying place the world is, and how I was a liar too, now, and should always be telling everybody that I'm ruined, and how I came to be ruined, especially the not-yet-ruined girls from the junior classes, when they come to ask me about it. And so all this made me so terribly sad that I could almost have volunteered for agriculture, or even for the army.

I made a point of looking up in the physics books about those Kaplan turbines, but even so I still don't understand. So what!

My Greatest Love

When we went on a hop-picking brigade, the last school holidays of our lives, we were already feeling terribly independent of school and everything else, and a bunch of us boys put down our tools and quit the hop fields early, at four o'clock, and went off to swim. When a fellow's put his matriculation behind him he can allow himself a few liberties. With his certificate in the drawer at home, and the adjudication interviews taking place as early as June. Hop picking is in September, and we'd all been through all that; those who were going to the university knew that they were going to the university, and those who had to go to work knew that they had to go to work.

We waded into the water, and for some time we were splashing about blissfully there, almost beside ourselves with satisfaction because we were so grown-up now, and could afford to ignore the teachers, and thumb our noses at them and their hop picking, and the competition for the highest number of quart measures gathered, and all that crap, when suddenly two girls appeared on the dike and caused a minor complication, because naturally we were there in the lake just like that, Adam's fashion, after all it was a very sheltered lake, well away from the village, in some kind of unused quarry, and then, who takes bathing trunks with him when he goes to do a day's hop picking? Anyhow, in the morning we hadn't known that we were going to get this mutinous idea of taking off at four o'clock, we hadn't known it was going to be a fine, sunny day, or anything like that. So there we were naked in the pool, and there were two girls from our class walking along the dike. And there's a big difference between saying to some well-developed coed in class: "Hey, Hanka, swear cross your heart you're still a virgin!" and wading out of the water in front of her just like that, without any bathing trunks, and carrying it off as though nothing out of the ordinary is happening. Especially as the girl who'd appeared on the dike wasn't one of those on whom anyone had ever dared try that cross-your-heart business. It was Šárka, with a friend of hers, only the friend wasn't nearly as pretty as she. That's something you very seldom find, a pretty girl with an equally pretty friend. At least up to now I don't think it's ever happened in my experience.

For some time we waited in the water and shouted various cracks at them, but it didn't seem as if that was going to inconvenience them at all. Calmly they spread out a rug on the grass, only a little way from where we'd left our clothes, and it looked as if they'd hunted out this particular spot with the intention of spending the rest of the holidays here. So that for a long while we just hung around getting very cold and beginning to turn blue, and then Jarda stuck his bare behind out of the water at them, or to be quite accurate, he did a handstand where the water was about three feet deep. Jarda Kovář had plenty of nerve for doing such a thing. For him it was like boarding a streetcar.

At that Šárka jumped to her feet and said that THAT was something she'd never forgive any of us, and she'd never speak to ANY of us again as long as she lived. Phew! Only then did it dawn on us that she thought Jarda, before staging his artistic act, had purposely slipped his trunks off under the water. That other girl wasn't really as upset as Šárka by a long way, but she went down among the reeds by the shore and scooped up handfuls of black mud, and threw them at us. Luckily girls aren't very good at throwing. And then they bundled up their rug and stalked proudly away.

It was a catastrophe. Absolutely the maximum catastrophe I could even have imagined in my worst dreams. For two years now I'd been head over heels in love with Šárka. Ad absurdum. The absolute and ultimate love of my life. And now this, just when I'd been promising myself so much from this last brigade, because in school it's a very complicated matter to start something with a girl, or at least so it had always seemed to me. I wouldn't even have come on this hop-picking trip if it hadn't been for this hope. Time to wander around in the evenings without any parents watching the clock all the while. And now a collapse like this, all because of Jarda Kovář's behind and swimming in the nude.

It took me at least two days before I managed to catch her at the pump in the yard, and convince her that I surely couldn't be blamed for what any Jarda Kovář did, that all boys aren't the same, and that I couldn't possibly have known that she would take it into her head to come to that particular dike to sun-bathe just when we were swimming there in our birthday suits. I said *I* could never insult HER by doing to her any such thing as Jarda had done. Then somehow, I'm not quite sure how it happened, I had to explain it to her all over again the next day, and there was still something left over for the third day, something she simply had to know, I felt I must impress upon her once again how strongly and severely I condemned what Jarda had done to HER that day by the pool, and that I certainly didn't think for a moment that she was accustomed to such behavior. Until all at once I was convincing her so forcibly that I heard her saying: "What are you doing?"

And I noticed that I was holding her by the hand, and I told her that I'd been thinking only of her for two years now, at least two years, ever since that awful school party when the Russian teacher was sick, and she wore that blue velvet dress with the pearls, and those big pockets down from the belt, and I suggested we could go out together if she was willing, otherwise now we wouldn't be seeing each other, because we'd both definitely finished with the loony bin. And I told her that at least six times already I'd invited her to the movies or somewhere, always hop-

ing that I should be able to tell her all this, and so on. So that
suddenly here we were, me really holding her hand, and she saying: "What are you doing?"

And I said passionately: "Šárka!"

And she said again: "What are you doing?"

And I said: "Šárka!"

And so it went on all the time, at least fifteen times around,
until at last it occurred to me to stammer out that I loved her,
and that I'd been longing for her an awfully long time and above
everything. Then she pulled her hand away from me, and I began
to talk in a terrible hurry (to this day I don't understand where I
got all this, but most likely out of books), saying that I knew these
emotions had many times been misused by unscrupulous people,
who didn't know how to value a pure relationship between man
and woman, and these things said even where there were no genuine emotions at all, but that I didn't know any other words
apart from these so often abused ones, in which to tell her that I
loved her, that I had loved her at least since the tenth grade, even
before that awful party, from the very first time I ever saw her,
when she had on that black sweater (and she was a DISH, but in
that black sweater especially, I tell you, that was SOME-
THING!), right from the time I first started attending that
school, in fact, when all on her account I began to go to the
French class, which wasn't compulsory (the worst thing about
this is that it was the truth, and I wasn't by any means the only
one who suddenly manifested an interest in that language), and
that I loved her, and loved only her, even though I'd never managed to pluck up the courage to tell her so, but all the same I
knew it was real and genuine love, though I couldn't say anything about what lay before us. But if I knew anything at all, it
was that this was the real thing, that I loved, loved, loved her,
desperately, wildly, above everything.

All this was certainly true, but the moment I said it, it became
something different from what it had been up to then, and something seemed to emerge from it that I hadn't wanted to say at all,
because inside me all these things were much better than what I

had managed to squeeze out. It was all the time only ALMOST TRUTH, although it was quite clear to me that I REALLY LOVED Šárka.

The boys always used to say that girls want to hear these things said, and I thought that she would be glad to hear them, too, though on the other hand all this did seem to me a little bit like Jarda displaying his behind, and I seemed to myself to have got into a tailspin, because she went on saying nothing at all. But when we're in a tailspin, that just suits the other sex, and if one can't be Belmondo it's better to be a unique idiot. Only that never actually occurred to me until much later.

At last she looked at me sideways, with such eyes, as though she were looking at me and yet not really looking at me at all, and she asked: "Do you just like me, or do you really love me?"

So I had to repeat all of it from the beginning over again, but this time I did truly love her DESPERATELY, and I could have told her so, if necessary, seven hundred times in succession, if I could have held her all the time as I was holding her now, because somehow in the meantime I found that I *was* holding her. So then she said: "You know . . . nobody has ever said this to me in my life before. I'm not worthy, really I'm not, to have anyone fall in love with me, because I'm not at all pretty. . . ."

Seriously! Never have I met a girl in my whole life who didn't have to be convinced that she's as beautiful as the sun, or something of that kind. So then I asked her if she thought she could ever love me, because I felt that if ever in life I was to be happy, then it would be with her and nobody else.

Then she said that she didn't know whether she could believe me, that she'd seen me with Irena at the movies, and she knew that I must have said these things to plenty of other girls, boys always do say these things, she knew that, and she knew a lot of girls who had paid dearly for it when they trusted someone who was only trifling with them. (My God, TRIFLING, she actually used that word!)

It occurred to me that she couldn't have seen us in the movies, Irena must have told her, the little wretch, she couldn't keep it to herself; and just for a moment I wasn't absolutely sure whether by some freak I didn't love Irena a little bit, too, but I said: "There was nothing between Irena and me, it was only a way of passing the time, because I didn't know whether I could ever find the courage to tell you that I love you. If I could have taken *you* to the movies, then I would never have gone there with Irena, especially not to such an awful Russian film. It was just chance— and I didn't want to be alone."

Then Šárka said all right, she did believe me, but all the same, it was DREADFULLY RUDE of that Kovář boy, standing on his hands like that with nothing on, she had never thought he could behave like that, but if I really wanted, then we could go out together.

So naturally I hurriedly said yes, I did want, and I was thinking to myself that thanks to Jarda Kovář's bottom I was now holding by the hand and embracing around the waist the greatest love of my life. And I tried giving her a kiss. She accepted it, but then she quickly retreated a couple of yards from me, and asked: "What are you doing to me?"

It was fine.

Naturally, our acquaintance was soon being talked about. It began to make a striking impression when I brought her dinners and suppers for her, and went with her afterwards to help wash up the dishes. Not that I did it with all that much pleasure, I don't suppose normal people ever tackle such chores with any great enthusiasm, but I couldn't let her stand there all that time in that stupid line in front of that idiotic field kitchen, that's all. Plenty of boys brought dinner and supper for someone else as well, but always in rotation, and I was the only boy who brought dinner for one of the girls, and not just once, but every day. But all the same, I think several people envied me the job.

Naturally they began to make jokes about us, too. For one thing, now I couldn't go swimming with the boys any more, because I went walking and swimming with Šárka, but the moment we went off anywhere, and supposing we met a couple of people we knew on the way, they began to sing:

> Avanti popolo,
> Into the woods we go!
> Vašek and Šárka, too,
> On a bicycle made for two, ta-ra-ra. . . .

This again, of course, was largely out of envy of us. Everybody who's ever been hop picking will confirm that there's nowhere you can go there, except one way or the other along the road from the village. If you're lucky you get a village with a crossroads, and then you have two more ways to go. Then at nine o'clock all the teachers are out rushing around the village green yelling: "Doležaaaal! Mazánkovaaaaaaá!" and shining flashlights into the eyes of everybody they meet to see if by any chance they happen to be Doležal or Mazánková, in whose places in the sheepfold they've found only empty mattresses. But personally I think there are very few things in the world that can annoy a person so much as when somebody shines a flashlight in his eyes. I'm not sure it isn't the very rudest thing I know. But from the whole race of teachers you can't expect ANYTHING DECENT. One of my friends, when somebody flashed a light in his eyes like that one evening, let fly with a tomato, and hit the person who was shining the flashlight on him straight between the eyes— afterwards it turned out that it was the headmaster from the neighboring school, who slept in the Sokol gymnasium on a mattress and covered himself with the red flag. Maybe he was out looking for some Doležal or Mazánková from his own school, even if he didn't happen to be bellowing at that moment. But then all the teachers from the whole village were going on in unison at this boy (and they didn't even know that the tomato was stolen!), demanding WHAT was he thinking of, and HOW could he dare to do a THING LIKE THAT, although I think that shining a flashlight in people's eyes is at the very least as rude as throwing and hitting somebody with a partly eaten tomato. I simply don't understand why they make such a distinction in these matters. On the contrary, not everybody can hit the target with a tomato, and especially not as accurately as that, while any fool can score a bull's-eye with a flashlight. He shouldn't have flashed it, and then he wouldn't have bought an eyeful of tomato.

Every evening after supper, then, Šárka and I used to go for a walk along the highway. Everywhere around us nothing but hop gardens, where you can't sit down, or walk around, or anything. On the ditch banks or under the apple trees along the roadside the boys and girls sat, most of them in groups, a few in pairs. When we passed a group, they always shouted after us that "Avanti popolo" song, but when it was a couple, then all you saw in the ditch was just a darker patch and a cigarette in the night. Somehow we didn't seem to worry those darker patches at all, but what the groups shouted after us wasn't always as innocent as that "Avanti popolo."

Šárka always hurried five or six steps past the place, and said: "Come on, please, those people are so DISGUSTING!"

So we pushed on in thoughtful silence until we were ten or twenty yards away, and she asked: "What do you think of Ehrenburg?" As if at all costs I had to be thinking something about him. People don't really read books in order to think something about them, or about the fellow who wrote them, or the ideas contained in them, or anything of that kind, but so that they can say: "Oh, yes, I've read it. I've got it at home. It's splendid." In any case there are plenty of books in which you won't find a single idea to think about. It's a kind of game. When two people meet who know how to play it, it's quite entertaining for any third party. It goes something like this: "Just now, I'm reading Dostoevski," and he draws on his cigarette. "You know, to me Dostoevski—well, there you've really got a WRITER. Only actually he's still waiting for a proper commentary."

"You're right, that's just the trouble," says the other player, slapping the back of one hand into the palm of the other. "The commentaries on Dostoevski today are absolutely incorrect." And they've played the first round, and both of them put on elevated faces as though no one but the two of them knows how to interpret poor Dostoevski properly, and only with the help of their commentary will the old boy really become a WRITER.

Only you could forgive Šárka for it. I think even Dostoevski and Ehrenburg themselves would forgive her everything, if they manifested themselves on an evening at the end of August, like this one, and she started regaling them with this sort of stuff: "You know, I think Ehrenburg is really a widely intellectual author," she said. "I think really he's the only living intellectual author we have now in modern Russian literature." And she added that for his sheer intellectual breadth she had to admire him.

Which was pretty well the end, because when someone begins lecturing you about intellectual breadth, then you can't very well steer them straight from that to kissing under an apple tree. And so I said that I had always thought Ehrenburg to be *intelligent* rather than an *intellectual,* especially in *The Ninth Wave* (which was the only book of his I could remember, because it had been in our compulsory syllabus for matriculation), but that on the other hand it could well be true that he was more an *intellectual* than *intelligent,* in fact he was quite a typical example of a writer of wide intellectuality.

Šárka thought for a while, and we walked in silence, and she said that when she came to consider carefully, perhaps in certain ways he *was* more *intelligent* than *intellectual,* especially in that *Ninth Wave,* there she had to concede that I was right, when she thought it over.

There was nothing to be done about it. Šárka was a DISH, even in the track suit she had on, the dish to end dishes, and by good luck *The Ninth Wave* had been part of my compulsory school reading.

Then gradually we ran out of things to say, so we sat on the stone coping of a kind of little bridge, to have a rest before we walked back.

I looked at the sky.

"It's beautiful, isn't it?" and I should certainly have gone on to say something about its being so beautiful chiefly thanks to the fact that she was there with me, if we hadn't gotten into such a groove in advance with all that intellectual and intelligent stuff. It didn't connect up too well.

"It is," she nodded, and pressed my hand a little. "Just look at that sky. I would so much like to live in the country."

I thought about how awful it was having to go to the pump to wash in the morning, and how you had to go on all the time pumping with one hand if you wanted to get even a trickle out of it, but I didn't say anything.

"Don't you know the stars?" she asked me. "I would like to know the stars, too, all of them. Absolutely all."

"Šárka," I started twice, and then swallowed it again, so that it shouldn't come too suddenly. "Šárka, come and sit down there with me for a little while!" Just below this bridge I'd seen a small level patch of field, with a stack of hay.

She shrank: "Oh, I couldn't!"

"Only for a little while."

She shook her head: "You won't—you won't take advantage?"

"I beg your pardon!" I said, and stepped back from her a pace or two.

And she whispered: "All right, let's go there. And give me your hand, I can't see anything. You don't think there'll be any nettles there, do you?"

"Here? Not a chance!"

So we sat down by this hay, I spread out half the pile, and we leaned against the rest, and I saw that the stars were really very beautiful, a very well-conceived thing, and I said to her—and now I managed to say it—that her eyes were more beautiful than all those stars put together, because let the stars be what they would, if half of them were gone I wouldn't even realize it, and it wouldn't mean anything to me, but her eyes were simply her eyes, and inimitable, just as she was she, and no one else . . . and while I was saying it I was almost crazy with joy, because it seemed to me that I was really going to have a girl, and it would be this DISH Šárka, the most beautiful and most unattainable girl in the whole school. And the hay smelled lovely, and the stars shone beautifully, and we could hear crickets singing.

So I kissed her, and told her how much I wanted her, and kissed her again, and she whispered: "You see, you are taking advantage!" and I begged her to forgive me, because now I simply couldn't help myself, I loved her so much, and a host of other things, too, that suddenly came pouring out from somewhere inside me. And then suddenly *she* began to kiss *me,* which was something staggering, and she asked me if I loved her better than Irena, which I did, because kissing Irena was like when a dog touches you with its muzzle, and not at all such beauty as this. She asked me about a lot of other girls from school, too, whether I liked them and whether I wanted them, too, but I said I wanted only her, because a man can love only one woman, as she knew very well, and she said that she did know it, but that a girl can give herself only once, and was I sure that nothing could happen? And by this time we were almost lying down, and I didn't know very clearly whether I was on my head or my heels.

"No," I said, "don't be afraid, nothing can happen."

And she asked: "Have you had lots of girls before?"

"No, of course I haven't," I told her, because I remembered that in that *Ninth Wave* of Ehrenburg's he writes about this very thing; when the boy goes to the brothel, there Ehrenburg writes that he saw what pleasure it gave her when he told her that he was still a virgin.

But the greatest love of my life asked: "Have you truly never had anyone before, or are you only saying that?"

"I truly never have," I said, smiling happily. "Really, word of honor!" And I have to admit that it also happened to be the truth.

"Truly not?"

I kissed her: "Truly not!"

"Then excuse me!" said my greatest love, and I felt her stiffen, and then she began to put on neatly the jacket which had gotten itself half pulled off in the course of our clinch. "But I'm not your guinea pig!"

And she let out a snort, and before I realized what was happening she was up on the road.

There was nothing left for me to do but take offense, and since that time I haven't got any greatest love. The most incomprehensible thing of all is that after that day it was Jarda Kovář who started getting Šárka's dinners for her.

The Problem

The whole afternoon we'd been lying by the river in Modřany, and what with the sun and the water, and the shouting at one another across the river, we were half out of our usual skins.

There were five of us, the same as in that novel they're reading on the radio, and we didn't really know one another all that well. We'd been raked together from all quarters, by pure chance, into the same army auxiliary course, which we had to attend once a week for a few months before our military service. We had special printed permits to be absent from work for that purpose. And a driving license, in any case, is a good thing to have, especially when you can get it this way, a good deal more cheaply.

But this particular day our instructor hadn't turned up. Obviously I wasn't going back to the factory, now that I was excused from it for the rest of the day. It wouldn't have been worth it, anyhow, I would only have gotten there in time to clock out. But none of us had any special ideas what to do with this time that had dropped from heaven into our hands. A couple of the boys from the course went home, and we five, who had hardly begun to know one another well enough to be able to attach the right name to the right face, decided to devote the rest of the afternoon to navigation, because it was a lovely sunny day, and none of us was at all eager to go out into the steambath of the streets, or even to go and sit over a beer somewhere indoors. On a day like that I don't think anybody ventures onto the streets or into the city unless he absolutely has to. God bless the waiters up there at Barrandov, running around in dinner jackets in that heat!

In the evening we were sitting in Braník, at the last streetcar station, swapping tales about the road crashes we'd seen, and when, and various bits of memorized driving wisdom, and discussing mixtures and ignition and brake fluids.

Honza and Kad'our were students, and great at name dropping. For instance, if they were talking about actors they'd always say "Johnny" or "Olda," by which they meant somebody famous like Jan Werich or Oldřich Nový. In fact they always talked like great experts about everything, to make sure everybody recognized them as two-thirds geniuses. To supply the remaining third they had various phrases like: "But of course, quite formidable!" and ". . . as you know, of course!" and ". . . actually . . ." and other similar general utility words—and the other party could usually manage that sort of thing even a little more expertly than they could. We used to have a lot of fun with them in this way, all we had to do was egg them on a bit and they'd pour out flowers of intellect like a fountain. But apart from that they were good fellows.

One very pleasant, sunburned boy was named Pešout. He was a gardener, and as it turned out, the biggest idiot of us all. He was one of those people you can tell at a glance for what they are, no timid souls, to be scared of a bump, but genuine thrusters who can stand up to anything, who know what they're doing, and aren't the least bit inclined to give themselves airs just because they're behind the wheel of a car. But what I envied him was that suntan, because to the end of my days I shall never be that chocolate color. I always have endless trouble getting sunburned.

Then there was Jirka, who worked with me at the Praga factory. We knew each other a little from playing table tennis, and then from the driving course and the streetcar. But I only had to travel three stations by streetcar, when I didn't walk instead, which I usually did when Mom managed to get me out of bed in time, while Jirka came all the way from the other end of town.

I was ravenously hungry. It was nearly eight o'clock, and the last time I'd eaten was a snack during the morning.

We sat on the plank benches and waited for the streetcar crew to bring the car out from the loop to the station. It was a fine summer evening, and they certainly weren't all that eager. The concrete of the pavement was still warm.

On Saturday or Sunday there were usually hordes of people here, rushing off to some hut in Pikovice, or boys going out together in a party for Sunday with their smoke-blackened camping kettle; but during the week there was nobody here but the people who'd come in by the buses from Modřany and Hodkovičky, and now and again some couple glad of the warm weather, so that they needn't bribe the porters somewhere, and put up with their bawdy jokes, but had time to come right out here instead of just as far as Stromovka, where there's a peeping Tom lurking behind every other bush.

The streetcar crew were sitting taking it easy in the lighted front car, reading each other the juicy bits from the evening gossip sheet. Then the driver looked at his watch and went to look at the schedule clipped behind a grille on the side window. For a little while they went on laughing at something. From our bench in the twilight we could see them there whinnying and stretching like silent puppets in the lighted streetcar, because at this distance you couldn't hear a sound. Finally the driver pulled himself together, put his cap on his head, walked forward, stuck his cap by the peak behind the window, tinged his bell out of habit, and sailed out with a rush to the station, where by this time there was a nice little crowd of us waiting.

The conductor pulled up the windows and put on the lights in the trailer car. We climbed straight into that one, and sat down just a little way in from the door onto the platform, to leave the corner vacant in case someone should turn up who must be given a seat.

The conductor clipped the tickets, we stuck them under the

straps of our watches, and gradually we ran out of anything to say. It's difficult to know what five people can find to talk about, when they're all sitting side by side, with half the streetcar staring straight into their mouths for want of any other entertainment. And the same goes for five pensioners on a park bench, when just one talks and the others crumble up half a roll for the sparrows, and they go on and on repeating to one another excerpts from their memoirs of the Galician front, and trumping one another's aces with tales about which of them has eaten the most frozen goulash and sawdust bread. They begin with how Brusilov took the offensive, and fall out about whether it was in 'fifteen or 'sixteen; and then, if they've been pensioned off long enough, they end by forbidding the grandchildren they're supposed to be minding to play with one another.

So we just gazed in front of us and shut up. At one of the next stations quite a lot of people got in, so we made room for them. Pešout and Honza stayed sitting down, and the rest of us got up and stood over them, dumping all our stuff in their laps, including our damp swimming trunks.

I had on a flannel shirt, worn outside my trousers. It was made to be worn like that, but the boys suddenly started pulling my leg about it and arguing that it was crazy. It was a kind of game we had.

The streetcar went scorching along the track, laid here between plowed fields, where they said there was going to be a good road some day. But up to now there was only the streetcar line, and electric lights on tall masts, lighting up the spectral, excavated earth, all black cinder, because most of this stretch was former embankment. Here and there a piece of wall stuck out of the ground, or we could see the hole left by the cellar of some demolished house.

On principle I argued with them in defense of the way I was wearing my shirt, and purposely left it that way. My back was a little sunburned, and when the air from the doorway curled around us into the car it was pleasantly cool.

On the platform there was some drunk, with his hat jammed

down over his forehead, reeling from one corner to the other and talking away indistinctly, the way drunks do.

In the corner beside us sat a tiny, crooked, wrinkled old granny, naturally wearing a black saucepan hat with a veil, with a comical handbag, and eyeglasses on her nose. She was ostentatiously taking no notice of us, and reading *The Daily Worker,* which had a part of some comic strip on the back page.

The tipsy man began to sway about a bit too precariously close to the doorway, and the conductor carefully shoved him inside toward us, so that he wouldn't catapult out among the piles of paving stones, and other materials just as hard and unsuitable for landing on.

He was standing right behind us now, clinging with one hand to a strap on which was an advertisement for one of those preparations that make your jams jell. "Sets in five minutes, keeps for ten years." With the whole weight of his beery belly dangling from the leather, the strap creaked rather unpleasantly.

Suddenly a hand came flying between us, holding a newspaper he'd extracted from somewhere inside his crookedly buttoned jacket. He shoved it under our gardener's nose and announced: "Here you are! Read!"

People looked at us curiously, at last even the old lady with *The Daily Worker* cast a surreptitious glance at us over her glasses, with washed-out, slightly owlish eyes, with strikingly black lashes and a black line on the lower lids. Sometimes there can be a lot of fun with drunks.

Pešout gently and placidly pushed away both the hand and the newspaper, and said: "Thanks, Uncle, but I can't read."

We giggled a little, and so did the few people who had also heard. For he'd spoken very quietly, as it was always his habit to do. But this man heard, all right. As he obviously wanted to say something, there was a minute of silence while he only mumbled: "You can't . . . you can't . . ." and swayed on his pectin-postered strap and his straddled legs. Then he suddenly jerked out very loudly: "So you can't read. All right, then, we'll teach you."

This was too much for us, we began to laugh.

The old granny with the *Worker* looked up at us again, this time reprovingly. But that didn't stop Honza from asking: "We? Who's 'we'?"

Everybody was now looking our way, and some fisherman with a rod case and a bait tin for worms said: "Must be the football team from 'The Gamekeepers.' " Nobody laughed this time.

Our drunk thumped himself excitedly on the chest and roared: "Us—the working class."

This was too much, even the old lady shook her head, and it's a wonder we weren't rolling in the aisle. That guy looked as much like the kind of people who really stand over machines for their living as he did like the overalled giant in the posters, the one with the well-pressed creases, just sweeping one pale-green imperialist off the face of the globe, while two others have gone head first before him, and all you see of them is their legs as they take off into space.

It made me think about one girl at school who provoked the teacher by asking if she was entitled to write in her questionnaire that she was the daughter of a worker, seeing her father was a fireman. And one boy's father was a sexton!

Only we didn't go on laughing very long, because all at once the hand came flying between us again, only noticeably faster this time and without any newspaper, closed up into a fist, and bashed our sunburned gardener right in the face.

He even tried to hit him again, only he didn't manage it, because we caught hold of him at once, and waited to see what was going to happen.

There was blood running from Pešout's nose. He held his handkerchief to it, and we clung on tight to the struggling drunk.

It had happened right at a station, and people were just boarding the car, and as we were only just inside the door we were in their way. Some fellow with a brick-red complexion and a bull neck—it looked as if his head grew straight out of his shoulders— let go of a good-looking, slender woman, flew at us and took a couple of smacks at Jirka, who was the nearest to him, pulling his hand away from the drunk's shoulder.

"You puppy!" he says. "You'd dare!—to an old man!"

Then all the people who'd been sitting inside and had seen what had happened, began to talk at once, and those who had pushed their way inside shouted things back again to the ones who were still pushing after them.

On the platform, where those who had just come aboard were all crowded together, somebody was already carrying on about hooligans, and about young people in general, and proclaiming that he'd know how to deal with that bunch.

The conductor rang his bell, and came struggling toward us, bursting with zeal for his duty, and before he even reached us he was asking what was going on here.

There was a brief moment of silence, and into it the old granny beside us announced: "That drunk struck this boy here."

The conductor and the man with the brick-red face began to be very embarrassed, the bull-necked one let go of Jirka, turned his back, and made as if nothing had happened. The conductor, too, was absolutely floored, and didn't know what to do.

And then suddenly somebody spoke up: "Then land him one, boys, right in the face!"

It may even have been the same brick-red man. The whole streetcar took it up, it was a wonder they didn't turn it into a chant: "That's right, bash him in the mouth, boys, give it to him!"

We were just going along under the ice house, in a part of the town that isn't very lively, so at once the conductor offered: "I'll stop here, then, and you can get off with him."

And he tugged at the bell, and the car actually did stop. The people began to make a gangway for us, so that we could get by with this drunken man. He disliked this very much, he grabbed at the door, and the grilles on the windows, but struggle as much as he liked, we hauled him along all the same, like a gopher washed out of its hole.

But now suddenly up rose our dear gardener, took his handkerchief away from his nose to make himself heard better, and announced that that wouldn't do, that he wasn't a brawler, and he refused to settle the affair that way.

"We're trade unionists and members of the army auxiliary, not hooligans. We're going to the police." He fairly radiated all the copybook maxims about good little boys and a perfectly regulated world.

I know a few people, both boys and girls, who are quite proud when somebody calls them hooligans, because it's the favorite term of abuse used by those thrusting people who've got nothing better to do than hide behind some slogan or other, and egg on other people in this style: "We know you're good fellows, so now we want you to do so-and-so, and such-and-such, and if you don't do it, then you're not good fellows, you're hooligans and that's that, and we're here to be the judges." And that's another case where they use this "we" as if they were speaking for the working class.

They can't get it into their thick heads that after work I look forward to some plan of my own a good deal more than to a meeting, where most of those present will be the usual lot, anyhow, the ones who go on and on forever bleating the same stuff. The only ones they convince, if you ask me, are those who haven't got a girl waiting for them at the porter's lodge, but only a sack of coal at the best. The religious bigots were usually celibate, too.

But Pešout was an honest boy who believed a hundred per cent in what he said, and it was a matter of principle with him, from which he wouldn't have withdrawn even at the price of another blow, in the eye this time if necessary.

What could we do? When it came down to it, it was his nose, and we all had our union and army auxiliary cards on us. But above all, it was his nose.

The conductor shrugged his shoulders, obviously this attitude affronted him: "Well, if you don't want . . . all right, then!"

The brick-red fellow shrugged his shoulders over us, too, we'd certainly sunk considerably in his estimation, and even in that of the other people in the car. Well, except for the wrinkled old lady, who was placidly reading her paper again.

We peered out of the windows and the doorway, keeping a watch out for the first cop. There wasn't anyone standing under Vyšehrad, or at Železňák.

At Jirásek Bridge the old lady folded her *Daily Worker* and got out. But there wasn't any uniform there, either.

We all got out at National Street, the five of us with our drunken friend well in the middle. He came with us quite calmly. You could see from his face that he wasn't afraid any more.

The light signals at the crossroads were switched over to the automatic system, and the traffic policeman stood on the pavement beside his little gray booth.

As we came near him, our fellow suddenly broke away from us and ran ahead. "Comrade," he shouted, "comrade, I've brought you these brats!"

We came along more slowly after him. The policeman looked at us sourly: "What is it?"

"A mistake," I said. "This man hasn't brought us, we brought him."

The policeman, a good-natured, anxious, middle-aged guy with gray hair, looked both us and the other fellow over, and caught the smell of the brewery from him. Quietly he said: "All right, then, what's happened?"

"He attacked and struck my friend here." In all my life I would never have hit on such a cultured word for a bash on the nose, if it hadn't been for the old lady in the black hat.

"Hmmm . . . and where did this happen?"

"In the streetcar."

"And where?"

"In Braník."

"My God, and you've brought it with you all this way?" Disgustedly he stripped off his white sleeves. "Well, what have you got to say to this?"

"I'll tell everything for the official report, comrade," said the beery one loftily.

"What can you do! Come on, then!" He looked at the lights working on automatic, and locked his little hut. And off we went to the station. Here it was actually the central city one.

They led us up to the first floor, and distributed us on chairs there. The traffic cop handed us over and disappeared. We waited some time.

Two plainclothes officers and a lieutenant looked us over. They didn't look upon us with any great favor, either, and it turned out that only one of us had his identity card on him, and the addresses of all the others they had to verify by telephone, somewhere according to the locality.

The fellow we'd brought placed in their hands a whole wad of documents; they nodded their heads over them and gave them all back to him, except his identity card.

The clock on the wall showed a few minutes after a quarter past ten.

Pešout told his story.

We confirmed it.

One of the plainclothes men sat down at the typewriter and waited.

Some head or other poked in at the door, leaned inside for a moment, looked us over, and vanished again.

"Well," asked the lieutenant, "did you strike him?"

"Yes."

"Why?"

"Because he insulted my honor as a workingman."

"How?"

"They were singing in front of everybody: May the Yanks come over soon!"

"*What?*"

"That's right: May the Yanks come over soon!"

We were all startled rigid, and then we all began to speak at once: "That isn't true! He's lying!"

They didn't listen to us. They weren't looking at the other fellow any more, either, their eyes were creeping steadily all over us.

"So that's how it was!"

"It isn't true!" I said.

"Look here," said Pešout, "we're members of the army auxiliary, and trade unionists."

"Were they singing?" the lieutenant turned to the drunk, who was looking at us triumphantly.

"Yes, they were, Comrade Lieutenant."

"He's lying," I said, "just plain, ordinary lies!"

One of the plainclothes men, standing between the lieutenant and the drunk, asked quickly: "And can you prove he's lying?"

"And can he prove we were singing?"

The lieutenant reproved me: "Don't be impudent!" But he said it in quite a calm and fatherly manner.

Honza said: "The whole streetcarful of people were there— Look at him, he's drunk!"

And Jirka said quite bluntly in front of them: "You see, you idiots, we ought to have just clouted him in the mouth there by the ice house, and we could all have been home by now."

They all looked at one another, the one at the typewriter turned the roller up, and the lieutenant said to Jirka: "Don't talk like that! It wouldn't necessarily have turned out to your advantage."

"Maybe, but it's the truth that if we'd done it I would have been home and had my supper by ten o'clock, instead of sitting here."

The lieutenant hesitated: "We know them all too well, these birds! Too well, the number of them we've had sitting here . . . ," and he indicated the row of chairs. "All too well, . . ."

"But can't you believe it, when five people tell you?"

The lieutenant wagged a hand. "Oh, I can see into you—all too well!" He liked that phrase.

We waited. I shut up, and so did the other boys, because it was no good arguing about anything.

They stuck their heads together and whispered something. Then they handed the drunk's papers back to him—well, actually he was hardly drunk at all by this time.

"Go on home, and the next time something like that happens, get some witnesses and don't get into the habit of bashing people."

He rang the bell, and a head appeared in the doorway.

"Take him out."

We got up from our chairs.

"You stay here!" We were like mice.

"We're workers, too," said Pešout.

The lieutenant folded his hands behind his back. "I don't want any brawling in the street, and it could turn out badly for you, too." When he moved his belt caught the light. His boots creaked and shone. In that rig it must be hell in summer, I thought. My feet were burning even in moccasins.

The plainclothes men sat down at the table and offered each other cigarettes.

The lieutenant allowed himself a sort of half smile, and began to warn us that booze, loose women, pubs, and moonlighting are the beginning of the end. Now and again he added: "And remember that, boys!"

The plainclothes men smoked, and one of them turned the pages of a newspaper.

"You stick to your work, youngsters. You know what they say, honesty is the best policy."

Finally he had nothing left to say to us. He looked at his watch, and said in an undertone to one of the two at the table: "Let them out at a quarter to." Then he went away without even giving us another look.

The plainclothes man who had been sitting at the typewriter earlier finished his cigarette, hungrily drawing the last whiff out of it, and stubbed it out in the bottom of the ashtray. It was a few minutes after half past ten.

He pressed a finger on the bell on the table.

"But honestly, we weren't singing," our gardener still wanted to convince him. He knew that nothing was going to happen to him, but he couldn't grasp that they wouldn't believe him when he was telling the truth.

The man didn't look at us, he said something like: "I see!" or "Sure . . . sure. . . ."

In the doorway appeared a sergeant with a bundle of keys in his hand.

"Push off, then, boys—beat it!" said the man at the table, and jerked his head toward the door.

The street was dark, silent and chilly.

Kad'our burst out, agitatedly but with conviction, that he would remember that man's face, and we would meet him again some day. As though he didn't understand that it wasn't so much the drunk who mattered.

The patrol looked at us suspiciously as we went by.

We separated at the subway. I bought a new ticket and went home. It was after eleven, midnight coming up fast, and I was on morning shift the next day.

I was thinking to myself what I should say to Father. Because I would have to account for myself somehow, and he'd never believe the truth if I told him.

Our family relations break down when I put on the phonograph.

Strength of Will

In the morning we'd been baiting Tom Thumb, and I knew that, understandably enough, he wouldn't forget it or forgive us for it, because for us the army was a temporary circumstance and more of a joke than anything else, and for him it was his life's mission and a desperately serious matter. Tom Thumb was Tom Thumb, and there was nothing to be done about it, just as there was nothing to be done about the fact that it had just begun to rain, we were nearly four miles from barracks, and in twenty minutes time, according to schedule, they would begin serving dinner for our company. Tom Thumb was a good guy, actually very good, when you considered the choice offered, but he couldn't bear to hear himself called Tom Thumb, or anything else that forced him to think how small he was. With him that was the end.

He was good, as far as it was possible for him to be good. On the gymnastic apparatus he went through his paces like a little god, but the trouble was precisely that he could never be anything but a *little* god, because Tom Thumb, or Second Lieutenant Komač if you prefer, measured from head to toe a mere five feet two inches, and it's always a misfortune when a small guy finds himself in a position of authority. He would make three immaculate somersaults—for instance—drop neatly from the horizontal bar, and say to some fellow like a mountain: "What, a big fellow like you, damn it, and can't do eleven pull-ups? Just watch me!" And hup! he was back hanging from the bar, and did twenty-two of them, straight out of the book, chin right up to the bar, and with his legs stretched out horizontally before him into the bargain.

Only now it was up to the guy like a mountain to say: "Yeah, but you've got some breath, Comrade Second-Lieutenant!" and everything would be in order, because then Tom Thumb could declaim: "Breath? That's strength of will. When I say I must, then I must, and that's that. And I do it!"

Yes, fine, only there always seemed to be some ignorant jerk on hand, who instead of passing Comrade Second-Lieutenant's breath control and will power, blurted out: "Yes, but look how little weight you're carrying!"

And good will went out the window. The clown might laugh, but two-thirds of us certainly wouldn't be laughing, we'd be spitting out our souls somewhere on the assault course, most of us inside gas masks, and anybody who didn't manage to open the valve in time was a dead duck. Because through that filter you couldn't get enough air to give you strength to read a newspaper. Luckily we discovered that trick with the valve quite early on.

Strength of will was Tom Thumb's speciality, like hanging up some recruit on the horizontal bar and baying down below him: "You must, you must!" Or: "Fight, man, fight!" While all the time the fellow in question was flapping about like a flag at half-mast, and was only too pleased that he hadn't yet fallen off into the sand.

Fight!—that was Tom Thumb's line. He wouldn't let it be taken from him. He was a fine gymnast, that's a fact, and I think he wasn't in any way particularly stupid, or perhaps he simply wasn't any stupider than one expects; but not even strength of will did him any good when we went on training runs, because what could he do, with his five feet two inches? Whatever he did, his legs remained the appropriate length for a man five feet two inches tall, and no more, and whenever we felt like it we could always run away from him, and pretend we couldn't hear when he bellowed some order after us. So that later on he was forced to accompany us on our route marches and training runs on a bicycle. And when it wasn't full military order, and we didn't have to run in army boots but could wear light running shoes, we very often ran away from him even then, because with his height he only had three-quarters of a bicycle. And naturally there was also always some joker to be found, who was willing to scatter a box of thumbtacks in his way.

Maybe he really wasn't a bad guy. Somewhere in Slovakia he had a wife and family. I remember the time—I happened to be on duty on the gate—when his fourth boy was born; he was quite a stallion, this Komač. He came back into barracks to sleep, a little bit drunk, and announced to me on the gate: "I've had a son for four days now, and I haven't even seen him yet!" Then he went on to tell me about his wife, and finally he announced that she was such a splendid woman, and he loved her so much, that he wouldn't part with her, no, not even for a million dollars!

But all this had nothing to do with why we were now standing here on a kind of flat, trampled patch of field just off the road. What had to do with this circumstance was simply Tom Thumb and the mood he was in; because in the morning, on the way out here, all of us boys had been playing a kind of silly game—seeing whether we could all burst out laughing together on the word of command. We'd been whiling away the time like that between breakfast and parade. On the count of three, everybody had to sound off together. In a little while we really had it so perfectly drilled that on the word "Three" we came in like a crack squad, absolutely simultaneously, and made it sound like quite natural laughter, too. Well—and then we were lined up in front of Komač, and he was expounding to us something about our morning program, which was on military preparedness, and Tonda Trnovec took it into his head to liven up the proceedings by calling "THREE!"

And that's why Tom Thumb was in a bad humor, and why we got the kind of morning training session very few of us could remember. But always, even at the most stupid and damnable moment, some idiot would suddenly say "THREE!" and instantly everything in the world was a joke to us, including what was happening to us at that moment. And Komač never fathomed and never got it out of us what we were laughing at. He thought we were making a fool of him in some way, and that riled him.

Now he seized his bike, and looked us over gleefully. We were all fed up with this morning, right up to the neck, and we'd gotten our uniforms all plastered with mud. And on top of everything, slowly but surely it was beginning to rain.

"Well?" he said. "How are you feeling?"

We were silent. Here and there somebody poked a finger in his ear; we were marching at ease, and smoking was allowed. Tom Thumb held his bike, and turned the pedal into position.

"We'll finish," he announced. "Dinner's in twenty minutes." He looked us over. "If anybody still wants to laugh, let him get it off his chest now. At the double, later on, he won't have time left for laughing."

Again nobody said anything, although my face was all screwed up with the effort it cost me to keep from coming straight out with that "THREE!" Or: "One, two, THREE!" That would be even better. This thought so delighted me that I couldn't contain myself, I burst out laughing. A few others around couldn't help joining in. Tom Thumb shook his little head over us: "I see, you guys, that you still haven't had enough of this." Then he gave me a long look, taking me for the cause of all this trouble, and said, "Málek, take that antitank gun from Doležal." My name's Málek, I should mention. And he pointed to Doležal. "Doležal, give it to him!" He waved his hand at me.

Doležal is the second biggest fellow in the company, but he'd had quite enough of the forty-four pounds that damn gun weighs. He took my rucksack from me, and placed the gun with its wheels on the ground in front of me.

Tom Thumb hoisted his bicycle across the ditch onto the road, and stepped after it.

"For reasons of training it's necessary that the soldier become accustomed to all kinds of arms—eh, Málek? Those who in the process still have time left over for fooling around will also get accustomed, that I can promise you. In war conditions it could well happen that the antitank gunner might be put out of action —eh, Trnovec?" He turned, casually as it were, to Tonda, who was standing beside me. "Take that other gun!"

Tonda took the second antitank gun from the boy from the first platoon, and shortened the strap on it to suit himself. As he was working on it, and had his head bent, he whispered to me: "Three!"

Normally, on longer marches, two of us always carried each antitank gun on our shoulders. For one man it's too big and awkward, and the weight too badly distributed.

Well, but still, during a war . . . he had something there.

"Everything is a matter of will power, Málek, Trnovec, that goes for you, too," lectured Komač. "Will power, that means not being lazy."

"But, sir," said Tonda, "but. . . ."

"Let's go!" Our second lieutenant threw his leg over the frame of his three-quarter-size bike with balloon tires. "Forward, forward!" He pressed his foot on the braced pedal. The first rank of three jumped across the ditch or scrambled down into it and up the other side onto the road. "We should be in the dining room by now. Come on, shake a leg!"

"But, sir," asked Tonda, "who's going to carry these with us?"

Tom Thumb let out a howl: "Trnovec . . . *who's going to carry them with you?* What are you thinking of?" He flung up a hand from the handlebars, and let it fall back again. "Man, you'll be the death of me!"

Meanwhile the boys had drawn up in threes across the ditch, on the road, only Tonda and I were still standing here on this trampled stretch of field.

"Strength of will," said Komač. "Everything depends on strength of will. When I see a boy who isn't afraid to exert him-

self, I make a note of it, and when I find one as lazy as a dog—
Trnovec . . . then he's got to learn!" Then he waved his hand,
as if beckoning us. "Come on, get on with it! We're not going to
stand here till we grow roots on your account."

We scrambled across the ditch.

". . . at the double, march!" ordered Tom Thumb, and
tramped on the pedals.

We began to trot. But right from the start we were left a few
paces behind the others. Not simply because we were carrying
forty-four pounds each, but rather because it's just about the un-
wieldiest forty-four pounds you can imagine. Though now I come
to think of it, I don't know that any forty-four pounds dumped
on a man's back would be all that wieldy.

Between the last rank of three and us the gap got longer and
longer with every minute. And the greater the gap becomes in a
case like that, the less heart a guy has for catching up again. Forty-
four clumsy, bumping, swaying pounds on your back at the double is an unimaginable thing.

Komač made a figure eight on the empty road behind the
trotting unit, and bellowed back to us: "Málek, Trnovec . . .
come on, come on, run!"

But we'd already stopped.

"Screw you!" said Tonda.

"Tonda," I said, "Tonda . . . THREE!"

"Screw *you*, too!"

It was now raining steadily, no longer a matter of single moist
spots from individual drops. The whole road was dark and glossy.

"Tonda," I said, "Tonda, think of dinner!"

"Screw you, and dinner, and all!" said Tonda, and spat at his
feet. "He's having some hell of a game with us, I tell you." We
were breathing heavily.

The sound of running feet grew steadily fainter. Once more we
saw Komač ride back a little way and call out something to us,
but in the meantime the whole company had vanished around
the bend of the road, and he had to turn around again and go
after them.

We tried to run again for a little way, but it was quite hopeless. The worst thing about the whole situation was that I was still dying to laugh the whole time, even when I hardly had enough wind in me to breathe at all. Strength of will. You try cultivating strength of will with a lump of iron on your back that thumps you at every step right down to your heels. It was all talk. Even Komač himself must know that it was all talk. And the whole company knew that it was all talk, it was only a question of who would be the first to recognize it so absolutely as to dare to say it aloud, so that all those who up to then had still believed that all this stuff, everything, everything, everything, was something more than mere talk would find it intolerable to lag behind, intolerable to continue pretending that these speeches were anything more and better than speeches. All that bull about a firm will, and the similar maxims for life.

Komač was a good fellow, and could be taken seriously, because when you came down to it, it was fine how he told me that he'd had a son for four days, and hadn't even seen him yet, and that he had such a good wife that he wouldn't part with her even for a million dollars, he loved her so much. But when he started talking about arms potential, or building up the chemical industry, then he couldn't be taken seriously, for the very reason that he himself knew that he was saying what he was saying because he had to say it, and not because it was what he wanted to say.

But to us, of course, out there on the road, this was all one, like everything else—such as, for instance, that I prefer the theatre, while Tonda finds the movies good enough, or that Tonda has an uncle in America, and my grandfather was a Jew. To us, straggling along the road with those hand cannon dangling on our backs, all this was a matter of complete indifference.

The boys had utterly vanished, we could no longer hear even the faintest echo of their steps, nothing but the quiet whispering of the rain on the road, and on the trees that bordered it. From the direction in which we were going a truck met us and passed by; otherwise there was nothing but this rainy silence.

"Something ought to come along going our way," said Tonda.

"That would be some use." But nothing did, the road was quite empty and we were alone.

Both of us, by mutual consent, dumped the guns from our backs at the same moment, and tried alternately shoving or pulling them along on their wheels. It's forbidden, of course, but the one place where things which are forbidden mustn't be done is in the presence of those who've forbidden them. And there was nobody in that category here to say "Don't you know that an anti-tank gun must not be moved along on its wheels?" Nobody like that was around at this moment. In any case, we'd never managed to find out why you mustn't run an antitank gun along on its wheels, seeing it *has* wheels. But the fact is that we got along a great deal worse, or perhaps not worse, but at any rate more slowly, than when we had them on our backs. They wouldn't maintain a straight course, and we were fighting with them all the time, because they insisted on running off to one side.

In the end we fixed it so that we carried them between us, one on each shoulder, so that although each of us was still carrying his full forty-four pounds, still it was better than when they were banging us over the heels. And we thought to ourselves that Komač was a bastard, and all sorts of similar things.

Then Tonda got the idea that we could overtake them by taking a short cut through the woods, but it was a stupid idea at that time of year, we would either have had to come back to the road before the bridge, or ford the river, which in this season was five feet deep. In the summer you can easily cross by the stepping stones.

Suddenly we heard a motor approaching us from behind. I believe if we'd had live ammunition with us, and if the driver hadn't stopped for us, we would have been quite capable of shooting him, truck and all, at that moment. But he did stop for us. The minute he caught sight of us and we waved to him. We heard him brake, and then he came coasting up alongside us.

He never asked anything and we never told him anything. I don't think we ever said a word except thanks. It was a big Praga truck. We hoisted our war department junk over the side, climbed up by the back wheel, and quickly crawled aboard after it.

Tonda banged on the roof of the cab, and the driver stuck his head out of the window, peered around at us, and said: "Sit down, boys!"

And we were on the move, and it was like being on velvet. When we overtook our running comrades, and Tom Thumb on his bicycle, we quickly lay flat on the floorboards. They hadn't even gotten all that far ahead of us, after all, and under the bridge just behind the barracks, where the driver stopped for us, we had to wait quite a while for them.

They weren't running any more, only gently trotting, and they all had faces like boiled beets. We crept out from under the bridge and joined on at the end. It wasn't any hardship to keep up with them now and maintain formation without any gap. In any case those smartly running ranks of three had lost most of their form by this time and it was just a straggle of breathless, sweating humanity.

The duty officer at the entrance lifted the barrier and we trotted into the barracks.

"Breathing exercises!" ordered Komač. We began to walk around in a circle. ". . . arms upward stretch, breathe in! Arms downward stretch, breathe out. . . ." and at last he noticed us.

"Well, and how are you feeling?" he hallooed. "Did it work or didn't it?"

We didn't say anything, though once again I badly wanted to say "THREE!"

"But you knew why you were doing it. . . ." He was filled with joy at the success of his educational methods. Almost as much as that time over the fact that he'd had a son for four days, even if he hadn't yet seen him. He grinned at us jovially. "Well, put them down now, don't wear yourselves out when there's no need!"

Then we went off to our barrack block. We dumped our arms in the store; we could clean them after dinner. Everybody hauled off his shirt and started washing off the sweat. Under the cold water steam rose from their skins.

When I got there with Tonda, Komač was already scrubbing himself with a rough towel. His gymnast's muscles rippled under his skin, and he beamed and beamed like a full moon: "I'll make soldiers of you boys yet!"

Tonda rubbed the back of his hand against his forehead, clutching the soap in his palm. Somebody had to make some sort of answer. We couldn't let Tom Thumb talk unacknowledged into the empty air. He deserved that much respect. We couldn't pipe up "THREE!" either!

"All it needs is a little will power, and no laziness, eh?"

"Yeah!" I said. "Yeah, that's right."

Expertise

In our old days in the Scouts we used to take proficiency tests, and ever since then I don't know anything better than to be an expert at something. I confirmed this basic principle definitively in the army. It doesn't even matter about being enough of an expert to have a real understanding of something, it's quite enough that people should think you have. Everybody always tends to be rather what people think about him than what he actually happens to be. Though as a matter of fact most people don't at all want to be what they really are or what other people think about them, but something which they themselves secretly imagine they are.

Take this army business. A guy goes into the army, and privately he thinks this or that about it. Partly about defending his country and all that, too, even though it goes without saying that nobody swallows the sort of bull they reel off to recruits everywhere in the world. At least, none of the normal guys I know ever swallowed it. But since he has to think something, every recruit remembers a word here and there out of all that nonsense, provided, of course, he doesn't happen to have it dished out to him by the kind of idiot who can only teach recruits one thing, that to view things his way simply means to be as big an idiot as he is. To come across an idiot, of course, is only too easy, anywhere in the world. Plenty of people all over the globe are missing on one cylinder. Like when you see somebody on a bus, placidly reading a newspaper, and you think to yourself: Yeah, just an ordinary fellow, what is it about him that seems queer to me? And suddenly he stands up, and you find yourself staring, because he's only got one leg. As long as he was lying back in his seat and half hidden behind his paper you never noticed anything, or to be more accurate, he did seem to you somehow a little bit queer, because a man with one leg even sits a bit differently from people with two.

So, for instance, you get Lieutenant Kubíček censoring the boys' letters home. Anybody who likes can wait to get his letter cleared, and then mail it immediately outside, but Kubíček loves to be busy with something, so he makes a thorough job of his censoring. I think army censoring ought to be like army cleaning. Slosh with a rag here, slosh with a rag there. What's wet's clean!

"Novák, come here! What do you mean by this? How can you pretend that you don't like it in the army? Can't you keep a girl's attention except by trying to make her feel sorry for you? You rewrite it. . . . Rewrite it, Novák, and don't write such stupidities next time, eh?"

Then all of a sudden Comrade Lieutenant drops on a letter with about forty-six military secrets in it, and on top of that, four whole lines just written in numbers. He glares at the address: "My God, Munich! And no signature!" He hurtles out of his office and howls along the corridor: "Who wrote this? Who wrote this letter?"

Silence.

"Nobody?"

Silence.

"Very well, nobody!" Two strides this way, two strides that. "The whole hut will assemble!"

Any other time that would really bother us, but now the word's gone around that something's up, and we muster like the wind, ready to be interested in and entertained by every mortal thing.

"Who wrote this?"

No answer.

"Duty sergeant, I'm asking for the last time: who wrote this?"

The duty sergeant shrugs his shoulders.

"Duty sergeant, I asked you a question."

"I don't know, Comrade Lieutenant."

"You don't know?"

"No, sir, I don't."

"Very well! Nobody—you understand, nobody!—is to leave quarters."

And he goes snorting off to the counterespionage guys like the wolf after Little Red Ridinghood. The counter boys undoubtedly smell a rat somewhere, but on the other hand they can't just throw a letter like that out of the window. So they have to get down to it, they stare and stare at it, and then start deciphering those figures at the bottom. It's no special test of genius. The first group is 11. The eleventh letter of the alphabet is K. And in no time flat they discover that what they've got written down there, in the most ordinary of numerical codes, is that: KUBÍČEK IS AN ASS. Somebody in the company obviously knew it already, but the next day, on the authority of the counter boys, all the officers know it, and from the boy who acts as chauffeur to the mess all the men in the garrison know it, too.

After that Kubíček, if he were smart, would cook up some story about testing the security precautions, or something like that. But he doesn't; Kubíček never thinks of anything that can't be read in the handbooks. So during political instruction, for instance, this sort of thing is likely to crop up: "Private Kvasnička, come here to the map and show me the divisions of the world."

Kvasnička happens to be surreptitiously reading *The War with the Newts,* and he's so deep in it that he says: "The divisions of the world are: England and the rest."

"Correct," says Kubíček. "Now come and show them on the map."

Well, yes, but that doesn't belong here. What I wanted to tell you about is how I became an expert on tank techniques. Shortly after Christmas, just when the sentimental mood is wearing off and discipline is beginning to harden again, Kubíček sent for me one day, and said, "Moucha, do you know why I've sent for you?"

I shook my head.

"No, Comrade Lieutenant." And I was wondering what could have leaked out this time, and how many days I should be likely to get for it. But off the cuff I couldn't think of anything. I hadn't even been out without leave for about five days. Nothing.

Kubíček lit up a cigarette coquettishly, and looked like Inspector Maigret: "You paint, young man, don't you?"

I started to say something cautious, like "Well, sir, I've played around with it a bit in private life. . . ."

"Don't fool around, Moucha! I *know* you paint."

I was getting nervous, thinking everything had come out about those parachutes and women and things I draw for the boys in their diaries—you know, it's the old story, everybody curses the draft, but at the same time he's busy collecting beautiful souvenirs of his army service. So I stammered out: "Well, yes, Comrade Lieutenant, now and again, if the boys keep pestering me, I do paint a little."

"Come off it, you were a designer in civilian life, weren't you?"

"Yes, sir."

"You see!" and he claps down his hand on some papers he has on his desk, and beams like a full moon, because he's read them through only ten minutes ago. "Now shake a leg and get over to the company commander's office, he wants to talk to you."

"OK," I said, nodding, and he said: "Don't you know how to respond to an order? Eh?" Because I'm still a rookie.

"Yes, sir," I said, nodding again.

"Then do it, and properly, or I'll fix you in a way you won't forget. The army isn't a kindergarten, you understand?"

So I stood to attention and said: "Comrade Lieutenant, the correct answer is: Very good, sir!"

"That's better," he growled contentedly. "Moucha, you could all too easily irritate me. We're never going to make a soldier of you, unless you pull yourself together. You know I can have you locked up if I see fit, don't you?" And he wagged his finger at me threateningly. "You've been through disciplinary orders with the divisional commander already?"

"Yes, sir."

"Good! So you know what the legal powers of a platoon commander are?"

I said nothing, just stood gawking like a half-wit. There's nothing better than gawking like a half-wit when you're dealing with a half-wit like Kubíček.

"Run along, then," he said, when he'd had enough of enjoying me gawking like a half-wit, and also because he knew the Old Man was waiting for me in the next office.

So I went.

The Old Man left me standing in his office maybe two minutes with my cap in my hand; he was pecking out next week's training schedule with one finger on the typewriter. Then he said, as though he'd just remembered: "Oh, yes!" He pecked out a couple more letters, and then swung himself and his chair around to me: "Moucha, can you paint a tank?"

"Just from memory, Comrade Captain, or from photographs?"

"Can you or can't you?" he cut me off briskly.

"I would have to try, sir, if you wouldn't mind," I said, because I was beginning to get the idea that some concrete relief might emerge from all this.

He looked at me and twisted his mouth up. It looked as if he wanted to spit, but then after all he only started piling onto the table a whole flood of orders, handbooks and magazines. At least half of them were marked: SECRET. SERVICE USE ONLY. CONFIDENTIAL. And I thought to myself: God, this really looks like something. Now what?

And in these handbooks there were photographs of all the tanks you can imagine, from the whole world, right from the First World War up to our own times. I've got a younger brother who's still going to school, and has to collect scrap metal and paper for salvage. He'd score a million points if he could haul half those tanks away to the salvage dump, and plunk all those handbooks on top for good measure.

"There you are," the Old Man was burbling. "There you've got paper, and this stuff, and if there's anything you need besides, get a pass from the supervisor and run over to NARPA, but don't spend half the day over there!" He liked to act in a truly operational fashion. Whizz, wham! Everything flies that has feathers!

So I got a pass from the duty supervisor and ran over to NARPA—stationery, fancy goods, gifts—for watercolors and three brushes, had a couple of beers at The Poplar Alley, which is our bar, and came back immediately, strictly according to orders.

Among the officers our Old Man was always quoted as an example of operational action. I guess I qualified as another example that morning, because in addition to everything else I managed to arrange a date with the salesgirl in NARPA—stationery, fancy goods, gifts—and by evening, before the Old Man went off to his family, I had a beautiful Centurion of British manufacture down on paper, just like life. I don't want to boast, but it was certainly a lot better than those figures on the educational posters for teaching recruits their chemical preparations, how to behave in case of an atomic explosion. And they PAY for those posters, and print them to distribute to the whole army.

The Old Man came in straight from the parade ground, saw it, nodded his head and called in Kubíček: "Look at that, that's the real thing, eh?" Then he pointed at me. "Don't let him stand guard duty! His job is to paint!" And it was clear to me in that moment that I had become an expert, that I had one foot in the stirrup, and from now on it just depended on me, and *how* it depended on me! Because the army isn't a kindergarten, and what you don't grab you don't get. He who hesitates doesn't eat. Every small boy knows that. As luck would have it we are the antitank company, and have to deal with tanks. If it should ever come to that.

After that they went away happy, and I waved a plastic ruler around a bit over my wet Centurion, to make believe I was still hard at work, in case they were hanging around in the doorway. Out there in the corridor I could hear the Angel, my section leader, yelling for me, because I should have been on fatigues that day, and naturally I hadn't done them. In addition to that, he was pretty sore because I'd been over to the bar in the morning, while he, what with all his military duties, had never had a chance to get out of barracks and go there, too, so that he was just looking for—and up to a point, let's face it, he actually had— good reason to be after my blood.

Kubíček heard him, and said like a shot: "Corporal Angel!"

"Comrade Lieutenant?"

"Don't allocate my duties to Moucha, and don't rely on having him at your disposal for some time to come."

"But the fatigues!" protested the Angel, mortified. "My God, those latrines are as filthy as the inside of a tank. . . ."

"I said clearly, did I not, don't count on Private Moucha!"

"But the latrines, Comrade Lieutenant. . . ."

"Angel!" blared Kubíček, and even through the door, which was now closed, I could just see him, and see Corporal Angel, too, standing to attention like a ramrod. "Be careful, Angel, I could have you put on a charge, too."

"But, sir, the old hands certainly won't do it," protested the Angel, still feebly resisting, but by this time he was in retreat on all fronts.

"I don't want to hear another word. You can go." And the Angel went.

Then the Old Man came down from the attic, all wreathed in cobwebs and the usual junk there is in every attic in the world, only in our barracks it's combined with layers of orange-colored antifire paint, and carrying a whole pile of glass and picture frames, with a lot of cast-off statesmen like Stalin glaring out of some of them, and others holding long since outdated tables of ranks, sharpshooters' badges, and similar bull meant for the natives. I could see that that Centurion of mine had completely hooked him. He stacked the frames in a corner, beat off the dust and the flakes of orange-colored paint he'd collected in the attics, and I asked him: "Which one should I do next, Comrade Captain?"

That embarrassed him slightly, but as he was an example of

operational action he went off and burrowed a little while in those manuals he'd left on the table for me, while I went on waving my ruler over the Centurion. Then the captain, to cover the fact that he had those manuals in his hands for the first time, said in a wise, considering voice: "Yes, Moucha . . . carry on with the most widely used types. That will be the best thing."

I squinted sideways at the Centurion to see how it was drying off, and said: "Yes, sir, the most widely used types. That will be the best thing."

And the Old Man went home, because it was late anyhow by this time, and his wife would be waiting for him with dinner, and he'd have to sign the children's school workbooks for them.

That was how it began. Every morning I went to work parade to get my job for the day, got rid of it right there on the spot, and then just went off to Kubíček's office, which I'd made into a studio, and rolled tanks off the assembly line like a one-man arms factory. Now and again, understandably, I had to pop over to NARPA for more materials. Those were my days. A tank a day. Sherman, Walker, Bulldog, General Pershing, Saint Chamond, AMX, US-M 48. When I ran out of frames the boys, who by this time had also caught the fever, went looting through the entire barracks, and every evening I went to hang up another new picture in the corridor or the lecture room. In addition I'd also started making descriptive tablets for them, with the tactical and technical data, and soon this information began to interest me more than the actual painting. Even the boys who had to do my fatigues for me, since I'd suddenly been withdrawn from all such duties because of this artistic commission, began to pride themselves on me, and in a frenzy of local patriotism went off stealing frames even from other units. Not one of them ever reproached me. If it had been one of the others who'd drawn this lucky ticket it wouldn't have been any different, except that then *I* would have been the one doing the latrines, not to mention having to go on guard and kitchen duties, and polishing equipment.

But in the meantime the commanders from the other units of

our battalion had started coming over to have a look at our pictures, and even all those boys who'd complained bitterly at first about my getting out of all the most tedious army chores, thanks to this painting stuff, suddenly started to be just as proud as the others at the exhibition we had hanging on our walls, and to egg on all the other fellows so that nobody would miss seeing it. The Old Man strolled around smiling behind his whiskers to see how eaten up with jealousy the commanding officers of the other companies were because they didn't have a single designer among their personnel. The fellows who did paint, in their lots, somehow couldn't manage this sort of thing, and in any case they wouldn't have been able to scrape up a single frame or a single sheet of glass in the whole barracks by this time.

The one bad thing, of course, was that just when this enterprise was really getting into its stride, I found myself running out of anything to paint, because I'd used up all the tanks, transporters and armored vehicles that were shown in all those books. But as luck would have it I hit on a brilliant idea. In one of the manuals there was a description of a tank called Ontos, but there wasn't any picture of it shown there. So I painted it simply off the cuff, according to the description. It was a somewhat unusual tank, that's a fact. When the Old Man saw it for the first time, he said: "My God, Moucha, what's that?"

I picked up the handbook, found the page, and read:

" 'Ontos A-1, belongs to the military equipment of the A.A. . . .' "—those capital A's stood for the American army. " 'It is provided with six nonrecoiling cannon, caliber 105mm. and one 12.7mm. machine gun, firing tracer ammunition, which serves as a range finder for all six cannon. It is possible to fire simultaneously two, four or all six barrels. The wire basket on the rear of the carriage serves to catch the empty shell cases. Firing is automatic. . . .' "

The Old Man stuck his head on one side: "Ah, yes, I see . . . I see!"

With that move I'd opened up a whole new field for myself, and I went on to invent the Ontos B-2. It's true there wasn't any mention of this mark in the book, but nobody worried about that. Technically I provided it with first-class equipment. Besides those cannon it had also an automatic rocket gun, and a special oscillating device which enabled it, while in motion, to leap from side to side over a range of thirty yards, to the total confusion of enemy fire.

I made plenty more such tanks, but my showpiece, on which I staked my highest hopes, was the Mark III, an elderly German veteran from the beginning of the war. There was a picture of it in one of those books. But I gave it much more massive tracks, such as we use now, and in case one set got put out of action, it had a spare pair, two mounted on either side; and at the rear there was a whole nest of rockets for destroying ground targets. In the little turret it had on one side I mounted, from the French AMX, a 100mm. cannon, with progressive rapid-action winding and selenium-activated homing on target. That progressive winding and selenium-activated homing got them most of all, though nobody knew what it was, and no more did I. On the technotactical data I'd spread myself around. I'd written in for it three kinds of drive. A motor running on naphtha, a sun drive on the principle of the use of chlorophyll green, and also an atomic motor, which, however, was only at the experimental stage so far, and subject to further development in order to achieve protection against radioactive fallout. Its speed I extended to ninety miles per hour, and its armor was of synthetic material which was twelve times harder than steel. Naturally it could also make those leaps from side to side. That was my patent, I couldn't leave that out. A crew of three men supervised instruments which governed the machine independently, according to a computer program modified by the radio-locational survey of the selected course. In fact, the whole barracks was agog when this machine of mine at last saw the light of day, after diligent labor, and was hung in the place of honor in our company gallery. That *proves* that military service is waste of time! It would never have entered my head in civilian life to think up anything so crazy.

About two days after this the Old Man came to see me again. I was just working on a still more highly developed type, the Mark III/C-4. He collected the bills from NARPA for colors, blocks and brushes from me, and said: "Moucha, leave these tanks now, in any case we haven't any more frames for them, or anywhere left to hang them, and do me a few good wall posters, will you? The battle for peace, and so on, eh? . . . A couple of actualities . . . colonialism, Africa, and all that."

And he walked off along the corridor, in the middle of the kind of pandemonium that always breaks out when some big shot is coming to visit, and thoughtfully studied the pictures of MY tanks as he went.

I showed the half-finished Mark III/C-4 behind the cupboard, and cold shivers ran down my spine when I thought what might happen if some general with eyes of steel also started thoughtfully studying my tanks. . . .

The whole garrison turned out on parade half an hour early the morning of the inspection, and plenty of the boys had gone so crazy with all this terrible uproar that even at assembly they were still polishing up their shoes with their handkerchiefs and wetting their pocket flaps and the points of their coat collars with spit, to make them stay straight. But I was thinking to myself that no flat pocket flaps and well-pressed coattails were going to save ME, the only thing that could save ME was if they didn't show the general around the quarters of the antitank company. But the antitank company and their quarters, thanks to my diligent and devoted work, were the pride of the whole group, and I knew only too well that they were sure to show them to him, they wouldn't for any money miss the chance of showing them to him, and even if he hadn't the slightest wish to see them, they'd drag him there against his will, like a bull to the slaughterhouse.

And then he arrived. He really had eyes like steel. He was the first authentic general I'd ever seen as close as that in my life, and the first one I'd ever had anything to do with, and I think he looked exactly as such a general is supposed to look. Immediately, as soon as he ambled out of the car, there began such a charade; first he stood back and waited, while all the majors and captains from the various companies marched up to report to the colonel, and then the colonel left them standing and marched up like a mechanical doll to the general, who all this time had been standing unobtrusively aside, looking like a pensioner out giving the dog an airing, and then the colonel repeated to him the whole rigmarole of reporting which all the commanding officers had been practicing for five days.

Then the general walked past the entire garrison right to the end, where the mine squad and the cooks were standing, and back again to the beginning, so that he could see everything, saluting all the way, and with us staring one after another into his eyes. Finally he halted there in the middle of the line, turned his belly toward us, and roared: "I salute you, comrades!"

And we roared back, as they'd drummed into us a million times: "Hurrah for our Comrade General!"

After that he spent about half an hour issuing a stream of commands, which the officers in turn handed down to one another; but we'd already been informed, of course, that when all this was finished we would have to march around the parade ground, and when we came to that bit of concrete in front of the staff building, where the general was now standing, we had to do a ceremonial slow march. So first the Old Man passed the word to Kubíček, and then Kubíček passed it on to us, and we began to stretch our legs in the approved manner. I was marching in the front rank, and if it hadn't been for those tanks of mine, so soon to explode into a world disaster, the whole thing would have looked to me like a scene from the film of *Fanfan the Tulip*. In the army you've always got to keep a careful watch on yourself, so as not to burst out laughing at moments like that. When you're looking straight at Kubíček's backside and stretched-out neck! I think it must be worst of all for a general, trying to keep from giggling even when he must want to more than anything. He's got a harder job than any comedian on the stage.

But it finished at last, and finally we were all standing to attention by our correctly half-opened lockers, in quarters, and the general paced from one to another, and said: "Hmmm, very nice!" or pointed a finger at some corner of a shirt that jutted a quarter of an inch too far out from the pile of folded clothing, and wagged his hand and shook his head weightily. Then he saw the first picture on the wall, and began to walk from one to another of them along the line. Evidently he was interested. Suddenly he turned to Karel Baštář, who was standing about two yards from me, and said: "And what types of enemy tank do you know?"

"Report your name," whispered the Old Man behind him, and Karel spoke up: "Private Baštář, Comrade General," but not a word more, because it's true we'd hung all those tanks up there, but otherwise we'd never studied or discussed them. The only person who could really tell anyone anything about them, out of the whole company, right up to Kubíček and the Old Man, was ME.

The Old Man was also beginning to get nervous, so he said quickly: "Comrade General means Western tanks, Baštář." And behind the general's back he stabbed a finger upwards at the wall. For just behind the general the Sherman was hanging. While the general himself was staring at the opposite wall, at my Ontos B-2.

"The Sherman, medium tank, weight thirty tons," said Karel, and the general went on studying my Ontos B-2.

"Continue, Private Baštář," said the Old Man amiably, and Karel read on: "One 75mm. cannon, one 12.7mm. machine gun, one 7.62mm. machine gun, speed up to thirty-four miles per hour, formerly also mounted with firearms of other types in various combinations, some having also a flame thrower . . . crew, five men." He coughed. "Private Baštář concluding, Comrade General."

The general looked at him and nodded his head.

"Excellent, excellent!" Then he turned toward the Old Man, and asked him: "Who painted these pictures for you?"

The Old Man paled slightly, he surely must have suspected there was something wrong; gradually he got the message, and started looking around for me.

"It was Private Moucha, Comrade General. . . ." His voice shook with anxiety, and although he was looking straight at me he couldn't find me, and rapped out: "Where are you, Private Moucha?"

I knew this was the finish, but there was nothing to do but to be a man, since you *are* a man, anyhow, and turn a proud forehead and an unmoved face to the thunderbolt. I took one pace forward and bellowed: "Private Moucha reporting! Here, Comrade General!"

The general looked at me, took a step or two toward me, and began to smooth down the flap of my breast pocket, which was sticking up. I waited to see if he would flatten it out for me with spit, but he didn't.

"Comrade Captain," he said then, slowly and quietly, and the Old Man made a leap like a lynx to present himself to view: "Yes, Comrade General?"

"Reward him!" said the general briskly, and stabbed a finger somewhere in the region of the top button of my blouse.

"I've already suggested to the battalion commander . . ." the Old Man started burbling eagerly—but the general made a motion with his hand that warned him to be quiet and keep his suggestions to the battalion commander to himself, because HE still had something to say. And the Old Man shut up like a clam.

"Keep up the good work, my boy," the general said to me. "What do you do in civilian life?"

"I'm a designer," I said, and the Old Man prompted me: "Comrade General!" So I repeated: "I'm a designer, Comrade General."

"I see, I see!" said the general, and looked us all over once more with his steely eyes. Then he called it a day, and left, with the Old Man a step behind him, naturally. He walked slowly to the stairs, and Corporal Angel, who was orderly officer that day, roared: "ATTENTION!" And when the general, naturally with our Old Man still one step behind, had gone down the stairs: "AT EASE! STAND EASY!"

They were gone, it was OVER, we closed up our lockers.

Expertise

"You devil, the LUCK you have!" the boys said to me, and slapped me on the back, as proud as punch that the general was so pleased with our company. "Boy, do you have all the LUCK!" It seemed to me that they were absolutely right.

The Mother of
the Regiment

The wicket beside the main gate hit him in the back just at the moment when he was buttoning his pocket on his documents after getting them checked. He heard the soldier and the two subalterns on duty there laugh, and he realized that from the moment he'd approached the entrance he had had some curious feeling of uncertainty, of something indefinite threatening him, tension, expectation, mockery, the trace of a smile on the faces of those fellows on the gate; or perhaps something even earlier than that, dating from the moment when he had been informed, although he hadn't been counting on anything of the kind, that he could simply: RUN AND CHANGE, AND HERE'S YOUR LEAVE PASS!

It was like the period before graduation, when everything had been put behind him, when he could afford to go placidly to bed without having to turn back in anxiety to take one more quick look into his books, on Marxism or any other subject. Quite simply, everything was now behind him, exactly like before graduation—though graduation had actually begun in some long-ago, lost moment when he had first learned to read and write by the look-and-say method, and later, when he had memorized his first chemical formula (he could still remember that it was K_2SO_3).

And it had continued steadily, and not only in the part of his life that was more or less official, but also in his ordinary life, through the experiences of learning to ride a bicycle, of first connecting a cable to the loudspeaker he had fixed up as an extension into the adjoining room at home, first kissing a girl, and first kissing, after some three months' acquaintance, his future wife. And just as with the formula, he could still remember the place in the park where that had happened, and then the moment when they had made up their minds to marry. They had been going out together then for three years, and this state simply could not be endured any longer; either they must live together, or separate for good. But they were accustomed to each other by that time, though they still had not slept together; for she was afraid, and he was firmly convinced that this abstention was an essential part of the image of an honorable man. In the end they managed to convince their parents that it was possible for people to marry, even without being what they called READY FOR IT; for after all they were their parents, and there was really no course left open to them but to be convinced.

Marcela was in her last year at the Academy of Musical and Dramatic Arts, and he had still two years of school ahead of him. But they were modest in their demands, and did not get used to living in a different way even later, when Marcela was already earning a salary, and Peter was getting 400 crowns a month from his mother, as well as his scholarship. Everything really went VERY WELL. She was allotted to a post in Prague—a piece of luck they hadn't even expected, but apparently she was in good odor with those who determined these things—and her mother handed over to them part of her apartment. So they had a home, even though it never was really home to him, for home is where one does not feel oneself a guest. Now they were ADULTS, the kind of adults who speak in deep voices, saying: THIS IS MY WIFE. Words like: MARRIAGE, WE'VE PAID THE RENT, ELECTRICITY and GAS, and such, belong absolutely to the adult world. He had, then, a home, though he never got used to the furniture with which that home was filled. He himself had received a piano from his mother, so he used to say jokingly that he had contributed two items to the inventory. For this was Marcela's home, full of her relations and her furniture, which was alien to him. But he LOVED her, and he knew that by comparison with that everything else was VALUELESS; for that was how people wrote in the books he read, and he believed them, and tried to arrange his life and affairs on the lines they indicated. However many things there were in this world, not one of them was good enough for Marcela, and for the life they had wanted to live together when they began, when they had hope and faith, and were eighteen, nineteen, twenty years old. He had been given a piano, and he knew that it was a genuine gift, something that would be missed by the giver and must be made up to her somehow, for his mother must be well aware that she would probably never again be able to afford a new instrument. She herself had taught him to play on it. But for Marcela . . . and as a matter of fact, the piano was the very thing that had successfully brought them together, when they had met at an evening party of all their former fellow pupils. Peter had volunteered to Marcela: "If you like, I'll play you 'Rhapsody in Blue.'" He didn't even know why he made the offer; perhaps it was simply because he had somehow contrived to fall out with a girl named Jana, the previous night, and Jana was present at the party among the rest. However, Marcela did like. In fact it gave her great pleasure, because everybody was looking on, and everybody knew that he was playing it for her. At that time she had already been accepted at the Academy of Musical and Dramatic Arts, and she loved to hear people say that she was going to be an actress, for she didn't have really sufficient confidence in herself. She was going into the puppet theatre, and she was not sure whether that was her real thing, and what she most wanted; but it seemed, on the whole, to be easy, since there existed for it—though she found that out only later—few criteria, and still fewer people who knew what those criteria should be.

Peter finished his playing, and then they went to dance. He asked her—it was shortly before the holidays—whether he might send her a postcard. He didn't really know why he said it, but he did; it fulfilled his conception of the proper way for people to get acquainted, and in any case he had to find something to say. Just as he could not imagine them living any other way than in an apartment house with a brass door latch and turn-of-the-century decorations around the entrance; even though he knew that in the event they would find themselves living in a quite different and incomprehensible world, of which he was a little afraid, because there the values to which he was accustomed were no longer valid: the values of good marks, gained by diligent studying and constant attention, marks which he affected to pass over with a wave of his hand, though in reality they had absorbed a considerable part of his life, and he was proud of them.

But after that encounter everything somehow got into motion; and in the end he became adult because he was THE HUSBAND of the girl to whom he had played "Rhapsody in Blue" that first evening. (And now he no longer believed that it had happened by chance.) They had their own four walls, they bought the first few essential things together, and the time of his graduation came. He was still playing the piano to her regularly. He got a special reward for good—indeed excellent—results in his studies, and they bought a vacuum cleaner with it. They also wanted to have a short holiday, for he had caught cold and contracted influenza. But then it turned out that he would have to go for his military service. He started his first job—he, too, got a lucky allocation in Prague—and immediately lost some of his illusions. Then he joined his regiment and lost still more. He found himself in a world with which he was willing to come to terms, and this also was a world about which much had been written in books, though such a different one. Here, too, common values held good; and here, too, they were repudiated by drunks, gamblers and bad characters. But as soon as a man grasped the essentials he could manage this as he had managed everything that had accompanied him through life so far. Peter also managed it. As he was not the most efficient of recruits physically, and was pigeonholed accordingly, he never got to know the joys of autumn exercises in muddy yellow puddles, and the saturated plough lands that from time immemorial, in the view of instructors, have been ideally suited to the novice soldier's first attempts at stealthy approach, entrenching, and chemical training.

He got through by dint of regular training, and found his place with the technicians, among the locators, radio stations and telecommunications instruments; here he had qualifications, and these were things he understood. He was not too happy to be serving so far away, but it had never been his habit to rebel vainly against things which he was convinced were fated. He got used to new values, and accepted without protest what even the regulations described as "the hardships of military service," though he did not take those sentiments about the duty of accepting hardships manfully quite literally. But he knew that you can't stop an express train with your foot. He took night duty gladly, which made him mildly popular; but he did it merely because at night he could telephone Marcela without being disturbed. And that in turn enabled him to ignore the hints to which he was often obliged to listen, when there was talk about wives and girl friends at home, who, it was granted, hadn't forgotten, but who equally certainly were not suffering from loneliness. . . .

At night he could listen to the radio, too, and through the day, thanks to night duty, he was spared small inconveniences like carrying coal, stoking, collecting ashes, and hundreds of other chores that involved a degree of discomfort.

And during the nights spent at the teleprinter switchboard or the locator screen he began to think about things which had never occurred to him before. To tell the truth, many of these things he understood only up to a certain point, after which they lost coherence for him, and there remained only an enumeration of various factors, about which he was certain that somewhere they connected and made sense, but he could never clearly determine how or where, the vital point was too securely hidden. There were things which certain people valued, and which were yet a matter of complete indifference to others. Occasionally something hitherto unknown and undiscoverable burst suddenly to the surface of his mind, and then he was always startled. Somewhere here, too, there was a connection with Marcela, who was helping to produce puppet plays, something he had originally thought of as belonging among the toys and hobbies of elderly gentlemen, or the occupations found suitable for those Pioneer groups not yet experienced enough for model-making or the Michurin circle. Something like being able to draw a horse in a single line. Yet suddenly this art was capable of providing a living for any number of mature people, who only a few years ago would never have been able to set out into the world with such genial simplicities as Špejbl and Hurvínek, or Mickey Mouse. He had gotten used to this in the end, and he pigeonholed the subject among debates on music and art generally, where he had ranged all such things from the moment he discovered that one can talk quite well even about a film one has never seen, without anyone involved in the discussion being aware of the fact. When he listened to Beethoven or César Franck he didn't need any definition to help him, he loved music just as it was, and needed no aids to its understanding; but it seemed that in addition to listening to all such things, everybody felt the need to talk about them. So he had provided himself with remarks like those he used when discussing films he had never seen in his life. He had begun to think all this very mysterious; for here again things lost their cohesion. There was this incomprehensible fact, that there existed people who had never been required to study so long and so laboriously, who had never known the misgivings and tension that could be exorcised only in the moment of meeting one's colleagues in corridor and foyer, completed index in hand, and replying to their questions with: "They've given me a B!" People who had never experienced anything of the kind, never needed to drudge away long days (and nights) on subjects which actually were not in the least interesting, never sweated away a single hour over Marxism, or learned to understand it in a different sense every time the doctrine changed. And yet all these people, who had never had to tremble for their work allocations, and who were in every way immune from most of his worries, ended up earning as much as he did, or even more, and obviously, where many things in life were concerned, they also knew their way around a good deal better than he did.

Perhaps this is how it happened that he began to esteem Marcela; for originally, of course, before they married, it had been mainly an ordinary, unfulfilled eroticism which had bound him to her. And these were the things which were all there within him, even though he could not think of them all in the same moment, when the metal wicket hit him in the back.

What did occur to him on the spot was simply that they didn't like him, that this little incident at the gate had been laid as a trap purposely for him; and inwardly he admitted candidly that they had some reason for this. Such duties as they were now performing, for instance, did not apply to him; but he could hardly help it that he had had tuberculosis as a child—he remembered the dark X-ray room, and his mother's anxious eyes as she stood behind the doctor, peering with him into her son's body—and that by pure luck life had placed him in another sphere from theirs, where circumstances happened to be more comfortable. But he rejected the idea of a personal dislike at once. It had been an ordinary joke; the wire spring that operated the wicket was there ready and waiting for everyone, as was the soldier who had held the gate with a bow the instant before he let it swing at Peter's back.

And now he was sure that the tension and uncertainty he had felt on his way to the gate, and all this ferment within him, stemmed chiefly from this leave pass dropped from heaven into his hands; for though he had certainly gotten a commendation for maintaining communications in unusually difficult circumstances, the person who had actually obtained this leave pass for him was the Mother of the Regiment.

This was the nickname of a certain staff sergeant, the former wife of one of the pilots from Transport Command, who was an excellent fellow (a pilot can hardly allow himself to be anything less than an excellent fellow), but whom she had nevertheless divorced. He still came now and again to invite her out for coffee or to dinner, or something like that. The Mother of the Regiment worked now in the secret archives, but as she belonged to the airfield personnel she appeared regularly at the communications center or the central switchboard. She knew that Peter's wife was named Marcela, and much more, besides, for it is hard to keep silent when you have someone to talk to and something to talk about. She was a handsome woman, who dyed her hair blonde to suit her uniform. Together they made fun of their own reputations, and sometimes, too, of the aide to the Chief of Staff for Mobilization, who for some time now had been paying her regular visits in her office, with a packet of Colombian coffee in the pocket of his tunic.

The Mother of the Regiment was named Jana. She could not compare in any way with Marcela, of course, and clearly she did not try; but regularly she listened to stories of how Peter planned to have a child with Marcela as soon as he got home after his army service. A girl, probably, and she was going to be christened Lucie.

Once, too, she had provided him with an opportunity to talk about the girl whose name had also happened to be Jana (now no more than a memory, which had nothing to do with Marcela), with whom he had once gone to a movie, and whom he had met afterwards on a couple of occasions. But it hadn't turned out quite to his taste, for she had known nothing about houses with turn-of-the-century decorations; so it had ended in "Rhapsody in Blue," played for quite a different girl, and in this case the right girl.

Recently, after his commendation, coming as it had at the end of exercises, which was reason enough for more than one celebration, there'd been one more opportunity for a conversation, but Jana, the Mother of the Regiment, had surprised him by simply asking how long it was now since he and Marcela had seen each other. And later the same question had been put to him by his platoon commander, and finally by the Chief of Staff.

Once, when he had first come here, and long before he had realized what role the pilot played with his visits to her, or what was going on with the aide to the Chief of Staff for Mobilization, Peter had wanted to pay Jana a compliment, and made use of one which he knew and had used on Marcela. Forgetting, of course, that Jana had never learned Latin or studied mythology, he called her "The ox-eyed Hera!" With an expression of profound respect, naturally. He would have liked to develop the theme somehow by way of explanation, although the Mother of the Regiment had shown no particular signs of taking offense; she knew that a compliment can be present even in something which doesn't appear to be one at all, and she was accustomed to receiving compliments. But he began to suspect her of trying to seduce him, and as a result he wrote Marcela several letters in rather more passionate terms than usual. Only later did he understand that the pilot was her husband, that although they were divorced they felt no animosity against each other, but were something like two friendly in-laws together. And now, only very shortly before the wicket gate hit him in the back, he had been informed that he had a leave pass, and that the pilot who was going to fly him home to Prague in the old Dakota would be none other than the former husband of the Mother of the Regiment.

He would have liked to swear when the gate struck him, but he realized that that would be exactly what the orderly and the soldiers, amusing themselves and passing the time away thus on their boring duty, wanted him to do, so he contented himself with saying privately his favorite: "You damn bastards!"—for he was not literary when talking to himself—and adding aloud: "A very good trick, too!" He buttoned his pocket and straightened his lapels. He had home before him, and what was more, his first trip by air. Home, that meant the place where a man belongs, and not just because he had a piano there. Getting married was something like joining a party, something that delivered a man from solitude and gave him perspectives which one way or another he must maintain. It meant, above all, that A MAN NEVER AGAIN BELONGED TO HIMSELF ALONE. It was the subtitle to all the other mottoes: TWO CAN LIVE BETTER THAN ONE, and A GRIEF SHARED IS A GRIEF HALVED,

A JOY SHARED IS A JOY DOUBLED. But here again there was a point at which cohesion was lost. The Party, to which he now also belonged, after a period as a candidate, had meant at school, first and foremost, a means of acquiring a better work location permit, an acquaintance with the professors, the privilege of sitting at the same table with them and addressing them in familiar terms of friendship, and the advantage of getting any problems that might crop up settled at first hand. Then, and only then, was there time to consider those things for which people ought to have been entering school, those things, indeed, for which they claimed that they were entering it. What with the Union of Youth, and all that, somehow the important things were always put off altogether or rushed through, and far too much attention and energy was devoted to trivialities. He had racked his brains over this. He was ambitious to get on, of course, for Marcela's sake, but he was also ambitious to act as an honest man. He had known a few people who could change their convictions as fast as the wind changed. But after a year, even marriage looked rather different from what doctrine would prescribe, supposing any perfect doctrine existed for marriage. In the end he came to terms with it; it was something of importance to him, but clearly it was possible to regulate life only up to the point to which coherence could be traced, where perhaps it was even possible to stop an express train with your foot.

He was looking forward to his first flight. He wouldn't have to be bumped around for ten or twelve hours in a train, and all that time saved would be added to the time he could spend living with and loving his wife Marcela, who was young and pretty, who had caused a sensation in the barracks when she came to visit him in the autumn, bringing him security and everything else he found essential to life. It WAS ESSENTIAL TO HAVE SOMEONE TO THINK OF. He had heard more than enough about girls who were beloved and necessary, and had left behind them a few letters, and then only a desert of bitterness, such bitterness that when they reflected upon it men turned aside and spat, or gnawed wordlessly at a straw or a match stick, plunging their hands into their pockets and shrugging their shoulders, with a smile which was meant to indicate indifference to the whole affair. Everyone knew the indifference was assumed, but everyone accepted it at its face value. He was glad that he was going to arrive home by air, fly home to Marcela and surprise her; he was glad that he had someone like Marcela waiting for him—though that SOMEONE LIKE was a silly phrase, because NOBODY else could wait as loyally as she.

When it came to the point there were some good boys here, (at this moment he was full of benevolence), good boys who, even without any graduation, had earned more than he when they were working as drivers of diggers and bulldozers, railwaymen pickax wielders, layers of concrete, and saxophone players. Most of them knew nothing about César Franck, not even the saxophonist, and never played Janáček or even "Rhapsody in Blue" to wives like Marcela before going to bed. And although they were forever breaking out into some rhythm or other, they could never remember any name except Armstrong or Duke Ellington, and even those they got from newspaper photographs or phonograph records, whereas he could discourse on bebop, cool style, and much besides, and talk of Dizzie Gillespie and Ella Fitzgerald, and conduct a fluent conversation about them, too. It might be thought, of course, that this was hardly something one actually needed for living, yet it belonged to his life as surely as quadratic equations or lectures on sex hygiene.

Here, of course, all these things came to an end. This was the world of Jana, who was called the Mother of the Regiment, who got on well with her divorced husband (perhaps because he was divorced), who had arranged for Peter to be flown home, and who was also, to a large degree, responsible for that leave pass—the degree to which the aide to the Chief of Staff for Mobilization had not been actually obliged to pass on the word she had spoken in his ear to the platoon commander. She had told Peter to be at the airfield by three o'clock; and this had even saved him 100 crowns for train fare. It was kind, and he was grateful to her, even if she was known as the Mother of the Regiment. He had said thank you to her for his flight home, and she had said to him:

"That's all right, ask me out for coffee some time." But "some time" could also mean NEVER. He knew her, he knew how she talked to the aide from Mobilization, and it could equally well really mean SOME TIME. But the main thing was that it had enabled him to be with Marcela, so he answered: "Gladly!"

It occurred to him to wonder whether half of what they said about her was true. In his opinion they talked a good deal of slander about her, as indeed they did about women in general, gossiping idly before they went to sleep. . . . And Jana was handsome. Once he had heard her say that men are all cowards, since they're attracted by striking and beautiful women (she was speaking of making love), but devote themselves much more to the plainer and less striking, where they're more assured of success. She had also asked him, once, if he knew anybody at school with the initials K.H. But he didn't, and after that nothing more had been said.

It was two o'clock, and by this time he had reached the bus stop. He knew that Number Six went to the airfield, and after a while a Number Six actually came along. At the airfield he passed by the civilian entrance and went to the barrier pole, not striped here, as was usual, but battered and rusty, made of iron tubing with a complicated counterbalance arrangement with pulleys and levers. Behind it a captain in dress uniform and airman's cap was pacing impatiently, looking a little like a motorist in his Sunday best. As soon as he caught sight of Peter he waved a hand imperiously: "Jana—my wife—sent you, didn't she?"

"Yes," said Peter. He noticed at once that there was a plane already rolled out on the tarmac.

"Quickly!" said the captain. "Come on, move, man!" It seemed to Peter that he ought to have found something more to say, but it was evident that the captain was not particularly interested. They ran together to the Dakota. It dawned on him that perhaps he should have sent Marcela a telegram. They had an agreement, Marcela could have got someone to take her place at the performance if she had been expecting him, but it was no use thinking about that, he couldn't do anything about it now.

The captain closed and secured the door. Peter said in embarrassment: "I'm so sorry, I was delayed. . . ." But no excuse occurred to him, it had simply happened so, he had arrived at about two minutes past three, no help for it. Here it was no good thinking up trolleys fallen from their cables, or buses turning from their routes. That's the kind of thing we cook up in school, before we're adult. In any case there were no streetcars in this town.

"Don't make a song and dance about it," said the captain, and strode with long, reverberant steps up to his place in the forward cabin, whistling "St. Louis Blues." He looked like a good fellow, and plainly so he was (for a pilot would find it hard to allow himself to be anything less than a good fellow!). Peter went after him, and sat down in some agitation. It was a military machine, and the seats resembled aluminium chamber pots, because they were intended for men wearing parachutes. There was a general sitting there, with a briefcase which had once been yellow, and a major in a three-quarter-length field coat with a fur collar. Peter didn't know whether he ought to salute them, or how to do it, since he was already seated. The general and the major took stock of him.

"Going home?" asked the general.

"Yes, Comrade General," he said, rising.

"Sit down, sit down!" said the general, nodding his head.

Peter sat down again. The plane was already in motion; it was an informal flight, and the door into the pilot's cabin was not closed, so that the crew and their instruments were visible. They stopped on the edge of the runway, the motors roared ever more intensely, filling everybody and everything with their vibration. Nobody could any longer hear what the captain and former husband of the Mother of the Regiment was whistling, but now they knew by the way his mouth moved that he was speaking. But as only the crew were on the internal telephone, nobody overheard: "I reckon I'm carrying Jana's new *amant* for her." Nobody in the main cabin heard, but they all saw how the navigator leaned to look over his shoulder.

At last they moved from the edge of the runway, as the order was given from the tower; it was a solemn moment. The general groped in his briefcase and made a conspiratorial face, then drew out a flat bottle with a celebrated label, poured a drink for the major, and offered one to Peter. Then he himself drank. The whisky burned Peter's mouth, he was not used to it; he neither drank nor smoked, it had always seemed queer to him that there were people who needed such things. He and Marcela. . . . The general made a face at him. He recalled hearing stories about some general who ordered the soldiers who came to baby-sit, when he wanted to take his wife out dancing in the evenings, to take off their boots; and he thought to himself that this must be the man. He tried to imagine it, but he couldn't, there are some things which simply cannot exist, a minister in ceremonial dress riding a bicycle, or a general who ordered soldiers to take off their boots. It even occurred to him to wonder whether a general of a Socialist army could drink whisky, and without any soda at that, but evidently the answer was yes, he could. It came into his mind that he had not seen Marcela for exactly eighty-five days, and he told himself that he would compose a poem for the occasion, though he had never composed one in his life so far; but for that matter he had never in his life, until now, tipped a shot of whisky down his throat.

The general winked at him again, for Peter was glowing with the ardor of his mood, and the general probably attributed it to his bottle of whisky, still practically full. But Peter had not the least idea how one should respond to a general's wink; after all, he was young, younger than Marcela, he had started school a year earlier, and she had lost a year when she was ill. HE COULDN'T KNOW EVERYTHING—a sentiment he considered among his better sayings, along with that: I GOT WRITTEN INTO THE INVENTORY ALONG WITH THE PIANO.

But the general said to the major: "It's terrible, these boys nowadays can't take anything!" And the major, of course, agreed, for the general was celebrated not only for making soldiers take off their boots in his house (he did it for the sake of the parquet floors), but also for enjoying embarrassing as many people as possible. For instance, at all the ceremonious lunches and dinners he had to take part in as a general, he always ate poultry with knife and fork, and therefore all the others had to do the same, or at the very least all the lieutenant-colonels and majors who were sitting at the same table. The major was thinking of this as the general asked Peter: "Are you married?"

Peter agreed that he was, and the general nodded his head and poured another shot for everybody, as though that followed logically from the admission.

At this same hour the Mother of the Regiment was already at home. They did not let the wicket hit her in the back. Now she was sitting and reading, for the last time, a letter which had come into her hands half-ungummed. Her attention had been caught by the handwriting, so different from Marcela's, with which she was familiar. In the letter someone who signed himself with the initials K.H. informed Peter, with a wealth of detail, that his wife was being unfaithful to him. She checked by her watch whether the telegram she had sent would arrive in time to forestall any unforeseen catastrophe, scratched her head lightly, and looked in the mirror, thinking: I SHALL HAVE TO GET BUSY WITH THE PEROXIDE AGAIN. She went into the bathroom, lit the hot-water heater and turned the water on in the bath. Then she held the letter to the flame, and let it burn away completely into ash.

Afterwards she lit a cigarette without a filter, took a look to see how long it would be before the bath was full, felt the central heating, closed a thirty-year-old detective novel that lay spine up on the table, took off her uniform and hung it in the wardrobe built into the wall. Over the telephone she booked a place in some establishment, the director of which she addressed as Joe, tested the heat of the water, took a look at herself in the mirror to see how she looked without her clothes, and said in an undertone: "Ah, well, that's education for you!" And it occurred to her that here in her dwelling it was rather empty.

Then she turned off the hot-water heater, closed the door and discarded her cigarette. The holder she laid aside among her combs, perfumes and brushes.

Mood Indigo:
Extracurricular Thoughts Between Seven and Nine A.M.

If you ask me, this is one thing in which most people are absolutely the same. Oh, I know plenty of stories of men of the world, and noble ladies with the hearts of angels. And I also know that most people take very good care when they open their mouths, and try to talk as if their lips had never been soiled by a single word that would have to be printed in dots in the newspapers, or even in books for children, and to look as though they've never in their lives called their wives bitches. That's civilization. Me, too, I always say to people: "Please," and "You've been very kind," and "Oh, that's awfully sweet of you!"; and I go to listen to Tchaikovsky, or to join in discussions about Tchaikovsky and Rachmaninoff. But inside me I'm exactly the same as that deliveryman with the coal cart, whose mare stepped on his foot this morning in the street where I live.

He bellowed: "You cow!"—although it was a mare. "I'll kick your teeth in till your guts drop out!" And he took the whip from a hole in the floor of the cart, and began to beat the horse with the stock of it, like a kulak beating the collective cows in some social realistic literature from my school days.

I've got a reader at home that I inherited from my elder sister, and there she had all the photographs with Masaryk, Beneš,

Štefaník and the legionnaires, all stuck in from the time of the Protectorate, but this reader is also full of moral tales about misused dogs and horses and tortured cats, and in every case there's always some good little Frank or Tony who calls a policeman, so that everything turns out happily, at least for the horses and dogs involved.

But in our street there was never any policeman in sight, and even if there had been, I would have had to have a good deal more courage than I've got, to dare to speak to him, so all I did was go up to this carter who was beating the mare with the stock of his whip, and I had a twenty-crown bill ready in my hand, and I said to him: "Listen, do stop beating the horse now, please," and I stuck the bill in his hand. "Here, this is for you!" As luck would have it, it was just after payday, so I could afford to do it. Twenty crowns isn't really much money, and I so terribly wanted to do something to help that horse.

But the coalman went on hammering the mare, who was plunging and weaving between the shafts, and all he did was stick my twenty crowns into his pocket, and nod at me, and say: "Just a minute, ma'am, till I even up accounts with this bitch, then I shall be able to attend to you."

Only then it occurred to him that he really ought to look how much he'd gotten, so he hauled out the bill again and stopped hitting the mare, because my twenty crowns made such an impression on him.

"If it's coke you're needing, then I'm sorry to say it's no use, ma'am," he said, sticking the money back into his pocket, "but with briquettes we might come to some arrangement, or if you prefer I've got some best nuts here." And he groped with one hand inside the cart, pulled out four or five bits of some repulsive coal, and held them out in front of me on his palm. "There, look at them, ain't that beautiful coal?"

"Oh, it isn't that," I said, and I was thinking how lucky I was to have that gas heating in my tiny apartment, after all, just as I was lucky to have an apartment at all. "I don't want any coal, I just felt sorry for the horse." And then I went on, because who knows what a carter like that may say to you? And anyhow, who can be sure when the next bus will be running, and which route, and at a quarter to eight I had to be at the Hotel Krach to pick up forty miners' children from Wales, and one elderly lady who was looking after them, and making sure they didn't come to any physical or moral harm after traveling all that way. She always called me LITTLE BABY. She wore an impossible black straw hat, a whole armory of silver chains around her neck, her wrists and even her waist, and looked rather like some medieval penitent from some odd sect, only I don't think penitents used to have such a thick deposit of make-up on their faces, and I doubt if they wore wigs.

When she called me LITTLE BABY in some place where there weren't any Czech people around to hear, I used to smile at her sweetly (at least that was something I'd learned how to do!) and say straight into her face—in Czech, of course—: "And hell and blast and shit to you, madame! I'll kick you in the ass, you silly old bitch!" and other things like that. Not that I had any intention of insulting her—and of course I never actually did kick her in the ass. I'd known her son, too, he was a clergyman, and had been here as leader of a party from California two years previously. I was only saying to her the sort of things one always says to foreigners, things which unfortunately I can't allow myself to say among normal people, although it would be a HUGE relief to me if I could.

I started my periods at eleven, at fifteen I had well-developed breasts, at nineteen I could speak English well, and at twenty a boy from the university, whom I idolized, and with whom I'd spent three months freezing in the streets, and drunk a dreadful number of dreadfully bad cups of coffee in still more dreadful inns, called me a whore, just because it so happened I was no longer a virgin, owing to one accident in a Young Pioneer camp —and maybe two other similar accidents from a school in Roguesville, where I taught for a year before I managed to get this job as guide and courier. And the same year, only in the summer so that there was no freezing involved this time, one beautifully built and exquisitely stupid swimming instructor, who taught the ladies water-skiing at Karlovy Vary, wrote me off as a bluestocking, but absolutely blue, with whom no reasonable man could possibly experience anything enjoyable. Not that he seemed to me any brighter after that, but at the time when he said it those words still meant something to me.

When the foreign tourist traffic came to be respected and valued, and I began to interpret, it was a real stroke of luck for me—like winning the lottery. It was a great gain for a girl who, only a short time previously, had been allowed only to go and teach in a wretched village in the back of beyond, and even that with a very unfavorable report, and only after three appeals to the presidential office had at last been allowed to enter the university. Just a few years ago I'd had to take care of the mongoloid son of the chairman of the local District Committee. Naturally, out of all the teachers, it would have to be me, I was his class teacher, too! And if he hadn't done well in his examinations, all my hopes would have gone down the drain. At the same time, of course, it's equally true that I should never have been told I was a whore, or kept the pollen of my innocence for that idiot whom I loved as only a twenty-year-old can love, or frozen in the streets with him, or drunk disgusting coffee because we had no money for anything better. And I shouldn't have learned that I'm a bluestocking, either, from that other idiot with whom I slept out of pure pity, I was so sorry for him, such a good-looking man and such an utter idiot. In fact, most probably, I shouldn't have experienced a great many things, I should just have gone on teaching in Roguesville, and married the worthy headmaster there, an eccentric who played the violin and kept bees, and led an amateur group of cooperators. Now, instead of that, I usually had a Mexican parliamentary delegation around my neck, since I'd managed to learn Spanish as well, or this old dame with the children from Wales.

The name of this village wasn't really Roguesville, but something quite different, but I always called it Roguesville and always shall. The only man I had anything to do with there apart from the headmaster, was the assistant master in our school, who was a bachelor. He was an odd case, because he was the kind of teacher who went out with the children to collect old paper, or healing herbs, and took part in the ceremony of presenting scarfs to the Young Pioneers, and other unpopular chores, and yet with all this, and even when they were always holding him up as an example, still somehow he wasn't repulsive. A sort of aging Youth Union star, who'd never noticed that in his enthusiasm he'd let ten years slip away from under his feet, and grown a belly, but nothing else. In the end, of course, he ran wild and fell in love with the cow-woman in the local agricultural cooperative, a heroine of Socialist work, a clumsy lump with a turned-up nose, a homemade blonde with a patchy bleach job and a badly painted mouth which was always getting smudged and coloring her teeth pink. They say you can live anywhere, and I suppose there really are people of some kind living everywhere, that's true. But if they've got nobody to sleep with and nothing to eat (or nothing they'd like to eat), and nowhere to live (or at least nowhere to live as they'd like to live), then they should get out of it and refuse to go on living anywhere. This teacher—his name was Ladislav—found himself a bleached blonde who poured water into the milk to make it go further, and got a medal for it, too. And I had no success with him, but I got away from that hole at the back of beyond, and went to the university, thanks to the fact that that idiot son of the local chairman passed his exams, and moved up, and another unlucky teacher had him around his neck. Which was just the same, I suppose, as if I'd poured water into the milk, too. So once again I could hope for everything possible in the world. That was when I thought up a beautiful sentence about love for Ladislav, who was absolutely infatuated with that agricultural cooperative beauty queen of his, and I still use it today, when Ladislav, and Roguesville, and the collection of medicinal herbs, and the local chairman's mongolian child are all vanished into the past: a beautiful epitaph:

> He loved her so much
> that he went to masturbate on her grave.

At the university there were hordes of people, new people, who had gotten in there as the result of various interviews and such, and I noticed that most of them were there because they hoped to master the art of saying "Thank you!" and "I'm so happy to have made your acquaintance," and of holding their own in discussions about Tchaikovsky, and other stupidities. Maybe some of them even hoped they might get around to learning to think that way, just as I did when I was little, and my parents took me to acquire a good child's social education from a serious-minded druggist, whose turnover of sales would have dropped if he'd ever stooped to unsocial behavior. Some had probably come there for the same reasons as I, out of hope, and because it was the only way of escape they had from some Roguesville or other. Because the whole thing was rather like spending a hundred dollars to gain ten, or tossing a ten-pound shot a terribly long way—something we know quite well has no real LUSTER, the lasting kind that can't be compromised and won't let you down, but still is always better than jumping down an elevator shaft. And a good deal better than brooding over how terribly many things in this world have no luster, and how our difficulties arise from the fact that we ever got ourselves born at all, even more because we got ourselves born into a Great Age, and *then* going and jumping down an elevator shaft. That's if you're lucky enough to live in a house that has an elevator.

The Welsh children, along with this old dame straight out of a novel by Dickens or Walter Scott, had already been with me to visit Lidice, Karlštejn, and Saint Vitus' cathedral in Prague, including the royal treasury and the tombs of the Czech kings. Today we were going to Karlovy Vary, and all around the spas in that region with the exception of Jachymov, which by this time had pretty well lost its reputation as a spa. I had already conducted over the same route a party of young workers from Finland, some Rumanian officials, a Mexican parliamentary delegation, which got exuberantly tight there, and a YWCA party from California, led by Frank, the son of this same LITTLE BABY woman draped in chains. And Frank was the pastor of some church or other.

A lot of us from school went into interpreting; there was more interest in that than in going for practical experience in the scientific institutes. Many of the girls got things to wear and to eat from the foreigners they escorted, and plenty of other people held it against them, because they themselves hadn't got these things, and couldn't get them for any money in our country. Plenty of the girls even slept with these foreigners—but in the first place, the world's got big eyes, even here, in fact maybe bigger than anywhere else. And in the second place—well, for God's sake, try it! Just you try it! Try trailing around everywhere possible with somebody for fourteen days. Wear yourself out with buses and hotels, and end up hoping desperately that you'll NEVER see this fellow again. As indeed you never will, any more than you're ever likely to see that cross on the mountain in Rio de Janeiro. Fourteen days, and you'll either have had more than enough of him, and be glad you're never going to see him again, and even glad that you never want to see him again. Or else you'll be sitting, your last evening, in some hotel foyer with bulging walls, marble decorations of genuine plaster, and cardboard posters of young ladies from Air France, knowing that if you don't sleep with him tonight, then you'll never be able to do it, NEVER, and you'll be left with an empty place somewhere inside you after he's gone, and this night will be a dreadful regret to you at judgment day. WHAT IF HE'S THE RIGHT ONE? There are very few men who don't look like the right one, the minute you begin to feel you want to go to bed with them, THOUGH NOT AFTERWARDS. But *before* you do it almost every one of them has that look, as soon as you begin seriously considering such action. And you know that these waiters and porters, and all the rest of them, who look upon you simply as a prostitute selling herself for Tuzex[1] vouchers and nylons and leather costumes and

1 Tuzex is the Czechoslovak trading organization which sells goods and services only for foreign currencies. As the Tuzex stock goods, both home-produced and imported, of better quality than elsewhere, or even unobtainable else-

similar unimportant but enviable trifles, are in any case never going to believe, any more than anyone else will, that maybe you never slept with him after all. Whether you do it or whether you don't, that's what they'll call you, and that's what they'll broadcast about you.

So in the end you take a deep breath and walk out of that foyer with him, because if by any chance he should really be the right one—and you never can tell in advance—then this at last is something that really has LUSTER. These are thoughts women probably ought not to have, I suppose, but I know plenty who do have them, and not one of them could be spotted as a prostitute by the first idiot who happened along, because they're not as stupid as I am, going and blurting out something about myself in a rush of emotion and honesty. And the second idiot who happened along decidedly wouldn't be able to call them bluestockings, because they wouldn't sleep with him.

The son of this old woman who was now waiting for me with the children at the Hotel Krach had looked, at the very first glance, like a man quite good enough to make a woman want to sleep with him, even if he was a clergyman, and in charge of twenty-two twenty-year-old YWCA girls. In fact he was a man with whom most women in our country would like to have a child, and I can tell you he was the very first one in all those delegations and tourist groups I'd ever had anything to do with, who could make me feel as if *I* wouldn't mind having one. But I'd usually drawn nothing but ancient biddies like his mother, or paunchy granddads from parliamentary delegations, so that I spent a lot of time smiling into their eyes and saying those rude words. Not that I wanted to insult them. Most of them were REALLY VERY SWEET ladies and DELIGHTFUL gentlemen, but somehow with them I always wanted to say "Shit!" Maybe it's because they all call me LITTLE BABY, and other LITTLE things, or the mood I seem to arouse in them; and also, of course,

---

where, naturally money vouchers which are exchangeable there are eagerly sought after by Czechoslovak citizens, and foreign tourists are in a position to provide them. *Editor's note.*

they're just the kind of people in front of whom I can't even say a word like "brassiere" in their own language. Not that that's such an outstandingly good word, of course. Perhaps it's partly because I've got all my own troubles, too, which are not and never will be their troubles; and then, of course, there's also the fact that I'm utterly spoiled and cynical, as my mother says, and all the nice trips go to the girls who know how to fawn around the chief in the office and make themselves pleasant to him, though he's nothing but an old frontier guard, and a pig at that. So I talk to myself, for the same reasons that make that whore in *The Three Penny Opera* sing her song about the three-master:

By noontime the dock is all swarming with men
Coming off of that ghostly freighter;
They're moving in the shadows where no one can see
And they're chaining up people and bringing them to me,
Asking me, "Kill them now, or later?"
Asking me, "Kill them now, or later?"

When I say those rude words at the right place and in the right intonation, that's the same thing, only a little shorter. In any case, you can be sure you're not going to get the offer of a pirate today, even if you were like Jenny. More likely some tepid film director or an idiotic athlete. And he'll be as proud of you as of a car that gives him thirty to the gallon and does a hundred! I know!

I reached the hotel, and the bus driver was already waiting for us. The children from Wales were breakfasting on very light coffee with croissants and jam, and it still seemed as queer to them as when they had their first breakfast in our country, though they'd been here ten days now. The old girl was also drinking light coffee, and standing by her plate was a champagne glass smeared with egg, and on the whiskers around her mouth she had egg marks as well as powder and make-up. The minute I'd said hello it began to pour out of her: "Ah, here's our BABY. Good morning, BABY, I've missed you! How well you look today,

CHILD." And after a minute, when she'd finished her ten or twelve rolls and four cups of coffee with cream, and just as I was offering her the first series of smiling, whispered "shits": "I think it's going to be really beautiful weather today. I'm sure everybody always has good luck with you, BABY." She beamed at me, showing her false teeth in a bountiful grin, complete with croissant crumbs, and I laughed and said: "But it's all thanks to you, madame!"

What I was remembering was the good luck her son Frank had had with me—incidentally I'd like to know what devil transported an English clergyman into a YWCA in California!—and also, and in particular, the good luck I'd had with him.

After about twenty minutes we had the children packed into the bus, and began to move off out of the town in the direction of the Karlovy Vary road. Which was all just as I'd seen it so many times before, including that time with the YWCA and Frank. All because certain people considered it had LUSTER for them to send their fat, immature ducklings from California to Czechoslovakia, and long ago somebody had held that it had LUSTER to build a certain Hotel Pupp in Karlovy Vary, and for Frank there was LUSTER in escorting those twenty-two girls over here, and for me and for him, later, there was LUSTER in going to drink a bottle in the Florentine bar, that last evening, and afterward to sit downstairs in the foyer of this Hotel Pupp, not knowing where to go from there.

After a host of English novels and thrillers, he was the first clergyman I'd ever seen in the flesh in my life. He didn't give any noticeable sign of wanting to start something with me, and yet I knew he did want it. But also I knew this was not the man for a decent girl like me, who wants to marry and have children, a canary, a dog, and an aquarium full of fish, if there's a man to be found with whom all this would really have LUSTER, and if there's an apartment to be had big enough to hold all these things and him, too, and enough money to keep everything functioning as it should. But even if I knew all this very well, nevertheless it dawned on me that I was busy reconsidering my decision that I DIDN'T WANT to sleep with him, and why. And since it seemed I was reconsidering, and had at least gotten as far as admitting the possibility, maybe after all I DID WANT TO, because the kind of feeling that was building up inside me could never have been aroused by the thought of sleeping with anyone if I'd really NOT WANTED TO. So we sat and veered from nothing to nothing in the foyer of the Hotel Pupp, otherwise known as the Grand Hotel Moscow. The girls from the YWCA had gone off to bed, they'd said good night even before Frank and I went into the Florentine bar. It was almost half past twelve, and into the reception office came some fellow and asked whether he could get a room, whether they hadn't by any chance something free for one night.

The man at the desk began slowly and carefully explaining to him exactly which room he could have, and how much he would have to pay for it. Maybe it was too much money for him, and so he began to stammer some excuse or other, because he was ashamed of not having enough money. Behind the counter of the reception office sat some woman in the hotel uniform, filling out some sort of register, and she began to laugh at this man who hadn't enough money for one night in the Hotel Pupp, so dreadfully rudely, and so violently, that the badly pinned hotel badge fell off her left breast. The more the poor man blushed and stammered, the more she laughed and laughed, so horribly that I longed to get up and reach across the counter and give her a terrific smack across her painted mouth. For laughing at the man like that. And also because she was making a big production of this laughter chiefly to attract Frank's attention as he sat there with me, fixed there as a witness, in fact, because of me, and because of this helpless wondering what to do next about our situation. Here we were in the hall, and hadn't the courage to go somewhere else, somewhere where we shouldn't have to sit like this with a table between us.

Yet at the same time I was suddenly frightfully angry with HIM. HE WAS THE ONLY ONE WHO COULD HAVE DONE SOMETHING ABOUT EVERYTHING. I got into that awful kind of rage when one says: HURRAH! at every head that falls, even though I knew he hadn't understood a word, and had never grasped what was going on at the reception desk. But I knew that woman wanted to detach him for herself, that she considered herself a DISH, and me a POOR THING. Frank was from the West, he had money enough for a dozen or even two dozen such rooms in the Hotel Pupp, he had an International Diners' Club card, and above all, he had a great fund of understanding and sympathy for everyone. There was nothing you could reproach him with; he didn't eat with his knife, he didn't pick his nose, he was always well dressed, always fair and always friendly, and his eyes behind his thick glasses were always attentive and sad. He always had a reason for everything, and there existed at least thirty more things that justified me in being angry with him, including that fact that he truly was, out of all the foreigners I'd known, THE ONLY ONE with whom I had any wish to sleep, and in any case THE ONLY MAN, that evening or any evening of the two years that followed, to this day, with whom I ought to have slept, because I knew how much of him was interested in me as a woman, just any woman, and how much as a special, unique woman, as myself, and I believe there was more of this second. I was so angry that tears came into my eyes, and suddenly I was absolutely determined that now I wouldn't sleep with him at any price or upon any consideration.

In the meantime that man who hadn't enough money to stay overnight at the Pupp had gone away, and the bitch behind the counter had stopped laughing. It occurred to me that if I left now I should be leaving Frank more or less helpless before her, and in that situation perhaps she might really succeed in getting him for herself. Actually she really was a very handsome woman, a DISH calculated to arouse bad thoughts even in men who had their wives on their arms. So when Frank asked me, just at this most crazily opportune moment he could possibly have chosen, if we shouldn't go upstairs, I nodded, and we went.

But the very fact that he could pick the one moment when it was impossible not to nod assent, and the fact that in spite of all her giggling and quaking that woman behind the reception desk hadn't attracted him away from sitting with me, although she really was a DISH, somehow made me break into new rage and tears and grief. On the landing between the second and third floors I began to act so stupidly, saying I wasn't going ANY-WHERE with him (though my room was on the same floor as his!), and I stood there making an idiot of myself until it began to get even on Frank's nerves, and if he hadn't been just the person he was I should probably have gotten a couple of sound English slaps in the face, and found myself left alone on the landing to think it over, because the show I was putting on right then would have held all the Hotel Pupp spellbound, and all twenty-two girls from California, too, including the one who shared my room— maybe her most of all.

But well brought-up Frank only said: "Hilda, please come along, please Hilda, we're in a hotel!" until it dawned on me that unfortunately I'm not a whore or a bluestocking, but just an or-dinary hysterical idiot, and at that moment well on the way to being drunk, too, because I haven't any great tolerance for alco-hol.

So I wiped away my tears, kissed the hand which had forgotten to slap my face, kissed him on the cheek, too, and crept up to the third floor where our rooms were, and went to his door instead of my own. Frank was glad that at last he could stop worrying about what I was going to do the next moment, and he began to hunt first for his key, and then for the keyhole in the door.

Suddenly it was utterly natural and normal to want to sleep with him, he was a fine, good-looking, normal man, he had no need at all to promise me heaven knows what, load me with nylons and underwear and I don't know what else, just for the hope of being in the same bed with me, as most men usually have to, to their own great expense.

For quite a long time he couldn't do anything with this lock, because we also had to go on kissing and embracing and holding each other tightly, and doing all kinds of things which had noth-ing to do with unlocking a door. It seemed to me that we were standing in that corridor at least half an hour. It was a patent lock with a dog's head on the key, and evidently it had jammed somehow. He blew into the keyhole, and tried again and again, and then, in the middle of turning, it suddenly went CRACK in his hand, and the key broke. He laughed, and showed me the broken stump he still held between finger and thumb; and when we'd recovered a little from our consternation at that CRACK, which might well have been heard as far away as the ground floor, he said to me: "I'm sorry, Hilda! A slight complication!"

He collected me from the wall against which he'd propped me a moment before, and escorted me to the door of my room, which of course opened beautifully, as if freshly oiled, only there was one of those YWCA creatures sleeping inside there. He kissed my hand, and said it was an evil fate dogging him, and then I only heard him going down the stairs into the foyer, where the girls and I found him sitting in the morning, dozing in the same chair where he'd sat when we were together in the evening. On the table in front of him he had two empty packs of Marlboros, an empty half bottle of souvenir slivovitz, which could be bought at the reception desk, and a glass of soda water.

Then there was just one sleepy breakfast, at which we had no opportunity to talk much, and in any case we hadn't much to say to each other about it. And then the Tournaglobus coach was there for Pastor Frank and the twenty-two YWCA girls from California.

I had plenty of work with bills, passports, receipts, checks and everything else that a guide manages for foreigners on a journey through her homeland; and in any case it was late, very late for any thoughts of love, or of the man with whom love would have had LUSTER. That key, and the thought of what might have happened if Frank's room had been mine, and a thousand and one other things—obviously it was no use worrying myself into the grave about all this. But even if I'd learned, in the two years that had passed since then, to say that: "Hell and blast and shit" very quickly and with a charming smile, all the same Frank's mother shook me badly when she opened her travel album to show me, and naturally there were all his photographs, too. Frank with his family, Frank with the dog, Frank at the aquarium, Frank at the wheel, Frank playing tennis, Frank at Christmas, Frank as a student, Frank as a child, Frank with everything else and everyone else—only I was missing. And what emerged from all this was that Frank, even before I'd known him those two years ago, had been married, the wretch, though he'd never boasted about that fact. And naturally, in spite of all these photographs, and because of them, too, I had to think all over again of that lost LUSTER our meeting had seemed to have, and the words we had forgotten to say to each other, and which now we would never say, and which would be the cause of endless regret and guilt for us at judgment day.

I made the acquaintance of Frank's St. Bernard, and I got to know what his parsonage looked like, but that wasn't what would really have interested me, I'd seen dozens of such photographs from all over the world. What would have interested me was to hear how things were with him; whether everything in that America of his had LUSTER for him, whether he was getting on well there, among those children and fishes, or whether it was with him as it was with me. As it is with me, when I sing that song from *The Beggar's Opera,* or recall that sentence of Fanka's, in Čapek's *The Robber,* about lost youth. For I, too, grieve over my lost youth. As time passes, everything becomes more distant and lost. Everything, everything, everything. Even those journeys along this Karlovy Vary road, when I was a young hitchhiker, and the school in Roguesville, and Ladislav, whom I might have loved if I hadn't gone away to the university and left the National Committee chairman's mongolian son, and if Ladislav hadn't fallen hopelessly in love with that blonde, who has surely lost her figure completely in these ten years, and borne him a litter of kids as grubby as herself, for whom nobody ever has any time. The university, and those months of freezing in the streets and drinking bad coffee in worse cafés, everything grows every day more remote, and the more remote the more lost, until there's nothing

left of it that one can get hold of. Not even this, that even someone like Frank can be suddenly left without any hinterland, in
spite of all the children, the dog, the fishes, and California, just
like me, just like us.

I'm twenty-eight, I'm popular, a first-class interpreter and
guide for foreigners. I know how to dress and how to carry myself,
I'm educated and cultured, I have an ocean of things which many
people have not and may well envy—but how many times has this
body of mine served me as a thing functioning to some purpose?
And how many times yet can it serve me so, before it becomes an
object merely of fond reminiscences, something for lubricious
thoughts? And where's the LUSTER in all this? I'm twenty-eight,
and never again shall I be a breathless adolescent, afraid of herself, to whom men plead out of pure tenderness: "May I kiss
you?" and haven't a clue how to answer when one asks them:
Why? Never again will any man ask me such an exquisitely stupid question, all I shall know will be men without LUSTER,
telling me not to make an unnecessary song about it; and if I do,
they'll take off and leave without a word and without pity into
the blue.

The sun shone behind us. It was full morning, at last we were
speeding out of the city on the Karlovy Vary road. I pointed out
to the children and their LITTLE BABY grandma the Star castle, the White Mountain, symbol of three hundred years of slav-
ery and of Frederick of the Palatinate and the twenty-one ex-
ecuted Czech lords, about whom I'd told them yesterday when we
visited the Old Town Hall. Then finally we were passing the last
bus stop. The sun leaned down to us through the glass roof of the
coach, the driver whistled some street song and winked at me as I
chattered English into the microphone. I would have liked to
sleep a little, after that morning encounter with the coalman, and
to escape from all those worries that were working only slowly
toward their close. Then I had nothing more to say, and the
driver switched on the radio, and went on whistling his street
song to its accompaniment. Then the first curb flashed by us,

where I'd taken my stand some eight years ago to wave to drivers in the hope of a hitch. And there came over me suddenly the feeling that always used to come over me here, the feeling that always possesses you when you set out in the morning or early afternoon on a good highway.

Setting out is the most exalting feeling, it's one of the few things in the world that have LUSTER—maybe, maybe it's the ONLY thing in the world that has it. The more I think about it, the more it seems to me that this is true. Not that it has to be in any sense a particularly gay feeling, and yet there is surely some special consolation in it.

Atheism

It was half past ten in the evening, and the bistro had emptied.
They were the only ones left in the place. The waiter folded together the two wings of the street door, thrust the bolt of the left
side into the floor, and reached up to push the second bolt home
into the upper frame. Finally he hunted out the keys from his
pocket, and locked up. He left the whole bunch dangling in the
lock, went to his own place behind the bar counter, and uttered
in the direction of George and Veronica: "Don't disturb yourselves!"

Then he put out the big light over the bar, and all the lights
over the tables except the one at which they sat together, and
then paid no more attention to them. From another table he carried a chair behind the bar, set it down beside the hatch through
which the food was handed into the bistro and the dirty dishes
handed out, and spread out on the counter his sheaf of bills and
drink chits, placed his waiter's wallet in the open drawer with the
money, cast a glance over everything, and called through the
hatch into the kitchen, to the cleaner: "All right, Mrs.
Macháčková, you can go ahead!"

He pulled the chair closer under his rump, and began to work
with concentration. His invitation to George and Veronica not to

disturb themselves was quite sincere, for George was a daily—and a good—customer, and as such had his unwritten but acknowledged rights, even at an hour when it was long past closing time, and the keys were already swinging inside the lock of the door.

In from the kitchen came Mrs. Macháčková, the cleaner, switched on the working light in the ceiling, and began to wipe down the shelves above the bar, and the stools under it, with some disinfectant solution.

"Now this is just THE problem," said George. He pulled at his lower lip and waited for Veronica to ask what problem. When she failed to do so he repeated, with recognizably accentuated significance: "This is just THE TREMENDOUS problem."

"And what's that?" Veronica asked. She withdrew her eyes from the mirror behind his back, tilted her empty, tapered glass toward her, and gazed into the bottom of it, where a circle of lemon lay despondently drying, reddened by the departed bitter.

"What to do with the evening that's just beginning," answered George.

Veronica shrugged her shoulders. To tell the truth, it seemed to her that with closing time boredom had overtaken them. She raised her glass as if she wanted to drink something more from it, and sucked the slice of lemon into her mouth.

"What to do with the evening that's just beginning, did you say?"

In a certain house in this town, admittedly, there was a woman waiting for George. Not his own wife, obviously, just a woman—one in whose apartment he had been a guest more often and for longer periods than would have been healthy for her reputation, if she had had the least inclination to pay any attention to such a consideration; and if, indeed, there had been anyone left, anywhere, to pay any attention to it. He had been a frequent visitor there over a period of some six or seven weeks, but as soon as he had made Veronica's acquaintance, this afternoon, he had begun to reflect that that little apartment where he was expected was, for one thing, just a little too far out of the way (to be exact, it was on the fifth floor of an apartment house which had no elevator), and for another thing, was just a little too airless, its single window being quite insufficient, by any standards, to give it adequate ventilation in this summer weather. And finally, and principally, it began to seem to him that by this time he had had just a little too much of the woman who was waiting there for him. She had begun to appropriate to herself rights which did not, when it came to the point, belong to her. The affair had already lasted all those six or seven weeks, in any case, and making love had gradually become an irksome duty, something he didn't like at all. The woman on the fifth floor had now become, instead of the passionate lover he had originally sought in her, and for a few days actually found, much more of an attentive housewife. She told him off when he left the refrigerator door open, and refused to go to bed until she had washed up the dishes. And of course there were all those five stories and a mezzanine to be taken into account, and the air, which in this place under the roof had grown steadily thicker and thicker as the summer advanced.

But in addition to all this, it happened that George had in his pocket the key of a houseboat, anchored only a little way out of town; and this afternoon, quite by chance, one of his many friends had introduced him to Veronica. So it arose that although he didn't know yet whether Veronica was going to turn out to be the woman he'd been looking for all his life, or merely (and at least) a woman for this evening, he was by this time quite certain that he was going to write off the laundry, books and phonograph records he had up in that fifth-floor apartment, all the things he had taken there or forgotten to bring away with him during the past few weeks. He knew that he wasn't going there again, that he would throw away the key he carried in his pocket, that the whole affair hadn't been worth a damn. And he asked Veronica: "Do you have to go on somewhere?"

She made a beautifully vague film face, vapidly gazing, rather like Lucia Boché dreaming of the weight of Philip of Castille's masculinity while making delicate pillow lace. Then this cinematic reverie was transformed into the embarrassment of a *gamine* who is in full agrement with a proposal, but doesn't quite know how to respond without compromising herself at the same time. She turned on George a furrowed brow, and lips pursed up into a charming little snout, like that of a very thoughtful piglet.

"Well, no . . . nowhere in particular." And she put into it all the pride and self-confidence of a lady who at eighteen years old is standing on her own feet.

She's younger, too!—thought George. His mind was still very much occupied with the affair of that fifth-floor apartment; and he said: "Come on, then, let's get out of here, before they throw us out!" He cast a last glance at the fingers of the hand which was still holding the tapered glass, at her suntanned neck and shoulders, and her face.

"Where?" she asked. She circled the rim of her glass with her forefinger, and all this time she was still being that lace-making lady waiting for a drunken halberdier. She dropped her game with the glass, sighed, laid a hand on the table, and then smoothed her dress at the waist. She knew quite well that George was looking at her, and knew also that he had (God be thanked!) something to look at. She was eighteen years old, and her profession was still uncertain. Up to this time she had slept with four men—one of them, of course, having taken the initiative and first slept with her—and she hoped that the world was going to prove progressively her oyster.

Each of those four, in his day, had meant in her life an enormous and exciting hope, in which she had believed absolutely; for she was by this time quite well adapted to illusion. Afterward, as a matter of fact, they had meant very much less than she had expected, but she passed that over with the reflection that every beginning is hard. The first had added up to the material for a costume, and some jeans with the LEE trademark, as well as a few dinners in a certain artists' club. The second had been worth a lamp for her room and a pair of sandals imported illegally from Italy. The third scored only a nonsensical ornament sculpted by himself from a piece of natural wood; later on she had given it to her father for his birthday. And the fourth, and so far the last, had provided another pair of sandals, though of Czech production this time, and the material for a dress. It was the dress she happened to be wearing now. In addition, of course, they had been responsible for a half a dozen tiny roles in films and television, a card in the registry of available "walk-on" players, two dozen advertising photographs, and a fourteen-day stay at a symposium on films designed for beekeepers, and discussions on the influence of powder sprays on the infestation of the countryside by insects. She had been taken there by a journalist, whose delegate card was filled in for two people; the same man who afterward gave her the wood sculpture. And finally the last one had also gotten her a six-month engagement to sing in a café, to the accompaniment of a semiamateur orchestra, the leader of which had introduced her to George this afternoon. Originally, they said, it had been quite a flourishing and well patronized café, but by the end of her six months, which by a combination of circumstances happened also to be today, no more than a dozen or so guests were normally to be found there, and once again a dreary emptiness extended before Veronica's vision. So dreary that she saw no reason at all for not spending a short part of it in George's company, which at least would mean one more substantial supper, although she had originally promised to call up a certain stage manager who had gradually begun to assume the right to help this young artist, since the last of her four patrons had flopped so shamefully in his attempt to make a café star out of her. She judged, on the whole correctly, that the stage manager wasn't likely to run away from her if she put him off until tomorrow, while George was playing for her the role of the finger of fate.

He was a young musician, whose name was being heard here and there in the debates of the initiated, and who for that reason was interesting to her. In the first place as an artist, naturally because of that illusion that he would offer her the opportunity for which, up to now, she had waited in vain; and in the second place, equally naturally, as a woman, for the world is as it is, and maybe he'd turn out to be one of those men who might sleep with her, but were not capable of asking that she should do the same with them. In addition, Veronica had a certain sense of fair play, or so, at least, she often said of herself, and George had spent part of the afternoon and a considerable part of the evening with her, time which she had certainly not wanted to spend at home.

She had sung her songs about Shanghai, and cowboy love, and later, in the bistro under the café, having reached this point in the account of her fate, she said to George: "Obviously one is throwing oneself away here, and demolishing one's standards. But then again, it does pay good money, and at the same time it leaves me leisure to do my own things." Yes, the stage manager could wait; and she was just about as anxious to go home as George was to go to that apartment on the fifth floor of the house with the mezzanine. So she simply stroked her dress at the waist, and allowed a frilly edge of underwear to peep out of her décolletage, and asked: "Where"

Although Veronica had not been at all precise when she spoke of "her own things," George had understood her perfectly. The woman in the fifth-floor apartment usually made use of the phrase as a discreet euphemism for the menses; but plainly Veronica's "own things" were to be looked for in a slightly different direction. And George also suffered from the illusion that as an artist he must, for his living, do something quite different from what he did for humanity and the future. When anyone asked how he made his living, George always replied that he "made music"; and it was the truth. He did make music. Quite ordinary music for children's fairy stories on the radio, music which he himself played in the studio. Now and again he wrote the music for a film, and in his life he had composed some ten songs, of which one had become the great popular hit of last year's season. And as a result of all this, here he was thriving, and making quite a decent living. Yet he, too, was left with time for his own things, which in his case were mainly houseboats. George built them. Building houseboats interested and amused him just as much as making music, maybe even a little more. In his lifetime so far he had built three, and of the last one, which was finished apart from a few minor details, he had the key in his pocket. It lay at anchor in the old river harbor, the glory of which had vanished with the building of the first river dam, and had moved away with the boatmen and raftsmen. Only a little way from the city, right at its rim, in fact, beside a soft green expanse of turf untouched by sun or dust, and in water still unpolluted by any drainage. Fifty yards from the anchorage was the rear entrance of an inn, where they had an upright piano, which was quite enough for George where his current work was concerned. So for food and cigarettes it was closer and more convenient there than having to go up and down five floors and a mezzanine. And in addition, he was a valued patron of that inn, though it was quite celebrated. At the end of the war it had played host to two colonels, three generals, nine majors and one German field marshal, all waiting for capture. But they had never had a composer there before, let alone a composer with a houseboat.

So in response to Veronica's: "Where?" George drew out from his hip pocket a flat little key with a pendent compass and a ring bearing an enameled representation of the winds, swung it on his finger, and said: "Houseboat!"

"*A houseboat?*" cried Veronica, every bit as ardently as he had expected, and as regularly happened, once the situation had ripened to this point. He nodded with satisfaction: "Yes, a houseboat, and pure-blooded!"

"But how . . . where did you get it?"

"I built it," George triumphed quietly. "With these hands!"

"But this, of course, is sensational!" Veronica decided. "Marvelous!"

George was adding to the positive advantages of the operation the fact that Veronica, as distinct from the woman in the little apartment, was an artiste, who need not get up early in the morning, and a trip by houseboat had thus become a much more practical possibility.

He called the waiter, who assured him that they could perfectly well go on sitting quietly where they were, for he not only knew

George, but also valued him highly. To tell the truth, in the estimation of innkeepers, waiters and taxi drivers George was a very much greater artist than the critics judged him to be. Once again the waiter assured him of his deep respect, sold him another bottle of bitters, and sent Mrs. Macháčková into the kitchen for paper to wrap up the bottle for them to take away. He was a perfect waiter, he didn't allow himself any sly observation, any lascivious joke; he was a perfect master of his own art, as opposed to many of the aforementioned critics.

She was pretty, she was forsaken, and she needed help. In addition, George liked her and found her sympathetic. She was even an enthusiast for houseboats, like himself; though that was nothing very extraordinary in women, as he knew. She did not have to get up early in the morning; she drank Dubonnet and bitters with gusto; and she also hated snobs and bourgeoisie. She held that rather than pour down any rubbish it was better to remain abstinent. She had, unquestionably, the soul of a child, together with visibly baroque curves. But the main thing, the decisive thing, was that he had sat with her until half past ten in the evening, when he had been dreading having to crawl up five floors for his lovemaking, as he'd done for the past seven weeks. She had relieved him of that duty, once and for all; for the evening had begun with her, and she had made plain her desire and will that they should also end it together, since there was nowhere in particular she had to go; no obligation, no home where one dines, washes the dishes, watches the television, and crawls into bed.

The waiter let them out, and locked the door again after them. They heard the key turn in the lock behind them; and George waved to a taxi driver who was just cruising slowly past. The car stopped, and they got in, George beside the driver because he always loved to ride beside the chauffeur, and Veronica in the back seat. To be sure it was not very polite, especially as he had not said anything to Veronica about it beforehand, and for a moment it distilled a mood of curious sadness and disharmony, so that he was forced to remind himself, in answer to a sudden wave of uncertainty: If it comes to the point, even if she were a prostitute, still it's better than those five flights of stairs and a mezzanine, that sweltering apartment, all that nagging about the refrigerator, and making love like a sort of postscript, after a program consisting of supper, and listening to some celebrated fairy prattling Brecht on a phonograph record.

As the taxi drove away he realized afresh that this was a new adventure beginning, and he tapped a finger on the dashboard in a rhythm that transformed itself into a melody within his mind. And as he was not given to forcing himself to do things for which he had no appetite, he devoted himself to thinking about this melody, instead of to the labor of making spasmodic conversation, such as is normally conducted in nocturnal taxis ferrying couples from inns to nonnuptial beds.

For a long time now George had been engaged in composing a quartet. He had first gotten the idea—indeed it was the first time he had ever thought of composing anything in this manner—a year and a half previously, at Christmas, when he had gone to the midnight service to hear Ryba's *Christmas Mass*. All around him he had seen young people who had escaped from their parents and homes at such a late hour perhaps for the first time, by virtue of this religious occasion; and in the porch of the church, Ryba, Jesus Christ, and eternal damnation, neither here nor there as far as they were concerned, they were rushing to embrace their first rendezvous, their first kisses and stolen caresses. And the best thing of all was that neither Ryba nor Christ were the losers by it. That was when George got the idea of writing something more worthwhile than an attempt at a hit song, something about this church and this mass, and Ryba, and these budding young men and blossoming young women.

He had no contract, however, for the quartet which he had then begun to sketch out on the basis of this idea, no agreement such as he had for the music he made for radio or television, no deadline to goad him into working. Also this was to be something more than a bit of routine craftsmanship such as he regularly delivered to radio and television, and the purity and clarity of the idea engendered in the church porch got lost out of his head before he even got home from mass. If he had not made a few notes on the spot, on one of his own visiting cards which happened to be in his pocket, it would have vanished completely.

He had been working on it all this year and a half, in such moments as had visited him now in the taxi. Whenever he said to himself: I'm going to work on that quartet—he knew that it was really no more than a kind of excuse, to avoid admitting to himself that what he was actually about to do was idle his time away. The quartet had so captivated him that for several months he had not even touched his work on the houseboat, but he had not made the slightest progress. He had even made the acquaintance of the priest at that particular church, and had gone there again the following year to midnight Mass. But this time no idea came to him, though all those adolescent sprigs were there again, trying their best to behave like lieutenants in an operetta.

The priest, in addition to being a servant of God, was also a demon for motors, and even repaired sickles and flails; for after the death of the deacon, and through the general shortage of clergy, some parish in the country had been added to his cure. George had learned from him that all these hopeful young men and bright-eyed and permanently-waved young ladies came fairly regularly to church, though not one of them was actually baptized as a member of the flock. They came to church just as they did to the lectures of the atheistic circle, where devoted enthusiasts from the Socialist Academy (for a fee of eighteen dollars) hammer into the heads of all interested parties the principles necessary to a recognition of the scientific basis of the world.

All of which was worthy of consideration, and ought to find its place in the quartet.

But George simply could not recover the thread he had first grasped during that Christmas Eve service.

In the meantime he had been compelled to produce music for two dramatizations of Jules Verne. He had also acquired a contract for two songs, which were more or less written, though he still had to do a fair amount of work on them.

So it gave him astonishing joy when suddenly THIS came to

him again in the taxi, and he quickly took out his notebook, without which he never went anywhere (oh, to have had it with him that time in the church!), and began to scribble down his ideas as well as he could in darkness and in motion, tapping out his leading rhythm meanwhile on the edge of the door, or the dashboard. In all the year and a half since he had first begun to think about the quartet such an inspiration had visited him only once, when he was walking home across the city from a party, on foot and in the rain, because they'd extracted from him for drinks even the money he'd put by for a taxi. Home, of course, at that time, was not a little apartment on the fifth floor, but a solid citizen household with two reception rooms, the place where he actually belonged. There was his mother, the miniature Chinese bulldog Amor, his father, and his baby grand. The main part of this household, however, consisted precisely of his mother and the bulldog Amor, so that all his life George had been glad to escape from there whenever and wherever he could; and in recent years he had always managed to have on hand—the independent apartment supply being so hopelessly inadequate—some place like the fifth-floor flat he had abandoned today. This had not been at all complicated to arrange, since the inhabitants of such dwellings feel much the same as the proprietors of that inn outside the town, where they'd entertained a field marshal and plenty of colonels, but never before a composer. Though to distinguish between a man who composes music and a man who repairs refrigerators must be quite a problem in bed.

During the taxi ride, then, George was jubilant not only because he was traveling with Veronica, who was a dish, but also because he felt that his quartet was again on the move.

They drove along the road to the inn beside the houseboat; it stood just on the spot where the town lighting ended. George let the driver turn the car, and before the man could name some fantastic figure as his fare, gave him the exact fare due, plus a tip. Then the taxi was gone, and Veronica, still quite affronted and aggrieved at being shut up in the back seat like a carton of crockery, walked after him along a path which had been trampled out to the anchorage. It was not, in fact, very much trodden; all the way along it there was grass underfoot, wet with dew and pleasant to touch, so that Veronica took off her shoes and walked barefoot. Above their heads shone the amazing summer sky of a moonless night, and upriver an excursion steamer passed, hung with lanterns; and just at that moment some band on board was playing to the passengers that celebrated song hit of George's from last season. When they reached the gangway to their boat, the wash of the steamer had just touched the houseboat and set it rocking slightly. The gangway scraped against the shore. The chains stretched taut with a rattle, and again relaxed.

"It's beautiful here, isn't it?" said George, once again more the attentive host than the composer of a quartet which still had to be written. He was very much aware that here she was, Veronica, decidedly a dish (though that, of course, was not the end of all problems), and he drew in the fresh, moist air, and thought with relief that he had gotten that woman and her flat and her refrigerator and Brecht off his shoulders at last. He noticed, too, that the water level had risen a little, due to the rain in Šumava, and made a note in his own mind that he would have to shorten the chains in the morning.

Veronica, with her shoes in her hand, stood inhaling this SIMPLY MAGNIFICENT air; and when George suggested that they might even swim she agreed at once and with enthusiasm, though she had no bathing suit, and during that taxi ride she had been promising George, in her own mind, that she certainly wouldn't sleep with him, since he'd behaved so impolitely. But now this had begun to be interesting, as interesting as that affair with the journalist, who had afterwards got her a small role in an advertising film for electric mixers. She had had her own small dressing room in the studio that time, and when her partner came there to comb his hair, because the mirror in his cubbyhole was broken, she had been able graciously to allow him, and to observe: "Really, it's impossible to work in such conditions!," in order to demonstrate in what circumstances SHE was accustomed to work. That moment had been one of the peaks of her existence. She was extremely grateful to the journalist for it, and he would have had a real hope of becoming THE man in her life if he had managed to come up again quickly enough with some new idea—and if that fellow who had got her the six-month singing engagement at the café hadn't put in an appearance. . . .

George lit the spirit lamp on board the houseboat, and drew up on the mast a carbide lantern with colored signal windows on the sides and a white light in the middle. It looked as romantic as the song about faraway Shanghai, and Veronica began to sing it in an undertone.

She crossed over the gangway to the deck, and went inside; and there she had to exclaim aloud: "Oh, it's lovely here!" because it really was lovely there. So lovely that because of the impact it made on her she forgot all about that studied pose, gazing a yard to the left and slightly above the level of the tip of her nose, and all about opening her lips to respond only after a half second delay. And now it was in the balance whether she should string George along tonight, or relent and sleep with him. After all, though it was certainly true that the summer night, the house-boat, the lights on the mast and the steamer on the river, plus the scent of the grass, made up a very delectable whole, yet a six-hour stint in the café, afterwards extended into the bistro, could hardly be considered a schedule guaranteed to keep a girl fresh as a daisy and wide-awake.

George opened the bottle of bitters—for there's a right time for everything—and put on water to make coffee. He waved a hand: "We've got gin, vodka, vermouth and rum!"

"Could I have a gin and lemon?" Veronica ordered.

George was a little saddened at that; evidently he had no lemon. So she accepted vodka, and then another vodka, and one more for courage. She was again beginning to view that spot a yard to the left above the tip of her nose, and to react with a careful half-second delay, as they talked about the possibilities George was thinking up for her, and about all the friends he had in radio and television, and his comrades in the theatre, and all those others with whom he proposed to exchange a few words

ABOUT HER. The vodka was running out, so Veronica began to dilute it with bitters, as the bottle happened to be open in any case.

"This one's certainly got some floodgates somewhere," George said to himself, while she sat thinking about those four gentlemen and all the thousand possibilities of sweeping the world off its feet, once one was a woman of the world, and found such an enterprise amusing. But she thought, too, of how all those splendid possibilities had always, for some reason, evaporated out of her hands. Of the emptiness before her, with which she didn't know how to cope. And also of how desperately grazed and painful she had been, down there, that time when she got her role in the advertising film for mixers. And that other time, when they'd offered her the singing job in the café. And of how she had borne all that, in order to FULFILL HERSELF.

They didn't swim after all, they had forgotten about it. She liked George well enough, and she was drinking in order to bolster up her courage to sleep with him. She drank bitters, vodka, and finally even the gin, and in the end it made her ill, though luckily that hardly presents a problem on board a houseboat, and the water carries everything away.

George was very tender and considerate, he wiped her mouth and washed her face, he even went so far as to kiss her immediately afterwards. For one thing, he hadn't kissed anyone all that day, up to then, and for another he was still overjoyed at having shed that fifth-floor apartment from around his neck, and still made sure of his pleasure, and he wanted to prove that he didn't despise her in any situation, let alone just on account of a tummy upset. She really was a dish.

Then the excursion boat came back, just as beautifully illuminated as before, but this time without music; maybe even on the steamer everybody had had enough of it.

Unfortunately Veronica had drunk to such an extent that nothing came of the lovemaking, it wasn't even worth an attempt; and the notes which George had made in his notebook during the taxi ride were drowned out with spilled bitters, and in the morning even he couldn't read them. So that at noon the next day he was in a pretty wretched mood.

But after lunch, which was at the same time breakfast, they finally did swim. He was still playing the host, at any rate. Their debates on art and life somehow faded out, this was simply a houseboat, blessed with water, sun, a gentle breeze, and the sweet pleasure of *dolce far niente*. He went to the inn for food, and brought it back in a casserole, still beautifully hot, and there was coffee, which he made himself. Then, quite involuntarily and just in passing, as sometimes happens to men, he found that his arm was round Veronica's waist.

She swelled and stiffened.

"Take your arm away, please," she said then, and George thought: "Never lay hand on woman or flower—but I shall surely bust this sweet cow in the jaw yet. . . ." And then he laid his empty coffee cup gently and carefully in the safety shelf with the rim, and said aloud: "And what if I should ask you for your hand, contessa, . . . thus?"

Veronica gazed a yard to the left above the tip of her nose, allowed her eyes to blink with confusion, opened her lips slightly, and pronounced: "Really? But you can't expect me to answer a thing like that immediately! That doesn't wound you, does it, George?" And with delicate sensitivity she took him by the hand.

Stabbed Ophelia

*Motto: A ball is a ball,
and a bed is a bed.*

"And what's going to happen now?"

He was silent. He swallowed consideringly, shrugged his shoulders, and shifted his glasses to the left, to the right, and back again, pushed them up to the bridge of his nose, coughed, looked for a moment as though he was about to say: "Well, I don't know. . . ." and then shrugged his shoulders again as though to say: "Why pester me, it's your body, your problem, your misfortune." But finally he coughed once more, put on the wise face of a man who is prepared for anything, and said: "The main thing, little one, is that you mustn't be afraid!"

"No!" She shook her head, and the hair whirled across her puckered forehead. "No, that's impossible! Why don't you say something? I need, really I *need* you to tell me what's going to happen now. I need to know, do you understand?"

He caught her around the shoulders and drew her close.

"Above all, you mustn't be afraid. Plenty of girls have had the same worries before you. You'll see, it will all turn out well." And since she still seemed unsatisfied, he even became slightly pleading: "No, really now, be a good girl! You tell those nerves of yours to go quietly about their business. After all, they're only nerves!"

Yes, of course—she thought to herself—*of course, plenty of girls,* nothing special, what you've done to me, you calf, *plenty of girls,* it's nothing out of the way, just a normality, nothing more than a mild intoxication and a slight indisposition at the conclusion of a gay evening, and really it wasn't anything more than a gay evening, an evening on the town, a ball, only it lasted four months; and that's all about it. A splendid ball, like something out of a film, during which she had become acquainted with this hand that knew so well how to caress, this hand that was caressing her even now, molding her flesh in its palm, and making her feel as fine as a heroine in a film. All the people around them knew that bespectacled face, and could envy her, as the girls from school envied her. A magnificent face, and a magnificent hand. A sympathetic face. A face from the stage, from films, from the picture magazines.

"Best thing I can do is kill myself . . . at least if one even knew what was going to happen!"

"Now, honey, there . . . please! You simply mustn't talk like that! I know it's hard for you, but don't lose your nerve. You've got to trust me!"

She remembered this hand, and the head of this man to whom the hand belonged, in her lap and on her breast, without his glasses now and snuffling like an untrained puppy, affectionate and defenseless, looking for protection. But she always had trusted him, why speak of that now? Who, who can hide us so that the hunters can't get at us? Such a perfect life! The sun on the cottage in the morning, and the expert driver manipulating the wheel with hands gloved in worn deerskin. She remembered Schubert and Mozart, the concert hall, and one cello solo during which she had almost burst into tears (at that very moment she had been recalling morning in the cottage). And the American film version of *War and Peace,* the greatness and the agony of love, the suffering of those men and horses hurtling impatiently to their death even as they were reflecting on the beauty of life. O

God, how happy she'd been then! How sure she'd been that she knew now why she was in the world! How trivial everything else had seemed then, when she had glowed in that dress remodeled by her mother, and her mother's silver wedding slippers, which in the meantime had come back into fashion, while this hand—this same hand—had held her caressingly during the interval, among the creaking, woven cane chairs in the old concert hall.

Only today's sorrow was more enduring. Dread of maturity, terror of the child in her belly, drowned out even the cello, dimmed the vision of the student couples who had crept into the concert hall because they had nowhere to sleep together while it was still winter, defaced even the proud fact that *we have,* the creaking chairs, and the smiling emotion. Everything was suddenly turned wrong-side-out. Surely in the novels, at moments like these, the gentlemen concerned uttered wonderful words to express their joy at the thought of the child that was coming. And suddenly it dawned upon her that she had not the least idea whether she wanted that child, or whether, in fact, she even wanted this perfect young man, whom her father had praised so highly on the television: *Now that's what I call an actor!* While her mother had done nothing but sigh, and look at Father's paunch. A riot in *Faust and Marguerite*, heartbreaking as the young Werther. And tomorrow she had an examination in mathematics.

It stands to reason! Glasses first this way, then that, then up to the bridge of his nose. The meditative forehead, the movements that she loved. He spoke with emotion on music, that time. Music which outlived its own day and ours, but which was always valid for those who knew how to preserve the power of feeling, those in whom the force of our civilization must survive. And again the glasses moving this way and that, and an appropriate quotation from the Bible: "The just man is merciful also to his beast, but the heart of the godless is without pity."

And then a no less appropriate and gracious quotation from Engles, from an article on free love. Free love, the love which is free and escapes us, the love which is free to us, yet before we expect it goes off without us, walking somewhere in the valley of Šarka, or withdraws into the darkness of a movie theatre. All these thoughts, together with the admirable and complex sentences in which they were expressed, she had managed to commit to memory, and had written them all down in her midsummer essay for Czech language, which got her an "Excellent," and the Czech language teacher talked about it as if it were the essay of the century.

Her tears were flowing again; but the hand was always here, positive and firm, though not providing any answer to the question that interested her so much: WHAT'S GOING TO HAPPEN?

"You mustn't be afraid, sweetheart, you mustn't get hysterical, that isn't going to help you—that isn't going to help *us.*" The hand moved upwards, and turned her face toward him, and his lips kissed her on the other cheek. "Above all, no tears, I can't bear tears. You're beginning to look like a little quenched lantern. You've got to be reasonable."

Reason, splendid sweet reason, in glasses that can be flexed into various positions, and employed as total enchantment, in interesting and decorative ways; glasses to be cleaned with deep concentration when we discuss music, the one and only thing that is felt right down HERE, in our most inexpressible depths, and which we reach after with outspread fingers, but never capture, like that free love. Such a minor, minuscule adventure, on a night excursion roving between three inns and one theatrical premiere, a girl who knows she's looking her best, and wants to be envied for something a little more than merely the way she looks. She had wanted to lead him out a little from the formal concept of a young, successful and self-confident man, and she had been able then to ask: "Why"—wantonness withdrew from them somewhere, over the cobbles of the pavement, and took flight into the distance toward the Bethlehem Chapel.

"My wife, you know, Jarmila—my wife is very intelligent, and I'm very fond of her, very fond, I couldn't. . . . But she doesn't understand me. It sounds like a cliché, I know, but please do believe me, she doesn't understand me at all. I know it sounds very peculiar, but for me today she's a complete stranger—*a complete stranger!*"

A summer sky full of stars, gas lamps in the street, an English sports model with the hood lowered, medieval façades all around, a mildly intoxicated game.

"If I'd realized, if I'd known, that there existed a person who would understand me, whom I could trust a hundred per cent. . . ."

My God, he looks just like that idiot of a Russian teacher, when he takes the girls off into his study for their *viva voce* tests! The thought had entered her mind even then, and in great haste, because she had not wanted to lose her dream, and her night on the town, about which she was going to have so much to tell the girls, she had said: "Come and have a drink!" exactly as she had read it somewhere in Remarque. But perhaps, even at that early stage, she should actually have said: "—before you make a complete fool of yourself, even a bigger fool than our Russian teacher, my beautiful boy with the sympathetic glasses pinched from Arthur Miller!"

And they went to the fourth inn, and wantonness came back to them on tiptoe, very softly, they drank it in by sips with their well-cooled Valtické wine and their unusually assiduous waiter, who knew all about theatrical gentlemen, and indeed about life in general. At the end of it they were in debt by some trifling sum; they left a silver dollar with Kennedy's head on it, and then it was time to go and live. High time to think about some sort of living, somewhere. A few telephone calls, a trip somewhere, with a performance of *Berenice,* a bathing place with too-cold water and too-warm lemonade. *MONEY HAS NO VALUE FOR ME.* Wantonness came back constantly, by this time it had shown no disposition to leave at all; not until last week. It was surely quite fair, he had first inferred and later avowed, she knew perfectly well what she was getting herself into, and it's a fine thing in this world when things make sense, when we have a man who knows how to handle us. And here was this wantonness, and somewhere beneath it was also that astonishing recollection of how it had withdrawn on tiptoe toward the Bethlehem Chapel, and how he had called it back. "Come and have a drink!" A marvelous night, steeped in maturity, by the side of a man who was famous, and knew his way about.

He lit a cigarette, and had to release her shoulder for a moment to do it. The place his hand had warmed there felt suddenly cold.

"Now, look, naturally it isn't pleasant, but I'll help you out of it, only for God's sake you must be reasonable and not lose your head." He took a long drag, and thoughtfully expelled the smoke toward the high ceiling of the half-empty hall. "I've spoken to several of my acquaintances who're doctors—but it's no use, they're afraid. You'll have to go before this commission. They'll surely allow it in your case, you're young, and I'm married." He felt everything in her grow rigid, and he clasped her around the shoulders again and turned her warmly toward him. "Now wait a minute!" The soothing hand caressed her. "There are people who're definitely in the establishment, and people who're only in a state of hope. You think it over slowly. Do you remember how you burst into tears that time, over that Mozart thing?"

"Oh, no!" she said. Again she had to wipe away her tears. Don't cry, you idiot, she said to herself inwardly, don't cry, anyhow it was Schumann.

He was clever; he had those glasses which she loved; he recalled for her the concert hall, the cello, Natasha's agony, about which he had never known anything—*be reasonable! REASONABLE!* When day by day and minute by minute there's a baby growing in your womb, a baby nobody wants, a baby who's of no benefit to anyone, a baby who means the end of being envied, the end of splendid experiences, but no end at all to the explanations, and no wantonness dancing between four inns, no premieres, no dust of the wings mingling with the smell of the wardrobe. If I could find a creature I could really trust. . . . A thousand merry tales. "Mr. Cohn, that fish stinks. . . . Maurice, I'll give a party, if you'll bring your wife that'll make three of us." The feeling that it's time I got myself a steady boyfriend.

"You know I'm more of a playboy than a marrying man."

My God, yes, I knew that even then. From the beginning. He's an idiot. With the Russian teacher, at least you can be sure of graduating in Russian by way of acknowledgment. An idiot from the theatre, who got me into trouble and now tells me he's really a playboy. I'm going to have a baby by an idiot, my mother'll break me in two, and the girls will kill themselves laughing, after the way they've envied me. For all those beautiful stories from the cottage, and the English sports model.

The hand was consoling, the only support in this world full of snares. The only hope.

"I'll get hold of the money, you can take that for granted. Now what we've got to discuss is how to present them with such a set of circumstances that they'll simply have to do what you ask."

"You've said it already—I'm young, and you're married."

The glasses moved this way and that, and back to the bridge of his nose.

"Well, that's the point. . . . Look, at first I didn't want to add to your worries, but I see you've calmed down now. I simply can't figure in any way in this affair. You'll have to be reasonable about it. It's a very complicated matter, and I can't explain it to you very well." A glance at his watch. "It's already late tonight, and in any case you need time to calm down completely. But tomorrow you must go and make an application there, like a good girl. Yes? You promise? After all, you must graduate!"

She wiped away tears, and nodded. Yes, she had to graduate.

"And then we'll go and buy that sweater, the one you liked so much at Tuzex."

She nodded again. Tomorrow, she remembered, she had that examination in mathematics.

"You know where it is?"

"Yes."

He took the handkerchief from her hand, and wiped her face for her once again.

"You women, ready with tears at the drop of a hat!"

"You ox," she said. "You crazy fool, you painted clown, you

lump of rotten stuffing, you idiot with the brain of a gutted pig, you upstage cretin!"

"Yes," he said, nodding at her slowly, "yes, if a few insults will relieve your feelings, go ahead. By all means . . . yes!" He did his trick with the glasses, and the remaining half of his cigarette flew dramatically in the direction of the ashtray. "You know, it's a fact I've had plenty of crazy ideas about you, it's lucky there's always something to bring a man to his senses in time." His face contracted with pain. "And I thought I should find a support in you!"

He looks like the stabbed Hamlet!—the thought came into her mind, and she rubbed at the place on her shoulder where the hand no longer lay, and which was again growing cold.

"You know what?" she said.

He gave her a wary, dubious look; he hoped she wasn't coming out with the bright idea of being an heroic, unmarried mother. But all she said was: "Do you suppose the people there at the commission would give me a note to excuse me from school? There's a math exam tomorrow, and I'm absolutely unprepared."

Boy with a Rose

When the girl had drawn so near that the individual features of her face were distinguishable, and it was possible to watch the expression of her eyes as they raised briefly to take note of the figure before her, and then again lowered, the boy took a single step forward, but not so far as to prevent her from passing by, and said: "Good morning, Miss!"

And when she stopped and looked at him—but only after a momentary delay, to prove that he would not have added a single word to his greeting if she had not chosen to stop, and by doing so made it clear that she was giving him the opportunity—he added: "Could you do me a small favor, please?—if I may delay you just for a moment, Miss?"

He had a placid face, but nonetheless it was a face that seemed willing and likely to break into laughter the very next moment, almost like an obliging waiter, with some hint of unintelligible malice in his very obligingness, confronted with a country guest. In his hand he held a rose, an Indian tea rose with thorns as fine as hairs, and the rose, his hand, and he himself jutted sharply in the air like some enigmatic trick performed by a wandering fakir.

This happened beside the wall of an old cemetery, several centuries old, in fact, where scores of generations had moldered into dust, and where the most celebrated of all Jewish rabbis is buried, and in front of the windows of an empty and massive ministry institution, which has a large number of entrances, but every one of them provided with a pointing arrow and the inscription: EN-TRANCE AROUND THE CORNER. Within the wall of the cemetery there were still some trees growing, but otherwise the street was only a stony desert parched by the sun, and so it re-mained even beyond the end of the wall, where the space contin-ued on across a street intersection. There was nothing green here except threads of moss and a solitary blade or two of thin grass between the stones, where some careless workman had left, and time perhaps had also helped to gnaw out, a wider crevice. The shadow of the trees behind the wall never fell as far as the street, still less could it reach the boy, who stood in his black Sunday suit (cut, perhaps, in an almost extravagantly modern style, or at least decidedly more modern than elegant), in the middle of the pave-ment, exposed to the steep and merciless rays of the sun, always with the same expression on his face, and always projected with the same sharp precision before the startled and astonished—but again not so completely astonished—eyes of the girl. He was look-ing at her rather fixedly, though not more noticeably so than is normal in all boys when gazing into a girl's face in early summer, and at the same time he was watching some place behind her head; for in spite of his detachment and his strikingly modern clothes it appeared that he was a little shy.

At first she was slightly alarmed, although in some unsuspected part of herself she had expected him to address her, and indeed she could not be quite sure that she had not even wanted him to; for although when she first became aware of him her intention had been to walk straight past him, nevertheless she had re-mained on the same side of the street, the sunny side; and as she had approached him she had become conscious that somewhere at the edge of her personality there was a mounting tension, of the same kind that makes children hold their breath as they listen to thrilling fairy tales, and sometimes, in movie theatres, takes away the breath even of adults.

Then the tone of his voice reassured her. The silence had lasted

more than a minute, and she was wondering why she didn't simply step forward and continue on her way, although she had her
hair done up in a clasp, and an imported brassiere from Tuzex,
high-heeled shoes and a chunky handbag, in which she carried
her glasses, five exercise books, two textbooks and eleven borrowed ponies—all of which greatly exalted her value as a woman.
Only then did it dawn upon her that it was her turn to speak;
and she tried her best to withdraw that bubbling tension and the
wonder and curiosity in her eyes inside the demure shelter of her
peachbloom complexion and jet-black lashes. She transferred her
weight to the other foot and her handbag from one hand to the
other. It's a good thing I'm not wearing my glasses, she thought to
herself. She knew that glasses didn't suit her. And she said: "Why,
gladly, but I really am in quite a hurry. What is it you need?"
And immediately afterwards she smiled, because she had sensed
that there was a note of impatience in her voice, and she really
was quite anxious to find out from this boy why he had stopped
her; she even found herself rather liking him, and she wanted to
behave charmingly. Also the rose in his hand interested her, and
a yard or so behind him on the pavement stood an attaché case of
cracked leather, such as doctors used to carry when they visited
our ailing great-grandfathers. It was so forsaken there that it
could belong only to him. This case, too, interested her, and
therefore she smiled at him once again.

The boy inclined his body slightly; an insignificant movement,
some minute flexing of hips, or shoulders and arms, relaxed his
position, and the rose bowed in front of the neatly fastened but-
tons of his black jacket. Actually the material had some delicate
pattern in its weave, but in the vehement sunlight everything
merged into a single blackness.

He moistened his lips and half opened them once or twice, as
though he wanted to say something he did not quite dare to say,
so that the word already half-formed always halted and died on
his lips. Then he shook his head lightly, and smiled in a manner
which was no longer in the least ironic.

"I only wanted to ask you to accept this rose!"

Behind their backs the truck that sprinkles the streets with water went clanking by. He was silent, perhaps unwilling to have to make himself audible over the racket it made, and thus deprive his voice of the only correct and appropriate intonation. He was no longer looking simultaneously at the girl and at some place behind her, but directly at her. At her peachbloom complexion, her nose, lips, eyes and chin. But he did not say anything more, even when the sprinkler had passed, and over the asphalt in the middle of the street, and the pavement at its edge, now steaming in the sun, flowed a fine, diffused stream of water, and the normal city dirt of a none too frequented and none too well-maintained street at the rear of a gloomy ministry, the old Jewish cemetery, and some totally uncommunicative institute. He had nothing more to say—no "please"—not even a word about why he wanted to give her the rose. Precisely her, and precisely this rose. He merely held out the flower in his hand toward the girl.

She was delighted. For though all her feelings and thoughts were subordinated to the subconscious longing to accept happiness whenever it came her way, yet on this particular day, which was only just beginning for her, neither on her way to her first lecture nor, indeed, at any other hour of the day had she allocated time or place to the charmed act of accepting a rose from a man. So she smiled a little more widely. The flower also smoothed away all her uncertainty about what this encounter in a parched and sunburned street was to bring her, an encounter which by its very promise had contrived to detain her on a pavement without a morsel of shade.

"Thank you," she said. And she stretched out her arm in a single direct movement from the shoulder, her elbow unflexed, reaching toward the boy's face and the fragrance of the flower he held out to her. She took the rose, and since her original smile had flagged a little, she smiled at him afresh, breathed in the scent of the rose, heaved a deep sigh, half closed her eyes, and smiled once more.

"It smells heavenly. . . ."

At that the boy retreated a step, like a well-trained footman from an old house, but without the precisely calculated position of the hands which is characteristic of the breed. He stumbled slightly against his own battered case, and smiled, half as though he wished throughout to remain simply a pleasant companion, and half like a man smiling to cover up his own clumsiness. The girl stood facing him, the tip of one toe pointing toward the boy's case, and thus determining the position of her body. She studied her rose, turned it in her fingers, and waited.

"Do you like it?" asked the boy.

She nodded quickly, saying with animation: "Yes!"

"Good-bye!" responded the boy, and at that moment his smile was at its softest, and his eyes were again fixed only on the girl's face, quite oblivious of the wet asphalt, the overgrown, unused path and the oppressive sun.

She continued to gaze at him, in somewhat greater wonder than when he had first stepped into her path with the rose in his hand, and uttered his: "Good morning!"

"Good-bye!" she answered slowly; and then her pleated skirt whirled round her thighs, and with a sharp tapping of the metal tips protecting her heels, she walked away.

He looked after her as she receded into the distance. In the hand that was not carrying her bag, she held the rose poised before her. She had slender, beautiful legs, and as he looked after her, the swaying skirt, belted tightly at the waist, called forth only the best and pleasantest of thoughts. Then he stooped, lifted his old medical bag, snapped back its fastener, and as it opened, took from it one more, and again only one single rose. He remained standing in the same position as when the girl had first caught sight of him, with the trace of a smile which could well appear very ironic. And he stood without a single movement to suggest the presence of any impatience or dissatisfaction at continuing thus in the blazing sun and the heat, penned between the stone of the paving and the stone of the old wall. It seemed that he was not paying very much attention even to the rose he held.

On the asphalt the first dry patch appeared, and broadened steadily; and in a little while there remained in the whole street not a single damp spot to recall the passing of the sprinkler.

Part Two

And as the evil man is unable to believe that man, as man, is not inevitably evil, so, on the contrary, our nations have shown their better part precisely in this, that they contribute everything, shrinking from no sacrifice, when they are faced with the necessity of proving that they believe in their own immortality—that they believe in the immortality of the conception of liberty.

Vítězslav Hálek.
National Leaves, 17th September, 1863.

So long as we do not give up hope on account of one unsuccessful Spring, we have not despaired of Spring itself. And though the nightingales may still be few in the naked grove, yet we shall never on that account take our delight in owls. Let one sun soar into the sky, and though the bats now celebrate their heyday, they shall never put out its fire, nor cover its face.

Vítězslav Hálek.
National Leaves, 5th May, 1864.

In our country ability is persecuted, and inability protected. There is only one thing virtue must possess—the art of enduring!

Vítězslav Hálek.
National Leaves, 3rd August, 1866.

A Pancake Memory

Dedicated to Mr. Polcr, sometime functionary of
the Ministry of the Interior prison at Trenčin.

In command of the shift that day was Father, a sturdy, limping
sergeant who was said to have spent the war years in England,
and had earned his nickname mainly because he actually was
more or less of a real FATHER, and when he was on duty the
retributive process went along recognizably more pleasantly for
us, that's if anything in prison can ever be called pleasant; at any
rate, very decidedly nearer to being pleasant than when his simi-
larly uniformed colleagues were on duty. Maybe because of this
England thing. Father knew, and in fact he didn't try to make
any secret out of it, that he would remain a sergeant to the day of
his death (also precisely because of this England thing!), so that
he had no incentive to go hunting promotion at the convicts' expense. But all the same, I don't think it was just solely because of
this, for even the floor orderlies in his shift were more like ordinary people than guards. Most likely that was his good influence
on them. When Father was on duty we had a glimpse of something that the old hands call "prison de luxe."

He took me out of my cell still completely shattered after the
court proceedings, changing clothes, being marched across the
yard, signing the clothing lists and other mysterious registers, and
all that madhouse that was evidently going to continue without

intermission and for a long time without reaching an end. *C'est la vie,* as our French teacher used to say. First of all, immediately after they've awakened you on this court day, they take you to be shaved, then they dress you again in your own civilian clothes, and shove you into the transit cells, where they're absolutely certain to forget about bringing you any dinner, if some case in front of yours in court gets dragged out longer than expected, and you don't come into the picture until afternoon, as happened to us; but on the other hand they have two guys at a time instead of one on duty in the corridor there, so that you're hardly ever without an eye glaring in through the spy hole in the door. If you're doomed to be really out of luck, then in the morning the barber gets to you just at the right time to displace your breakfast. *C'est la vie,* as our French teacher used to say.

We went down three floors, to the main gates. Father opened the grille, and the duty guard opened the metal-plated door for him; and then up again, past the corridor by which you go to the court, or for any outdoor exercise, through the corridor where the interrogators have their offices, into a number of spot checks, and around a corner where I'd never been before. Father halted at a padded door beside which there was a bell, and a lighted notice in red letters saying NO ENTRY. He took off his cap, took out a handkerchief from his pocket, wiped his forehead, pressed the bell, and while we were waiting he said, "One and a half you got?"

I nodded. MY GOOD GOD ALMIGHTY, one and a half years! When I get out I'll be nearly nineteen, and I'll go headlong into my military service. It was as if the full force of it had only just hit me. Yeah, one and a half years! My God!

I suppose I must have looked pretty depressed, because Father waved the hand that held his guard's keys, a fine rattle they made, too, and he said, "Oh, you mustn't take it like that, being put inside, why, you're young. You've got plenty of time, you can still be a policeman yet . . . or Prime Minister for that matter." And again he waved the hand that held the keys. "You've got your whole life in front of you."

When you've flown straight from school into prison, that sort of advice doesn't cut much ice with you. Or usually it doesn't. All the same, I was glad that Father had said it, mainly because of THE WAY he said it. It made me feel a lot better.

Then the little light on the door went out, and another one went on in green, saying ENTER. So then Father tapped on the door, just to make sure, reached for the latch, and pushed me in ahead of him.

"In you go, the Chief wants to talk to you."

He opened the door, uttered some sort of announcement, and left me alone in the office.

They took us into court after dinner, of which, to be exact, all we saw or heard was the rattling of plates overhead, on the floor above us. The sun shone into the courtroom through terribly dirty and dusty windows, for it faced south; and among the public there, in his worn and shabby bus driver's uniform, sat the father of my comrade and accomplice Bret.

They began on our case at once, and you could hardly say that they went into it very profoundly. It only took a few minutes. In any case we were all anxious to get it over with. They read over the charge, and a few quotations from the depositions, which we'd heard a hundred times already, had repeated over and over, and over and over admitted. We admitted them once again, then the prosecutor and our counsel made speeches, and we had the last word.

Thomas said something about how bitterly he regretted everything, and that he would do his best by hard and diligent work for the national economy to atone for the crime he had committed, and be able to take his place again among our decent, law-abiding workers. Then I said something to much the same effect, and then Bret; only Bret was interrupted from the public benches by his father. You could see how agitated he was, that he wanted to help Bret, and that all this was a matter of great grief to him. In the end he thumped himself on the chest and roared: "I'm a worker, give me my boy, and I'll straighten him out myself!" On which he burst into tears and flopped back into his seat on the public bench.

It looked so idiotic, Bret was dreadfully ashamed, all of us felt a bit uncomfortable; but evidently this bit of theatre had its effect. Though it needn't have been just theatre. No father feels good about having a son in prison. It's true the chairman of the bench reproved Bret senior, and said he should restrain himself from emotional exhibitions, that he was in court now and not on board his bus. But afterward, when it came to stating the grounds for the judgment, that emotional exhibition of his, which he ought to have restrained in court, hit the spot. And so, though we all got one and a half years, in Bret's case it was conditional, so that his bus driver-worker father could straighten him out himself.

Immediately after that the proceedings ended; the bench rose, and when Thomas and I were led out a few minutes later, across the yard and back into the prison, the whole bench of judges, the girl secretary, and the prosecutor were in the yard playing volleyball. Only the defense counsel was missing from the party. My God, the boys and girls from school were probably enjoying themselves in much the same way at this very hour, playing Ping-Pong at the beach.

In the middle of the yard there was a wall that divided the court from the prison. When we'd been taken into court five convicts on *our* side of the wall had been busy shifting a gigantic heap of coal from the street gate to the shafts into the cellar. For security reasons, most likely, they wouldn't let the coalmen into the far side of the yard. On the way back, that heap didn't look even the least degree smaller. Perhaps just enough to be visible to the naked eye.

The commander had the window open in his office. It was hot. The window must have faced directly toward that side of the yard where the coal was. I could hear the scraping of shovels on the concrete of the yard, and even the sound of spitting, as the convicts hawked up the dust from deep within their throats. Somewhere outside, too, you could see the tops of trees. The commander was in civilian clothes, sitting behind a table on the far side of the room, and writing something with deep concentration.

For perhaps a couple of minutes there was silence. I stood inside the door, on the same spot where Father had posted me. Then the commander, who looked astonishingly small behind that table, raised his eyes and said languidly and ironically, "Well, what happens next?"

I had no idea what happened next, or what ought to happen next, and told him so. He turned blue, and flared: "So you don't know what happens next, eh? YOU DON'T KNOW? Nobody's taught you, I suppose? Well?"

I shrugged my shoulders, and this time, to be on the safe side, I was silent. There isn't even much you can say in a situation like that. But he hadn't expected that, either.

"You don't know? How long have you been here?"

"Four and a half months."

"Four and a half months. . . ."

"Yes, Commander."

"And nobody's ever told you that you must report in the proper form?"

"No, sir," I said, "nobody."

He studied me narrowly, and shook from his head to his waist. "You're Šotola, aren't you? Jiří Šotola?"

"Yes, Commander."

He rocked his chair on its back legs, and linked his hands under his belly. It was a solid little belly of the type the bricklayers on the building site where we went for practical work from school used to call a "socialism."

"And what if I should have you put in the punishment cells, Šotola, eh?" He relaxed his legs, and the chair crashed back on to all four legs. "You have the insolence to tell me to my face that in four and a half months nobody's told you how to report properly to your superior?"

"Nobody has, sir," I said again. "On my word of honor, Commander."

He giggled.

"You can keep YOUR word of honor to yourself, Šotola. Just keep it! Words of honor from people like yourself are worth a great deal, aren't they? I've been sitting here for a good long time, you know. Nobody's going to make a monkey out of me!" He rapped on the table with his pencil, and pressed a bell on his desk. Something buzzed somewhere, and after a moment in came Sergeant Father. Evidently he'd been waiting outside in the corridor until the commander would have finished with me.

"Mister Sergeant," said the commander—all the guards called one another "mister" instead of "comrade" in front of us—"teach this prisoner here that he must report properly when he's brought before his superior!" And he pointed a hand toward the door.

The sergeant made some alarmed response; we crept out into the passage, and there I listened to a short course of instruction. As the light sign on the door had been left at the green ENTER, he pushed me back inside again.

"Commander, Convict Šotola, 55 212, reporting on your orders, sir."

The commander listened to this contentedly, with his little head cocked on one side, and pointed me to a corner of the room: "Sit down!"

In the corner there was an iron stool screwed to the floor; absolutely the same, only not screwed down, as we had in the art room at school. The commander slowly wrote something down in some register.

"You know what you are, don't you?" he said; and when I didn't answer he continued: "A student, you understand! A typical student. How many such I've seen already! Here!" and he slapped a hand down on the desk in front of him, and wagged his head as though it caused him grave anxiety. "You won't get far this way . . . well, that's why you've ended up here." He crossed to a table with a typewriter on it, and inserted a sheet of paper into the machine. With obvious effort he tapped out a few letters. "This is where you all end." And again he looked at me very gravely. "This is your image!" And he pointed a hand at the place beside his typewriter on the table. Only then did I notice that my briefcase was lying there, and all the things I had had on me when they picked me up. Apart from the textbooks and exercise books and all those trivial things, there were four detective novels which I'd happened to borrow that very day when they arrested us: Edgar Wallace, *The Brotherhood of the Frog;* Edgar Wallace, *The Green Archer;* Alain Gordon, *Shadow of Gold;* Samuel Lewin, *The Mystery of the Scrimshaw Family.*

We'd gone to have a shower after gym, and then we'd run into Bret and wanted to go to a bar. One always has to go somewhere, sooner or later. But the bar where we'd thought we might go happened, quite by chance, to have its closing day that day, and it also happened that somebody'd left the lavatory window open. We climbed inside, got drunk, and went to sleep. In the morning, in the most ordinary way possible, they'd simply found us lying there.

The commander took out the paper from his typewriter, picked up some kind of form, put a carbon and another sheet of paper behind it, and fed the whole thing into the machine. For a moment he went on pecking laboriously at the keys, then he pushed those four detective stories a little further from the rest of my things.

"Come here!" He showed me with a pointing hand exactly where. He took out the form and its carbon copy from the machine and placed it before me, got up from the typewriter and went and sat down in his former place; joining the tips of his fingers, he gazed into space somewhere out of the window. The convicts in the yard were still shoveling coal steadily, and cursing and spitting.

The paper was a preprinted declaration, filled in with my name, prison number, and date of birth. There it was announced in my name that I did not wish those four detective novels to be placed with my personal things, and confirmed by my signature that I had been present at their destruction. I couldn't understand this very well. They weren't even my books, I'd only borrowed them during the break before gym.

"But, Commander. . . ." I would have liked to explain to him that these books were not mine, that all this stuff by Wallace and Alain Gordon and Samuel Lewin belonged to somebody quite different. But then it occurred to me that I might be dragging into this affair even the boy who had lent them to me. After four and a half months of living in a functioning prison thought up by people for people, one thinks very carefully before mentioning the name of one of one's comrades to anybody connected with the Ministry of the Interior.

"Well?" said the commander. "What is it?" He raised his eyebrows and bulged his eyes at me. "Well, go on, sign it!" And he let his brows and the wrinkles under them drop back into place again. "I mean well by you in this matter, Šotola, don't you know where this reading has led you? Do you realize how your mother's probably crying for you? And do you know what your father would most likely have to say to you, if he were sitting here in my place?"

Father and Mother, and I was glad of it, had not taken it into their heads to come and look on at my trial, as old Bret had done. In any case the affair had made Mother ill, so that fellow who interrogated us told me. As soon as anyone spoke of them I was near to breaking down. But now, after the court hearing, I would be able to write to them. In all this business about the bar we'd drunk dry, and prison, and everything, my parents were the worst thing. But every idiot seemed to take a delight in asking what my father would have to say to me. If you answered something about getting a few good slaps, or a beating, then the fellow questioning you always made a very grave face and mouthed out:

"*There, you see, you see!*"

This time I didn't say anything.

"Go on, sign it," said the commander again, when he saw he'd failed to get any satisfaction about slaps and beatings from Father, though he'd obviously been waiting for that. He tapped the Edgar Wallace that lay on top of the pile. "Nobody is going to misuse these books again. . . ." He sighed. "So much evil this stuff has on its conscience . . . so much evil!"

I was already holding the pen in my hand—but then I put it back on the inkstand.

"I would like to keep these books, Commander!"

I knew that he wanted to steal them from me. Now I knew it!
The court had confiscated from us one dirty poem by Vrchlický,
but that had been recorded. There hadn't been any mention
there of these books.

That was when he hit me.

I don't know how he did it, he hadn't even moved, but suddenly I got it. Sometimes when Father was very angry, or when he
was pretending that he was, he used to say: "I'll give you such a
clout, you'll get the second one from the ground!" But I never
did get that second one FROM THE GROUND. Never until
now. It was a wallop like a house falling on me. Like a town
falling on me. Like the kick of a horse. The boys in school had
another saying: "You'll get such a blow, that you'll fly like a
crow!" That was just the kind of blow I'd gotten.

As long as I live, I don't suppose I shall ever understand how
he did it. Even when he was standing up, the commander was a
head shorter than I was—and he'd handed it to me right across
his imposing official table. But obviously he'd had plenty of practice.

I sat on the floor and stared in wonder. Like every boy of a
certain age, I'd taken boxing lessons in my time, but I'd never
found myself sitting down after any blow. Until now.

The commander stood up, leaning on the table with his left
hand. Then he straightened up, pulled out a handkerchief, and
slowly wiped his right hand with it.

"Get up!" he said. "You see! Did you have to make that necessary?" And when I'd clambered to my feet he only shook his head
wonderingly. "Stu-dents . . . stu-dents. . . . You're all the same!
You know you'll have your conditional parole coming up later,
don't you? You'd surely like to go home, wouldn't you? And
yet you do such things!" He laid his hand on the books. "So much
evil these have on their consciences, so much evil!"

He must certainly have attached a high value to those detective
novels! He dipped the pen and handed it to me.

"Here you are, and no more nonsense!" He turned to the window, and all the time he was still shaking his head in wonder, as

though still pronouncing that: "Stu-dents, stu-dents!" or "So much evil, so much evil!"

CONDITIONAL PAROLE. The prisoner who by his work and his behavior shows that in his case punishment has already fulfilled its educational role, can be released conditionally after serving half his sentence. . . . So much evil. . . . And that blow like the fall of a house. . . .

I signed the declaration. The commander separated the original from the copy with satisfaction, and stuck it into his desk among his papers. Then he opened a table drawer and tossed the books into it.

"We're still going to have plenty of trouble with your generation, boy!" He sighed deeply, as though all that trouble lay solely upon his shoulders. "You've had too easy a youth, that's what it is. You've had everything handed to you on a silver platter, and then all at once we've got you in here, and I have to put right everything they haven't taught you at home or in school." He stared deep into my eyes. "And still you're ungrateful!"

He covered up the typewriter with its shroud. Then he lit a cigarette, pointed me to the stool in the corner, and went to look out of the window into the yard. He wagged his head a few more times at everything, and over everything, and sighed. Then in came Sergeant Father. The commander merely waved a hand at me, and went on staring outside, perhaps at the convicts who were shoveling coal from the gate to the cellar shafts.

I began to mumble the formula for departure, as Father had taught it to me a little while ago in the corridor, but the sergeant jumped in and stopped me. "When I'm with you, you needn't report." And outside he told me that it was simple, really, just like in the army.

"Have you done your army service yet?" he asked.

I shook my head, and Father said, "Ah, well, at least what you learn here will be some use to you there!"

As we'd been through the court process now, he brought Thomas out, too, and then we were allowed to carry coal to the kitchen and talk to the cook, a woman who was in prison for murder; and as we hadn't had any dinner, and Father was a good guy, he let the cook make us some pancakes in return for the coal. They were the first and the last pancakes I ever ate in prison, and I have the best possible memories of them. Before they took us away to a labor camp—though to be really correct one says ON a labor camp—we carried coal a good many more times, but it never again happened to be on Father's shift, and we never again got anything for it, either; and never, never again did we see that cook who had killed her husband.

C'est la vie, as our French teacher used to say.

The Last Possibility

We'd locked ourselves in the washroom on the second floor. In the whole hostel, maybe in all the hostels put together, this was most likely the only door that could still be locked, and probably the only place where a man could be alone, when it was worthwhile, or when he found it necessary. The hostel stood on a hilltop, and this floor was too high, the waterworks couldn't stand the pressure. The water ran only on the ground floor, so that nobody ever came into this upstairs washroom, and a little while ago Joe and Danny and I had turned it into a kind of small private gymnasium. Out of two concrete building blocks and a piece of one-inch piping we'd made ourselves a dumbbell, and from a steel plate layer's wrench for track screws, pinched from the mine, a slightly crooked and shaky horizontal bar. It was no good for anything elaborate, somersaults and such, but for pull-ups and arm exercises it did us very well.

"Have you thought it over?" asked Joe.

I nodded. I had thought it over. In fact I'd been thinking it over for a long time now, and many times, and since yesterday evening I'd thought about it all over again. It seemed to me now like something I'd really known all my life, and been keeping in reserve all my life, as the one possibility remaining to me when there was absolutely nothing else left. Obviously there's always some possibility left for a man, only sometimes it's worse than what he hopes to avoid by resorting to it. When they wouldn't release me from the factory, I was left with the possibility of volunteering for a year's service in the mines if I wanted to escape, but escape into the mines isn't really any escape, even if it is only for a year. I had a cozy job all promised and waiting for me through my future father-in-law. In Mototechna. People are crazy about cars, and in Mototechna you can earn good money.

And in the mines I was left with the possibility you're left with in any kind of work. *To go on sick call.* To go on sick call when you don't want to go down into the mine, or when you've got your own reasons for not going down into the mine. Or the possibility of breaking a finger, or an arm, when all your ailments and all your schemes for going on sick call fail you. I'd been trying mine on the works doctor all this morning, and they'd failed me. They'd let me down. And I didn't want to go down into the mine, and I even had my own reasons for not going down. That was why we'd locked ourselves in the washroom. Joe and Danny were my men, and I was their man. Any one of us could turn with confidence to the other two.

Yesterday, on the afternoon shift at the Johanka mine, the machine room for the main elevator had caught on fire, and although it was hardly more than a little smoke and fumes, yet it had been enough. One miner and nineteen convicts had stayed down there. Either they hadn't had their gas masks handy, or else the masks had failed them.

I didn't want to go down. Not at any price.

I'd had a broken arm once, when I fell off my bicycle. I could remember that there hadn't been any specially acute pain. I went to ride out onto the path, took the corner too sharply, and wrecked a beautiful, export model collapsible on the curb. It hurt when I fell, but it wasn't any unbearable pain. I'd known worse. And Danny had a pillow under his arm. Just to make sure. I was hoping that this business with my arm wouldn't be any worse this time, but I wanted a pillow to bite on, just in case. I'd thought of it yesterday, when we were crawling out of the Johanka by the ventilation corridor ladders into the neighboring Bernarda mine. And I simply didn't want to go down into the mine. It was *an honor*, it was *money*, but all that stuff was a bit like those slogans: "If you can't stand the heat, get out of the kitchen." These were things somebody else had thought up for us, and *I'd had enough of it*. Just as after a time it stops being amusing, having to keep saying "I love you!" to a girl you merely want to sleep with, and even that only because you want to sleep with *someone*.

Joe and Danny had talked at least a hundred times about how somebody somewhere had led the world by the nose, just by breaking his arm or burning his skin with a welding flame. I'd heard the same sort of thing plenty of times before, but Joe and Danny told it as if it was something really easy to master, and they'd promised me they'd do it to me today. I wasn't interested in leading the world by the nose. I didn't need that. All I wanted was not to go down into the mine but to get safely into my own little mine in Mototechna. Half a year of it, and yesterday afternoon, that was quite enough of mining for me.

Joe took hold of the latch, and tested it to see if the door was properly locked, then he took out a packet of cigarettes, and offered them to us: "We'll have a smoke first, eh?"

Apart from our gymnastics, we used to come to the washroom to have a smoke.

We lit up, and gathered at the window. Outside it was raining. Along the ground rolled a greenish-yellow mist from the chemical works, and above trailed gray-blue clouds, with a half-darkened sun peering out now and again. Just like always, or nearly always, in this region. I doubt if there's worse weather anywhere in the world than in this region, and for that matter I don't suppose there's a worse region anywhere in the world, either.

Opposite us jutted the sorting plant of the Johanka, and all around were the slag heaps from the Katherine, the Bernarda, the People's Government, and the Hedvika mines. The People's Government used to be called the Saint Barbara, and the miners still called it the Barbara much more often than they did the People's

Government, so that even we who couldn't remember the time when it had been the Barbara knew about it, and called it by that name, too. In any case, I don't think the People's Government is a very good name for a mine.

We smoked and looked out at the rain, as we had done at least a hundred times here. Joe said something about the weather, and about life, and Danny and I said something else to much the same effect, something that suited this weather and this life we led here. Then Joe and Danny repeated what they'd already said to me the day before, when I'd made up my mind that I simply wasn't going down into the mine again. They said I ought to leave this arm breaking business until we were on shift, because for injuries sustained at work the sick pay is much better.

You could see that Danny was scared by the whole thing, though he'd been the one to tell all the best stories about leading doctors and insurance companies by the nose. The people who spin the best yarns usually turn out to be no good when it comes to action.

"You'll lose your sick pay," he said. "I would wait until you're below ground."

"The hell with the sick pay!" I said, shaking my head. *"I'm just not going down again!"*

"Just because of that accident yesterday?" asked Joe.

I shrugged my shoulders. That miner and the nineteen convicts were certainly a reason, if one absolutely had to have a reason. But mainly, and simply, *I didn't want to go down.* I'd never liked it, but that was of no interest to anyone else, besides Joe and Danny. That miner and the nineteen convicts were a perfectly good reason, if I needed any. Like when they ask you at the permit office: "Why do you want to go to Yugoslavia?"

"I want to go to Yugoslavia because they've got a seacoast there."

"I don't want to work in the mine," I said. The cage had fallen. The shift was over. Maybe it had amused me a little at first, but now I'd been at it for half a year. Mouth full of dust, helmet on head, arm stretched from carrying the lamp, and fumes

137

trailing for miles through the passages. With my arm in plaster I would be out of action probably for six weeks or so; I had a month's leave to come—that meant still three and a half months of my contract. But there was always appendicitis and a host of other possibilities, once I could get away from the works doctor and into the hospital. In any case, plenty of things could happen in the world in six weeks. I simply did not want to work in the mine, and above all, I didn't want it *today*. When I remembered the slimy iron ladders of the ventilation plant by which we'd had to crawl out yesterday, that was quite enough to convince me that I didn't give a damn for any of the things Joe and Danny were saying to me. Reason, security, money, honor and heroism, and all the rest of the "I love you, oh, how I love you!" And all the paragraphs of the law, too, and all the people who lived by paying attention to them. The arm was mine, and I didn't want to work in the mine. And this idea with my arm was the only possibility I had of not working in the mine.

Joe couldn't grasp that. He'd been working in the mines for four years, and he liked it. He thought I was afraid. He couldn't understand that I didn't want to go down.

"Nothing will happen, not two days in succession, it never does, you idiot," he said. "You needn't be so terrified."

Both of them were afraid of this thing with my arm. I could tell. It was they who were terrified, and that was the reason. I merely didn't want to go down into the mine.

"You told me you'd do it for me."

"So we will," flared Danny. "Of course we will, has anyone here said we won't?"

Nobody had, but nobody had said that it was a risk either. A risk for them, too, even though it was my arm. You can go to prison for a thing like that. We all knew it, even though we hadn't said a word about it to one another. At last Joe had finished his cigarette. He smoked slowly; he did everything slowly and seriously. He threw the butt between the window bars and out into the yard.

"You're a nervous old woman," he threw at me out of the corner of his mouth. And as he exhaled the last puff, he asked, "I hope you realize it may set badly? You could end up a cripple."

"Straight or crooked," I said, "I'm not going down into the mine."

"What if you tried something with your stomach—or your eyes?" suggested Danny, just as if I'd never told them about the crucifixion I'd gone through in the morning at the health center. It was grotesque. I'd tried stomach, gallbladder, bronchial tubes, syphilis, conjunctivitis, inflammation of the bladder and sciatica. All quite vainly. All I got out of it was some aspirin.

"Well, he'll take notice of you with a broken arm," said Joe, turning his back on us and going to the showers, to take down the plate layer's wrench from the partitions between them. "He'll have to!" He shook his head. "But it's idiocy! Wait a week! Imagine getting all steamed up like this over a little bit of smoke!"

"I'm not waiting. I don't want to go down into the mine, and *I'm not going down today.*" I knew he had an exaggerated idea about this, but I couldn't argue with them that I wasn't that scared. He had to break that arm for me, I needed it. "A bit of smoke was enough for that group yesterday," I said. "Quite enough for them, wasn't it?"

Quite enough for them. I'd expected something like an earthquake, but those men were nothing more than just 19+1. The only death I'd ever experienced before was my grandmother's. Curtain, finish, nothing, no words any more, no more beer, no more suppers. It was new to me. 1+19. 19+1. They were nothing now but 19+1, nothing more, they'd had no masks, they'd forgotten their masks, or their masks had failed them. 19+1. They had been people, just as I was a person, and yesterday and the day before they'd been doing the same work as I. Down there underground, they'd drunk the same stinking, tepid water from the casks, and those convicts had even done extra work we should have been doing, because we brought food in, and took their letters out. But they were only 19 + 1. And really I'd felt nothing more than that, that and the certainty that *I never wanted to go down into the mine again.* Nothing more. Neither grief for them, nor joy and relief that I'd managed to crawl out in time, and undamaged. I was like those people who get married one day, when they find life boring, and then, out of the very same boredom in reverse, get divorced again.

Joe lifted down the wrench from its place above the showers. It wasn't fixed there in any way, only laid across the partitions. He weighed it in both hands, crossed the chipped enameled trough to join us, and let one end of the wrench drop to the concrete floor.

"They were just unlucky." He meant those 19+1. "It won't happen two days running. It happens maybe once a year." Then he jutted his chin. "Well, now what?"

I rolled up my sleeves. Danny tossed the pillow aside, and began to swathe my forearm in a wet towel. We'd brought that up with us, too. In every story about fractures a wet towel, wrapped around the limb, played a great part.

Joe swung the wrench a few times through the air, experimentally. Danny watched him, and asked, "How much do you suppose it weighs?"

As it hissed through the air I felt a slight weakness in my stomach, and sweat broke out on my back and under my armpits. It's one thing to *say* to yourself that if it comes to the worst you've always got the option of breaking your arm, but quite another thing when you really have no other possibility left. Maybe this time it really would knit badly! They're two different things. I was petrified by the idea of that brown iron falling with merciless force on the arm which up to now had always served me well. On that very bar I'd done thirty pull-ups only last night.

Joe weighed the bar testingly in both hands, looked questioningly at the ceiling, tilted his head on one side, and said: "More than twenty pounds—maybe twenty-five." Then he handed the wrench to Danny, who held it and weighed it just as he had done, and even gazed interrogatively at the shabby ceiling as he had done. Then he belched gently, sank to his knees, shook his head, and corrected Joe: "It must be *at least* twenty-five."

"Do you want to do it to him?" Joe pointed at me.

Quickly Danny handed the wrench back to him: "You've got more wind than me."

And as a matter of fact, Joe had, and the admission soothed him. He didn't like it much when people corrected him.

"The left one?" he asked.

I stuck out my left arm, wound to the wrist in the towel, but Danny knocked it hurriedly down again.

"Idiot, it's got to have time to work." He pressed a fingertip into the back of my hand, withdrew it, and watched how quickly the indentation vanished from my skin. "Like that you'd suffer worse than a dog!"

Joe shrugged. "Plenty of time, isn't there?" He stuck the wrench under the water pipes, and laid it crosswise over the trough. "I'll do a few exercises while we're waiting." And he took a couple of strides toward the concrete dumbbell lying by the wall. He liked to do his knee bends with the weight to balance him. But then he stopped, because the wrench under the taps began to roll, took a crooked turn against the edges of the trough, and seemed about to fall. We all watched it with strained attention, all getting ready to grab it, so that it wouldn't clatter on the floor. But it turned in time, and stopped against the standpipe under the taps.

"Hey, you watch it!" Joe threatened it. "Lucky for you!" He went to the wall then, and hoisted the dumbbell to his neck, and began to do energetic squats. In a few minutes he was as blue as my hand, and his veins were sticking out just the same, only in his case on his neck. He did his usual thirty, then let the dumbbell carefully down again to the wall, and said: "Well, you say you've thought it over carefully."

"I'm never going down again!"

He picked up the wrench from the trough.

"Whatever you say, bambino." He had regained his normal color already, and his veins had subsided. "Then you'd better lay it down somewhere."

There wasn't anywhere to lay it. The trough had sharp edges, an arm was more likely to get cut off on that than broken, and I didn't want it cut off, even though I've read in the papers that doctors are clever enough now even to sew on a severed arm. But what I wanted was a clean break. It didn't even have to be both bones. Even with only one broken, it would be impossible to go to work. I pointed to the window: "What about here?" I laid my arm on the sill; but first we had to remove a frightful monster, a hanger for towels. But even then Joe couldn't stretch properly there for the blow. And there wasn't a table or bench of any kind in the washroom. In the end I laid my arm against the stove, though it wasn't comfortable. Originally Danny had wanted to take one pane out of the window, so that Joe could get at me, but we talked him out of that. We had to wait a little while again, because somebody saw him from the yard, and shouted up to him, and Danny answered him. We didn't want him or anyone else to hear me cry out, if that pillow didn't work.

"You warming up again up there?" demanded this guy below; and Danny shouted back: "Sure we are. Come on up and join us!"

"Who was it?" asked Joe.

"That idiot Kryštofek," said Danny. "From thirteen. The one who's chasing that lamp girl who comes with the convicts."

Thirteen was the thirteenth station on the cableway, just where the machine room had caught on fire yesterday; and the convicts who worked with us had their own lamp room and lamp woman, and also lamps with a red stripe around the bulb. Then Kryštofek went off somewhere out of the yard. It was still raining the whole time.

I leaned down to the stove again, and laid my arm in its towel on the cast-iron top.

"Close your eyes, or you'll jerk away," Danny advised me, and then he held the pillow to my face and I bit into it.

Joe drew in two or three labored breaths.

"My God I can't!" he said. Danny said something back, and I mumbled something into the pillow and opened my eyes.

I saw the flash as the bar flew, but I didn't jerk away, by that time I wasn't even capable of it. The blow fell on my arm. I curled up into a ball, and gripped my wrist between my thighs. My God, how it hurt! I hissed and whined, but my arm was still intact. When Danny asked me, I still couldn't speak, but I shook my head at him. They were surprised, but Danny less so than Joe.

"We should have heard it," he said. "It snaps, like when you break a stick."

In a few minutes I'd pulled myself together enough to be able to lay my arm on the stove again.

"You still don't want to give up?" marveled Joe.

"No," I said. It was the only possibility. A blister was coming up on my palm; what was under the towel I couldn't see, but my arm was still whole.

I got another blow, and curled up again, and the pillow fell. As I writhed and whined on the floor, Danny held it in his hands, followed me around, and stuck it over my face again.

"Yell, that's it, go on, yell!"

I was drenched in sweat. But still my arm didn't snap like a stick.

"Did it crack?" asked Joe, and I could only shake my head again. I moved my left hand experimentally, then took it in my right and twisted it about. It hurt, but all the fingers moved, and there wasn't any grating of broken edges of bone to be heard, rubbing against each other. I had a bruise on the back of my hand now, I could see it, and feel it even beneath the towel, and the blister on my palm had changed into an inch-long wound with torn skin at its edges. But otherwise nothing to put me in plaster for six weeks. *It was still intact!*

Joe shook his head incredulously.

"Again," I said, wiping blood from my palm.

"You have to hit it so as to get it crossways," said Danny, and pointed out the place on my arm where Joe ought to strike to take the bone crosswise. They argued for a minute, then Joe took the pillow offendedly, and Danny picked up the discarded wrench. I closed my eyes again.

This time the blow was stronger, and also hurt more, but the bone still didn't break. They tried to strike obliquely, but again there was no cracking noise, like snapping a stick.

"Is this the same arm you had broken before?" asked Danny, as if there was something going on here that he'd never in his life taken into account, and never could have.

It was, and I told him so.

"Then that's it!" He banged down the wrench and threw his arms above his head. "You've got a calcareous bone there, we could go on bashing that for three weeks!" He began to unwind the towel. "After that fracture the bone's set stronger." I didn't know whether he was right or not. My arm was swollen, the last joints of my fingers were beginning to disappear into the bruise. I had the pattern of the towel printed into my skin.

"That'll disappear in a quarter of an hour," said Danny.

Every minute my arm swelled up more. But it was swollen enough to get two days in compresses, not six weeks in plaster. I asked for a cigarette.

After half a cigarette I pressed the torn skin from the wound in my palm back into place, and laid my arm on the stove again: "Let's go!" *I wanted it broken.*

We laid into that arm on top of the stove, Joe, Danny, and I, too, when they offered me the wrench. But it was no good. Then I leaned it against the wall, Danny pressed the pillow against my elbow, and Joe hit out again at my arm. That way, they say, the joints of the wrist may be dislocated, and a dislocated joint is at least as good as a clean fracture. But we never got anything better than a bruise. The boys didn't want to go on trying any more. In the end they had to have a cigarette between every blow. It had really got them.

"That should do you for today. Tomorrow we could work on it a bit more," suggested Danny. And it surely would have done. For today. But tomorrow I would no longer have the courage or the opportunity to do all this over again. But I still had an idea of my own.

In the end I half crawled and half had myself hoisted up onto the trough, and wedged my arm between the hot and cold water pipes, which here never ran water. I had to take a minute or so off to pluck up my courage. It was the last attempt, the last possibility in all this theoretical possibility of breaking my arm, this chance that had soared so splendidly and purely through all those brave speeches, and then faded. Then I braced myself with my right hand beside my left, and did a side vault over the paired pipes.

I fell sprawling on the opposite rim of the trough, and skinned my side a little, the way my arm threw me. But even in midair, before I dropped, I felt the same hot, burning pain shoot through my whole arm as that time when I rammed my bike into the curb, and there was an audible crack, like the crack when you break a stick. Danny and Joe heard it, too, and immediately, as they lifted me back onto the trough so that I could get my hand loose, they were assuring me that this time it was certainly all right. And we were all glad that we'd put this job behind us.

So it was all right. This shift—we were on afternoons at the time—and many others after it were home and dry, they vanished from me in a rosy mist of leisurely walks with my arm in a sling. Two or three days of pain before one got used to it. I started composing the story I was going to tell the doctor, who would certainly remember me from the morning. I slipped and fell—but that wound on my palm was a bit of a snag. All right, I slipped and fell in the washroom—for in the washroom there was a slatted wooden mat studded with nails. There I could very well have ripped my hand.

At two o'clock, just when the siren went for the shift, I was already on my way to the hospital, with an invalid splint and a doctor's note in my pocket. At a quarter to three, just when the nurse, who had resolutely ignored all my attempts to fix up a date with her, signed my fresh plaster with a ball-point pen, the earth shook under us, and the windows in the hospital rattled, and so did the glass cupboards full of bottles and powders, and the bottles themselves. Half a minute or a minute later the alarm sirens began to wail through the whole district, and again a minute or so later still, the sirens of the ambulances joined in, rushing from the hospital toward the Johanka, where there'd been an explosion of coal dust—in spite of the tradition that disasters don't happen two days running—and the entire shift stayed down there, all 93 + 256. Or rather 92, because there'd been one possibility left to me, and I'd managed that tricky vault over the pipes.

Now I could say what it was I'd wanted. I could see, beyond the fact that *I had not wanted to go down into the mine,* what I actually had wanted. But there was nothing. Nothing at all, just as there'd been nothing in the case of those 19 + 1. Maybe there was still some possibility somewhere, but now there was only that nullity that makes us marry one month and separate the next, and beyond that nothing, except perhaps a kind of faint weakness, such as you feel when a one-and-a-half-yard length of two-inch steel whistles through the air. A weakness that stems from the realization that casual words about the pattern of a towel, or about bones breaking like sticks, can be somebody's last. But even this was a weakness without feeling. Only of wonder. Empty, void, ordinary, futile and good for nothing.

Everybody assumed that something terrifying was happening in me. Something frighteningly incomprehensible. *If he hadn't slipped in the washroom, he'd have stayed down there, too!* They made cautious circles round me. They thought I had about me some genuine touch of "If you can't stand the heat . . . ," some special providence taking care of me, some convulsion as great as love, but there was nothing, nothing, nothing, only a date written in ink on my plaster, a date I hadn't yet managed to rub out, jutting six weeks ahead into an unknown life. And the works doctor's distrust of my story about slipping in the washroom, now suddenly checkmated by disaster.

I could have been dead now. But I didn't know anything about what it was to be dead. I went to stand at the shaft, when the rescue squads went down with their oxygen apparatus, and when they laid the miners and convicts in coffins ranged around the yard, for want of space anywhere else. But apart from the thought that this wasn't a very nice sight, and apart from banal phrases such as everybody uses—"It's terrible!," "Such a disaster!," "My God, two days running . . . ," "What will their poor wives do?," "How could it possibly happen?," "Bad luck never comes singly!" —nothing, nothing whatsoever, came into my mind.

I even went to volunteer for the rescue squads. I knew they wouldn't take me with my arm in plaster. But I didn't do it for effect, nor to get myself presented to the government commission which had been sent to the scene at once. *He lost his two comrades down there!*

"I understand just how you feel," they said to me.

I could eat, drink, lift my hands, read the newspapers, watch people, including the people belonging to the government commission, and there were plenty of them all over the place, wanting to know everything. I could have gone from coffin to coffin looking for Joe and Danny, if I'd wanted to. And now, too, I could quite well have fixed up not just a date but a close acquaintance with that nurse from the plaster unit at the hospital, if I'd wanted to, if there'd been some sort of possibility behind all this. *I could have been dead now,* that was the possibility. I knew nothing about what it was to be dead. *People felt for me and understood how it was with me,* but in reality everything was all one. *This* was all one. It meant nothing to anyone, just as it meant nothing to me apart from the bare fact that I was alive. Just as it meant nothing to those who divined in me some sort of drama that wasn't there, or even to the prostitutes who used to hang around us when we got our pay, and would have come out with just the same "So young, too!" as they'd said over Joe and Danny. They'd have said it over me in exactly the same way. And the three-member committee would have gathered together the things I'd left in the hostel and packed them in a cardboard box, to be sent to my family. And I would never have arrived in that snug little mine of my own with my future father-in-law in Mototechna. All the same, maybe I won't marry that girl of his, after all. I was alive, but I couldn't feel the distinction in any way, and the only thing there was to be done about it was to keep silent. Because everything else it was possible to do, apart from that, was only talk.

The Request

On the twenty-ninth and thirtieth of November the expected frosts came. Somebody has said that in a labor camp the winter passes more quickly than the summer, but otherwise there's nothing pleasant about it. In the evening it began to rain, the whole muster ground was wet, as it had been for several days previously; about midnight the rain changed to sleet, and the yard into one great ice-skating rink, and at three in the morning the guards woke up the leavers' brigade. These were the men with sentences running only into months, or those who would soon be finishing their terms. They went out to shovel snow and spread gravel and salt over the roads of half the district. The huts chilled in the frost, and people began to wake up.

Perhaps two feet of snow had already fallen, and every moment more was still falling. The brilliant carnival lighting of the corridor between the two wire barriers was lost in the blizzard, the lamps vanished beneath hoods of snow, a clinging wetness draped the world, and everything was disappearing, the world, the slag-heap from the mine, and the lights on it. A little while after the snow brigade of leavers had departed, the blizzard set off the alarm signal on the inner wire. Even the rocket was damp; it burst feebly into the darkness and collapsed into the white void, but the lookout on the northern crow's nest, ever wakeful and on guard, managed to register its brief flare. In the confusion he lost his bearings and fired into the camp. In Hut B the shot passed through a window, a jar of lard standing inside it, a mustard glass, and the bed underneath former theological student and SS man Zelcam. God knows what the old guy was aiming at, but Zelcam was lucky. If you're born to be hanged you'll never drown, and apparently they'll never manage to shoot you, either. The bullet had embedded itself in the chimney, the only brick wall in the whole barrack hut. Half a yard one way, and it would have struck mere boards, and somebody in the neighboring room would certainly have gotten it.

Between the two wire barriers the bedraggled dogs waded through the snow; the shot had startled them, stupefied though they all were by this eternal coursing around the corridor. They must have been even more bored there than we in the camp.

Zelcam struck a match to examine the hole the bullet had left in the frame of his bed, the eternally hungry Franta Zajíc heaved up his 280-pound body and groped under the table after a stray crust, and several people went to the lavatory, for cold like that stimulates the bladder. Only one bucket of coal was allowed per room, and between the boards of the hut, long since captured from the Germans, there were gaps in places through which you could thrust your hand.

Someone roared at Zelcam not to be such a lunatic with that match, that crazy lookout up there might take another shot at the light. Who knows what goes on in a cracked brain like that? In the summer they had shot Tonda Smrčka the day before he was due to be released, and all he'd done was reach through the wire after a kitten. Though of course it was true that at that time the internal guard had still been in charge of camp security; some people had hoped for better things from the lookouts, who were pensioners belonging to the district, and hadn't any incentive to shoot down prisoners just to earn ten days' leave; but all the same, as they'd just shown, they were hellishly trigger-happy.

But defrocked priest and SS armored division grenadier Zelcam calmly held the match until it burned out, and pointed out of the window. Nothing but whirling snow, in which the thousand-watt bulbs in the wire corridor looked like will-o'-the-wisps, and the searchlight from the watchtower was only a paler streak. The guard could not possibly see anything, certainly not a mere match. All the men in the room went by turns to have a look at the bullet hole. Franta Zajíc had already dug out the bullet from the chimney breast with a clasp knife, and somebody cracked the inevitable joke that he only wanted it to eat. A few people were wrapping up some food for the shift, and Granddad Pytel was cursing because once again he hadn't been able to sleep the night through. He did the buying for the whole shift; they had recently gotten their issue of pocket money, and business was booming for Granddad, or it would have been booming if only the supervisor would take him through the wire to the canteen. But up to now, somehow, it had never come off, and Granddad was still perpetually calculating and writing down his orders.

From time to time the searchlight from the tower passed over the hut, as faintly and diffusedly as over milk glass. Somewhere near the gate a second rocket went off, but by this time it had evidently dawned on the guards that it was the snow causing it, and it passed off without a cannonade. Nobody called the building brigade to work, for the buses had not come to get them. But the siren sounded to rouse the mining shift.

Pytel yawned.

"All the same, we won't be going down, the civilians haven't come." He waved a hand and yawned again widely: "We know from last winter."

The seething white darkness enveloped everything. The leader of the shift came, white from head to foot with snow, looked at the hole in Zelcam's bed and the shattered jar of lard, and wagged his head. Somewhere one more rocket went off, and the duty man brought in from the kitchen the iron pot of coffee. It must have been standing somewhere in the frost for a long time, for the coffee was quite cold. Franta Zajíc lamented bitterly over the smashed pot of lard, and tried to pick out the splinters from it. It was his, and without fat it's a wretched life in prison, very wretched. Finally someone advised him to strain it through a cloth after the shift.

Instead of the usual rush, suddenly there was plenty of time. The night shift had finished their stint, and had formed a square for their roll call, but still the civilian workers had not come; maybe the snow brigade had done its work too slowly, or else there was simply too much snow. Plenty of time. Pytel took off his helmet, tore a page out of his canteen notebook, and began to write a note. The night shift was already above ground, and bearing down on Hut B from the gate came the Bottle Brush, alias Ginger Dick, a country bumpkin with watery eyes and a reddish, bristling head that really did recall the kind of brush used for cleaning a baby's bottle. He was stuffed into a three-quarter-length Security Police leather coat, with high snow boots and a cap with ear flaps, on which he had collected a very respectable snowdrift. He saw the mining shift in their working overalls lolling on their made beds, and drove them all out to the muster ground, although the buses still had not come, and they still had no idea whether they were to go down even without the civilian workers, or whether by any chance they would be sent out to help clear the snow, which was still falling without respite.

The wretched, wet, frozen hour of half past five in the morning, on the last but one day of November. Life. The last to leave the hut was Granddad Pytel with the brigade leader. He walked slowly to the far end of the yard, drew out of his helmet the note he had written, and threw it into the box provided. He put his helmet back on his head and went to take his place in the second rank of five. He had an old and low number, dating from the beginning of the camp. His neighbor cocked his head at him enquiringly, a question about the communication he had just dropped into the box.

"Some money off my account for my old woman," he muttered, and Zelcam, two rows further back, announced that he was fooling, it wasn't any request about money from his account, but a report against Franta Zajíc, who in all that snowy confusion had stolen from the boiler room by the kitchen the food put aside for the dogs.

The Bottle Brush kicked at the snow, trampled out letters in it, and now and again, to stop them talking, yelled: "Quiet, boys, damn it!" He had his hands in the pockets of his leather coat with the lambskin lining, and occasionally he spat between his feet, and watched the saliva eat its way rapidly into the snow. He had no instructions. Except the basic instructions, of course: "Silence, boys, damn it! And I mean it!"

The prisoners in their mining overalls were freezing; they stamped and muttered. The night shift had already been dismissed to their hut. Now and again someone shouted something; darkness and blinding snow covered everything. The Bottle Brush's flock was cold, and also bored, perhaps bored above everything. And straight at the eternally nervous Bottle Brush flew the first snowball. He whirled around and rushed furiously toward the place from which the missile seemed to have come.

"Stop that! Stop that! Who was it? Come out here!" For half a minute the shift ceased to roll snowballs; then the Bottle Brush got one slap on the ear.

"Cowards!" he shouted, and began to hunt helplessly for the assassin, scooping the snow from the back of his neck and inside the collar of his coat. He pulled out his truncheon from his sleeve: "Come out here, hero, don't hide yourself! If I don't find out who threw that, I'll make the whole shift sorry! Don't play games with me, boys!"

But he didn't turn his back on them again, and he was trying to grow eyes all around his head.

Before seven o'clock the snow brigade came back in a great hurry. Word went around that some crazy clown, who had already served four years and had only 240 days left before his discharge, hadn't been able to resist the call of the distance, but had picked up his heels and run for it. Thus the shift finally got back into their hut, where at least it was a little better than outside, even if there was no coal. But twenty minutes later the buses with the civilian workers finally arrived, and the shift went on duty.

At four o'clock in the afternoon the fugitive was back in camp, savaged by dogs and with his mouth ripped from ear to ear. They paraded him on a rope before the whole assembled camp. The sky had cleared a little by now, only an occasional flake of snow still drifted down; in places there were even stars to be seen, and withering frost was setting in. The delights of winter were unleashed in their full glory. Winter as on a Christmas postcard. An idyll. A somewhat chilly idyll. The punishment cells howled for help.

The first of December was a Wednesday; they took away the fugitive to prison and judgment, and the camp got a new commander. Everyone had known for some time that a new Heart of Gold was coming; the convicts who worked in the administration office had passed the word around in good time. The new commander immediately had a special small wire corridor set up around the punishment block, and even made the electricians fit up lights there, so that no one could get near the unfortunates in the cells. In the huts they hung up posters, invitations to all to offer suggestions for improvements; a great competition with prizes. First prize, an electric shaver. A pity there wasn't a single outlet into which it could be plugged in any of the barrack huts. After a long interval proper outdoor exercise was again arranged, most probably as a result of the snowballing. They marched, while the Bottle Brush recalled his sergeant major days in the army. In fi-i-i-ves . . . by the left . . . qui-i-i-ck MARCH! . . . ab-o-o-u-u-t TURN! On top of this, they still had not let Granddad Pytel through to the canteen, so that the tobacco situation began to be really critical, and at last even the means of smoking, like everything else, had to be smuggled in from the mine. After roll call the shift which was judged the best for the month of November had to stand in the frost while the camp broadcasting system played them a record as a reward. The shifts that hadn't fulfilled their quota were dispatched into the warmth of the huts as a punishment, so that they wouldn't hear a note of it.

On the second of December a little more snow fell, but the frost held. Throughout the day it was below zero by two or three degrees. The new commander showed himself for the first time in the camp; up to then the old one had merely left him his nickname. All camp commanders, of course, have Hearts of Gold, and think only of the convicts committed to their charge, and everything they do is done with the best intentions. This one was also a Heart of Gold. He made a brief speech about what he wouldn't tolerate in the camp, what a penal camp should be, what he liked and didn't like, and what he viewed with particular displeasure. He also announced that prisoners would uncover their heads for five paces in front of and three behind a guard, and other such things. And on top of everything else, he had all the Jehovah's Witnesses transferred from the building brigade to the mine.

There were not a great number of Jehovah's Witnesses in the camp, perhaps seventy, but they were an élite. Every one of them was in prison on account of refusing military service. They would not serve. All they had to do was report to the Heart of Gold, and say that they would go into the army, and in twenty-four hours they could have been at home. But somehow not one of them ever did it. They preferred to stick it out in prison, but here again they had one more extra hurdle to take. They refused to work in the uranium mine, because uranium is used for making atomic bombs, and the Witnesses' faith forbade them to do anything which would contribute to war.

The old Heart of Gold had tested their sincerity over this several times, as duty bound: ten days' punishment cells, twenty days' punishment cells, strait jackets, the drum treatment—the order varied from case to case—but finally he gave up, and sent all the Jehovah's Witnesses to work in the building brigade or in the camp administration office.

The new Heart of Gold evidently thirsted for recognition as a strong man who could do better than that. When the morning shift reported for the mine, about eleven people stood aside, all Witnesses. On the afternoon shift the same thing was repeated. As a beginning they put them in the punishment block. With the assembly of the night shift they had all seventy of them together.

Only this fresh contingent intended for the night shift was not thrown into the punishment block. The Heart of Gold had made a point of staying in camp. Again he made a little speech—all Hearts of Gold are comedians of the first rank—and then had the Jehovah's Witnesses spaced out on the roofs of the huts. The Bottle Brush and Quasimodo swarmed eagerly up and down the ladders in their three-quarter-length lambskin coats and their warm mitts, and posted the prisoners, in their wretched thin rags woven from nettles and their patched boots, without gloves or socks, at regular intervals, like ninepins: "Still two steps farther along. One more! Now you here. Come on up, the next man!"

The hole in the frame of the bed was no problem, and the broken window had been stuck over for the time being with paper. Franta Zajíc had strained his lard into a new jar, which for safety, in case there was any more shooting, he hid under his bed. Granddad Pytel thumbed and pored over his shopping lists, and they all listened to the croaking of Ginger Dick, and the stamping above their heads, on the roof of the hut. There was a misty ring around the moon, the frost tonight would be no joke. About an inch of ice coated the windows.

"You'll stand there as long as you go on refusing to go down into the mine . . ." Quasimodo hectored outside. "You heard what the commander said, you're doing this to yourselves—nobody's got anything against you, but you'll do your duty here. . . ."

On the roof of the neighboring hut was deployed another thin, regular line of figures. In the light of the moon the men on the roofs cast long, sharp shadows on the snow. Somewhere in the darkness below them hopped the light stain that was the Bottle Brush in his lambskin coat.

"This has stopped being a joke, boys," spoke up Pytel. "We've never had this here before."

"In Mauthausen there were other things," said Zelcam.

Then the door was pushed open, and the brigade leader put his head into the room: "Granddad Pytel! Here's that request of yours. I forgot to give it to you." The paper was passed from hand to hand across the beds until it reached Granddad. The old man struck a match. He read:

REQUEST.

Convict Josef Pytel, born 5/12/1899, Number 214, Hut B, Shift No. VI.

I respectfully request the commander to permit me to send 1000 crowns from my account to my family to buy coal for the winter. I have about 14,000 crowns in the account.

Thank you for your kind consideration,

Convict Josef Pytel

On the back of the request was written the commander's decision: "Granted, but only to the amount of 25 crowns," and a scrawled signature.

Pytel waved the match until it went out, and then tossed it toward the stove.

"What is it, Grandad?"

"Nothing. The commander has a heart of gold. Good night, boys. Time you were asleep."

Outside, the wind whipped up the powdery snow and hurled it into the dark, toward the Jehovah's Witnesses spaced out along the rooftops.

The Class Enemy

The day began slowly and stealthily, as do all clear summer mornings. The stars receding, the sky growing paler and paler, the vast, uncanny stillness of the great, unlighted houses, a calm disrupted only by the sound of an invisible bus in the distance, and the commotion of the birds in the orchards.

Sleep shortens a term in prison by entire long hours, and therefore everyone makes a habit of sleeping until the last possible moment. In any case the day itself is spent only in waiting for the evening, when it can be subtracted from the total number of days remaining, so it is very important not to awake before it is necessary. Within the closed eyelids of prisoners there is exactly the same peace and tranquillity as within any other closed eyelids.

There were four straw mattresses in the cell, but five men lying on them. Even if one of them had happened to awake, not all the portents of day would have been able to induce him to stir himself out of a state of deep, silent stillness similar to sleep. They refused to be shaken out of it even when a car horn began to blare in the corridor, the official alarm clock, and the day was no longer heralded only by the light, the birds, and one alien, distant bus, braking for God knew what reason.

Most of them tried simply to ignore the horn, to hide their

heads under the covers and obstinately salvage the last possible morsel from sleep and its tranquillity. If only they could have been a shade more soundly asleep they might have escaped hearing it at all; and as yet nobody had proved to them that they were awake. Nobody had caught them with eyes open. Therefore they could remain in the world of their own warmth and their own dreams, which would not permit the uglier realities to approach closer than the topmost layer of rumpled and tattered coverings. The world enclosed within twelve square yards, the world of broad, merciless daylight beyond the barred windows, of baked beans and porridge, will be held at bay, far away outside you, as long as you can still encase your body in the armor of sleep.

Only the stone deaf, of course, could actually claim not to have heard the bellowing of the horn. It blared so piercingly that some of the guards not yet hardened by the service were driven to drape a cloth over the machine, or stuff a newspaper into the horn; but even if it had been howling at full strength, and its power had been redoubled, still not one of the men in the cell would have allowed himself to give the slightest sign of having heard it. Distaste for the day was too great, it was easier for them to come to terms with the din. Then, even through the rending clamor of the siren, they heard a thump on the door of the first cell at the extreme end of the corridor, and the guard's voice, hardly distinguishable at that distance, shouting to the men within. The knocking and the shouting came steadily nearer, always the same number of knocks, repeated ever more loudly, like some cruel, convulsive echo in reverse.

When it had drawn quite close to them, and was hammering at the cell next door, Leichtner, one of the five, who slept at the edge nearest the door, kicked off his covers and sat up. The only bit of free space in the cell was on his side, and in any case he was the senior man in the cell, and had to get up first. But he also preferred to be first because he had only one arm, and before dressing he needed a little time to fasten on his artificial arm.

As he got up, the horn stopped. It brought a measure of relief and an unaccustomed silence, so surprising at this moment that it might almost have given rise to the hope that the authorities had forgotten about them, or that something else equally improbable had happened to postpone the onslaught of morning. But in a moment they heard, in contrast to the stealth of the regular daily inspections, the clumping of far from stealthy feet outside their door, and immediately afterwards sharp blows with a bunch of keys on the metal plating of the doors. They could even hear the soft slither of the Judas panels in the doors, and a voice which they recognized at once as that of the guard usually known as Horse's Mouth, though the circumstance that he had only one eye had tempted his charges to invent many other nicknames for him. In a persistent bellow this voice declaimed its invariable morning greeting: "Didn't you hear the alarm, eh?"

They waited for it, and replied to it in a mumble of "Yes . . . yes, sir!" They tossed among their blankets, and some of them sat up, for that was their lot, and more precisely, it was expected of them, and it satisfied the guards. Satisfying the guards was important for people in their situation.

Leichtner was already up. The elder of the cell always asserted that he had lost his arm as a partisan during the war; and his purpose in life now was to be sufficiently obedient to ensure that in the final reckoning his obedience would be counted to him as credit, along with that partisan arm. He looked back politely into the single guardian eye behind the glass of the spy hole, and greeted the guard courteously: "Good morning, Commander!" He had to shout it aloud if he wanted to be heard outside the door.

But the Judas panel had slammed shut, and Horse's Mouth banged blindly at the metal again with his keys, and a second later they heard his voice shouting and his keys clashing at the next cell. They did not take his rough awakening amiss. They accepted it just as they would have accepted diphtheria, or a wife's desertion that only confirmed a long held and haunting conviction that she was as good as lost. He quickened in them no hatred that was not already there; if he called up any idea at all, it was simply the rueful realization of how easy and pleasant it would be to fall asleep now that the horn had stopped its blaring.

But they knew only too well that in a few minutes the guard would have reached the end of the corridor, and would turn back. And this time it would pay them to prove that they had been listening.

Silently they moved about the room, shivering, displaying the yellowed dinginess of their underwear covered with black prison stamps. They folded up their covers, massaging the goose flesh on their arms and thighs. Morning was morning; it was no use any longer refusing to admit that it was here.

The thickset, taciturn Koval, covered with what seemed to be a scaly hide, went to squat over the zinc bucket in the corner. They had to take turns on it before seven o'clock if they didn't want the cell to stink all through the day, for the corridor orderlies emptied the buckets at seven.

Nineteen-year-old Zmola, with his hair clipped close to the point of baldnes, helped the waiter Čepitský, whose lean emaciation suggested cancer or stomach ulcers, to line up the straw mattresses on top of one another against one wall. Leichtner took his stewardship too seriously to help them with this job, even if he could have been much help with his single hand. He was too exalted to make beds; indeed, he had some secret and lofty view of his own mission in life. Every one of them, on occasions, was a small moth dreaming of being a death's-head; and according to prison protocol bed making and cleaning were no part of the duties of the cell elder.

Finally, when they had the mattresses neatly stacked in the prescribed place by the wall, and the coverings rolled up and lined up together on end, they lifted old Harfa, the little, gnomelike gypsy, and laid him on top of the pile. Harfa was said to be seventy years old, and was doing time for rape. In prison he had contracted pneumonia, so he had permission to lie down even during the day. They hoisted him onto the pile of beds so that he would not occupy the meager floor space they needed for their diagonal walks from corner to corner of the cell, and on his account they could now number the doctor's visit among the events of the day. He came in the morning, usually shortly before dinner, with the injection ready prepared in his raised hand, the thermometer in his pocket, and two guards treading on his heels. The custodian of the keys stood in the open doorway, and by the blank wall opposite the mattresses the prisoners stood to attention.

"Soon be dead, eh, old geezer?" one of the doctor's escort would say good-naturedly, and old Harfa, with his head wrapped up, and looking like a seated Bedouin on the frontispiece of some travel book about the Taurus, would grin with his battered mouth, hug the thermometer under his arm, and nod his head joyfully. Sometimes he even got out something that could have been an expression of agreement.

Sure, sure he'd die! How could he dare not die? A great, a mortal sin he'd committed with Marie, a terrible sin. If only they could forgive him for it, if only he dared hope that the commander would forgive him, he'd never, never do anything of the kind again!

Meantime the doctor—and he, too, was a prisoner—had completed his task, and tossed the syringe into a box in which he had the used wooden spatulas for examining tonsils, and the needles with which he lanced prison ulcers. He wiped his fingers on the same piece of alcohol-soaked absorbent cotton with which he had also rubbed Harfa's buttock, and said: "What d'you make of the old man, then? He's as tough as they come—eh, granddad?"

And Harfa nodded agreement to him just as stupidly as to the guard's remark that he would soon be dead. Of course, of course! He beamed with his worn lips, with his mottled face and inflamed eyes: "That's right, that's right, doctor!"

Then the doctor turned to the others, standing lined up against the wall, and in turn examined their ulcers, their throats, or whatever they requested. Finally he indicated Harfa: "Take care, don't let him get cold. Lie down!" He wagged a finger admonishingly at the old man. "No walking around, granddad."

They assured him they would be careful. The guards at the door were getting impatient by now, but at these warnings from the doctor they usually laughed, and either they or Čepitský

("Spelled with *t s*, Commander," he always said after his name when reporting) would then make some remark about no fear of Harfa catching cold when he had such a young sweetheart. Obviously he had plenty of warmth and energy. Harfa had raped his own eight-year-old great-granddaughter, who had been helping him herd the pigs in the pasture.

"Come on now, old man, tell us what it was like!"

But Harfa always stared in one direction with his unchanging stare, grinning out of the mount of his coverings with his toothless mouth and his face of an ugly dwarf. At the most he lifted one hand in a helpless gesture: "Aah . . . you know . . . !"

The doctor waited, silent and unsmiling, and when the joking ended he took leave of them all, one after another, and then of all of them together: *"Au revoir,* gentlemen, I'll be off now."

"Good-bye, doctor," they replied in a ragged chorus, and as soon as the door began to close they sat down on one of the two benches affixed to the wall, or continued their pacing from corner to corner. Everything was really only a form of waiting, even the stink of chloride of lime from the bucket, the stench of Harfa's sweat and the many times breathed and never renewed air. The feeling of never having quite enough to eat, the longing and the hope. The curiosity. Would events take some unexpected turn the next moment, or continue dragging along in the same slow fashion?

"It's today, isn't it?" Zmola asked Koval rather unnecessarily, as he took his place on the bucket. Every man has his TODAY, some time in his life, and they all knew that for Koval it was this very day. Zmola knew it, too, but he wanted to say something, and he wanted to know how a man feels when his TODAY comes. Zmola's TODAY was still somewhere in the unknown future.

"Yes, it's today," assented Koval drily. He was just getting ready to wash, slowly and gravely as he prepared for everything. "At ten o'clock."

"They'll come to shave you, won't they?"

Koval merely nodded his head. Obviously they would come to shave him. Everyone has the right to appear before the court looking as well as he can. He cared very much about these formalities, even though the barber had only one razor blade for twenty people.

He knew the feeling that bound the others to him. It was respect, the respect of schoolboys for a brother at the university. He had already served his eighth year, and the scaly hardness—still further emphasized by his unhealed skin disease—the unbreakable, granite rigidity of the farmer reigning supreme over his fields and his family, all this had become even more knotted and engrained in him as a result of his stay in the prison camp, his work in the mines, and everything that could press hardest on such a man as he was.

They had brought him here two days previously; and yet these four, drawn together by a common tenancy now extending to several weeks, had vacated for him the best place by the wall, where he could not fall into the gap between the mattresses. Just as tacitly they had allowed him to be first on the bucket. He was accustomed to the possession of strength, and still possessed it, though he was past fifty. When they wanted to see the church clock from the window, Koval could lift any one of them by the elbows right up to the ceiling of the cell. And then again, Leichtner, in spite of his partisan past and honorable diplomas, was a thief, who had robbed some freight trucks. The waiter Čepitský had merely been thieving in a slightly more refined way when he charged for Courvoisier instead of Stock, and Zmola had said farewell to his blameless life at nineteen by an unsuccessful attempt to cross the frontier, to evade responsibility for his part in a tavern brawl. Not one of them had to live with the intimate consciousness of a double number, signifying the years to which he had been condemned, as Koval had lived. The prisoner who is accompanied constantly by those two digits acquires wisdom, the feeling of an account in process of settlement. Nor could any one of them take comfort in a sense of injury, like Koval.

They were still, at this stage, standing in only their shirts. It was the same every morning, it lasted an endless time, so that sometimes they began to suspect that they had been awakened earlier than five, and doubted whether the cathedral clock, which they could see from the window if they looked from the right angle, was showing the correct time. There was a small, curtailed eternity before they heard the next sound of the day: the opening of doors, and somewhere beyond, even the bubbling of the kitchen cauldrons, and the motors of the buses that came to take the definitively and legally sentenced prisoners from the opposite wing to their work.

"Unlockings and lockings," said Čepitský reflectively, as the keys rattled in their own lock. This time they saw the whole of Horse's Mouth's one-eyed countenance, as he handed in to them quickly a galvanized iron wash basin, and said: "Hurry up, now, no stalling!"

Zmola shot out with the can in his hand to the water tap in the corridor, while Leichtner, with his real hand, took down from the hooks outside the door all their towels, and the bags with their soap and toothbrushes, those of them who possessed these things. Then they stood gulping in the freshness of the air flowing in from the corridor. The prison had been built under Maria Theresa, and their cell had originally served as a place of solitary confinement. Five people could exhaust its air content so completely that the air within was never changed at all. The current now flowing in from the stone corridor was for them one of the best things they knew, like the vision of coolness and consolation called up by the sound of water falling into Zmola's can.

"Did you ever hear, Commander, how Cohn invited Roubíček to a party?" asked Čepitský, and began to retail to the indifferent and genuinely equine face of the guard one of the many stories about how Mr. Cohn met Mr. Roubíček. Then the stream of falling water was silenced, and they heard the slapping of Zmola's slippers. He ran into the cell, and the guard slammed the door without waiting to hear how this particular encounter between Cohn and Roubíček ended.

Koval pushed the rolled-up sleeves of his shirt still higher, and began slowly to wash himself. At the first cell the door clanged again, and they heard the slapping footsteps of someone running past with a bucket to the latrine.

"Maybe we shall get some outdoor exercise today," said Leichtner, with slightly exaggerated significance, to show that Koval's TODAY meant nothing to him. Nobody contradicted him, and nobody agreed. Occasionally, of course, there were periods of outdoor exercise. When the prison governor made his rare inspection and report—they were about as punctilious about that as about shaving prisoners—Leichtner or somebody else regularly replied to the governor's question as to whether there were any complaints: "We don't get any outings!"

For some unknown reason Leichtner had a way of pronouncing some words like a Slovak, although he was a Czech.

And the muscular captain regularly replied, with confidential benevolence in his voice, that outings were rather a complicated matter, that he fully understood that prisoners had a right to them, but there were so few guards, and their first responsibility was to escort the working prisoners to their employment. This, in any case, was never more than a system of questions countered by known and expected answers. A duel between one wretched pawn on one side of the board, and the opposing queen and bishop on the other.

"Food? Any complaints about the food?"

"It's these beans all the time, sir. . . ."

"Well, you know, the norm here is a modest one, and in any case no one invited you here, did they? The diet has the perscribed calorific value."

That silenced them. It really could not be said that anyone had invited them here.

From the window, and from the right angle, the cathedral clock could be seen, but it happened that the right angle was near the ceiling. They could hear the clock strike, of course, and it was quite possible also to look out of the window. But it was necessary to wait patiently and with concentration to hear the hour strike, and looking out of the window was forbidden and therefore dangerous. There were guards outside, and anyone they spotted at the window was bound for the punishment cells. So after breakfast, when they had surrendered their cups, and wrapped up their daily allowance of bread among the bed covers, Koval lifted up

Zmola by the elbows. He was becoming a little impatient. The cathedral clock showed half past eight.

Koval drank some water from the can, and began to pace the floor. He was not thirsty, but he knew that in a little while the water would become tepid. It was better to drink at once, while there was still some refreshment to be got out of it.

"It drags, doesn't it?"

Some time before his imprisonment, Zmola had worked in Koval's native village. He had even, as they found out in conversation, lived in his former house. Perhaps because of this, they felt rather more trust toward each other than did their companions. All of them, of course, were FRIENDS. It was better to be friends than the opposite. Enmity would have been hard to bear. It was far easier not to be enemies, and not to hold against one another what society held against them. They were in no situation to determine which of them was better, and which more deserving of condemnation. Harfa with his eight-year-old great-granddaughter, Leichtner's stolen goods from the freight wagons, Čepitský's trick of charging as much for Stock as for Courvoisier, or Zmola's misfortune. Only the matter of Koval's concealed land remained for them far less concrete than the concept of the fifteen years to which he had been sentenced for it. They never thought of justice as a concept. It was not among the things they thought about at all. They thought about women, or small rogueries, about the life they would lead, or at least the life they wanted to lead, when this episode was over. They still believed that it was only an episode. But fifteen years was no episode, and could never be thought of as one, or simply measured against any other fifteen years. It was an inconceivable ocean of months, days and hours. It was a term which could not be imposed for any act of which they were capable.

Koval, too, found time dragging. He passed a hand over his face, for his beard worried him.

"They ought to have been here to shave me by now."

"You've got plenty of time before ten." Leichtner, on the basis of his partisan past, addressed everybody in the familiar second person singular, and would even have done the same to the guards if they had let him. He was one of those people—and rather proud of it, too—who take liberties with everyone, just as they invariably use, out of some never very clearly defined principle, the approved greeting: "Honor to work!" And he delighted in using the formula: "It's OUR affair—the WORKERS!"

Koval didn't answer him. He never had much to say on this subject, and never answered anything he didn't want to answer. He had said very little about it even when he found out that Zmola had lived in his former house, and the discovery had stirred in him eight-year-old recollections that were still familiar and everyday to him. He was still silent when the others got onto the subject all prisoners are so glad to talk about, provided they can display it in the light of their own particular truth. Čepitský's presence was due to an innocent mistake. Leichtner had happened on an open truck full of textile goods quite by chance, and merely wanted to have a look what was inside, when they had arrested him and charged him with the theft of everything that was missing. Harfa's eight-year-old great-grandchild had tempted him to sin, with her legs spread wide.

But Koval had replied only with short, hard, laconic sentences, exactly as he saw himself: "Why?" He lifted his shoulders and let them fall again. "They wanted to get me here, and they've done it."

That was his definition of his case, formed and a thousand times confirmed in the course of the past eight years. He was in prison for the crime of concealing land. Not one of the others knew what kind of crime that could be, or how it was committed, and Koval felt no compulsion to explain its basis to them. He had been before the courts three times. Two regular courts, which had acquitted him, and then one extraordinary one, a people's court, which had sentenced him to that double-figure term of years. When he and Zmola were talking about the village and the house, he asked: "What about that orchard at the back there?" It had always been his pride.

"Which one is that?"

"There behind the barn."

"There isn't any barn there now. They made a communal cow shed out of it, and then, when they didn't have any stock any longer, they turned it over to the machine station."

"They did?"

"Last time I was there we had a workshop there."

"But there must still be something left at the back there, surely?"

"No," said Zmola, "I don't think there was much left. There was nothing to keep the stove going with in the winter. And it's a long way to the forest."

"Oh." Koval couldn't understand that, but he didn't want to rack his brains over things he didn't understand. At least, not now. It was just the same with that concealed land. Two courts had set him free, and one, a summary and extraordinary court convened right there in the village, had rejected every offered proof of his innocence, indeed of the nonexistence of the land he was supposed to have suppressed. They had even refused to have the land register of the district rechecked at Koval's own expense, as he had offered, and had sentenced him to fifteen years. Someone had testified that several acres in the mountains belonged to Koval's farm. So they had imprisoned the farmer and moved his family away. He shook his head over it, though he could not understand it. The state witness and Koval's son had been courting the same girl. And then there was the social interest, of course. Yet later he heard that the land which he, and his grandfather, and his grandfather's grandfather had tilled, had been reduced to pasture.

"My God," he cried, and this time he was deeply disturbed by the thought of everything the words "land" and "farm" meant to such a man as he was. POOR LAND! PASTURE! He shook his head, indicating with an outspread hand: "I had rye there this high, THIS HIGH, boy!" And it was indeed tall and noble rye.

"And the potatoes!" Through his head passed a vision of all the agricultural exhibitions he had known, his medals for pigs, his blue ribbons for potatoes. This said nothing to Zmola. He had stoked the stove with the cherry trees from the orchard because he had to keep warm somehow, and nobody had bothered to supply him with any other fuel. Not even a hundred years of Kovals said anything to him. He thought along other lines and in another way. He was another man.

"The main thing is that they should let you go," he said. Leichtner grinned silently and wryly in the corner. He said of himself that he always took his stand behind THE CAUSE OF THE POOR, and Koval behind bars was, in his view, the cause of the poor. He also claimed to be a partisan, and looked upon that as something superhuman.

The cathedral clock slowly struck nine. Four deep and nine chiming strokes. Slowly. They listened to them, frozen in mid-movement. The barber really should have been here by now.

"I'm curious to see how it'll turn out for you," said Čepitský. That went without saying. They were all curious.

Koval shrugged his shoulders. He had filled up eight years with the effort of waiting for this moment in the same firm faith as at the beginning. Less than an hour now, and it would be here. He had had to pay for his own transport and escort, and make good the loss arising from his absence from work for these few days; but at last they had allowed him to go, and here he was. Fantastic words for any prisoner's ear: review of the trial.

"I think they'll release you, or you wouldn't be here." Zmola's thought processes were simple. And he liked and respected Koval; he would have liked to be a man like Koval himself. To have his strength, and be able to hold up a man by his elbows. Leichtner also reasoned in a simple enough fashion: "If they'd wanted to release him, they need never have put him in prison."

They heard the cathedral clock strike the quarter hour, then the half. It seemed the barber was not coming. They listened attentively and expectantly for every sound from the corridor that might indicate he was on his way. But they sensed, rather than heard, only the passing of a guard in his foam-rubber-soled shoes. At last, when the silence and tension had become unbearable, Koval banged on the door. There was a moment of silence, then from somewhere in the distance rose the surly voice of the disturbed Horse's Mouth: "What's up there?"

"Here!" shouted Koval, with anxiety in his voice.

"Where's here?"

"Here—number twenty!"

"Well, what's the matter, twenty?" The voice drew nearer, they could hear the slow, quiet steps of feet shod with foam rubber.

"I've got to go to court at ten o'clock."

The footsteps halted, they heard the slither of the Judas panel, saw a flash of light from the window in the corridor, and then the guard's eye.

"Who's got to go to court?"

"I do!"

"What d'you mean—I? This your first day here, or something?"

"Koval, 55567." He was quite calm now. Someone had simply forgotten about him. After all, they'd brought him here, a journey of at least two hundred and fifty miles.

"I have no orders about it, you'll have to wait." The eye behind the glass vanished, and nothing was left but the guard's voice: "What time do you have to be in court?"

"At ten o'clock, sir."

"Well, you'll have to wait."

Suddenly eight years seemed to Koval enough of waiting: "Commander—please. . . ."

"Well, what now?"

"Couldn't you ask?"

The Judas panel was opened again, and the eye reappeared.

"Where'm I supposed to ask?"

Koval picked up a document from the bed covers and showed it: "Here it is . . . at ten o'clock. . . ." He held the summons to the little window. Horse's Mouth hesitated for a moment, then the eye vanished, and there was a rattle of keys. The door opened: "Let's see that!"

The inhabitants of the cell lined up once more against the wall, and Koval handed his paper to the guard. But Horse's Mouth turned his attention first to Harfa, lying on top of the straw mattresses.

"What's he doing lying down?"

"He's got pneumonia, Commander."

"Oh, yes, it's the old chap." He nodded his head, and began to read the paper.

"And you're Koval?" he said after a moment.

"Yes, sir."

The guard folded the paper and handed it back.

"I'll ask the chief of the shift about it."

The door slammed, and they heard his footsteps receding. The cathedral clock was just striking ten o'clock, four deep strokes and ten chiming ones.

"They never begin on time, anyway," said Čepitský soothingly.

Koval was calm now, like a man who has done everything that lies in his power. He sat down on one of the benches. It occurred to him that they ought to have asked for some fresh water, since the door had been opened. What was in the can would soon be undrinkable. The sun was now shining straight into their cell. In defiance of all the danger incurred in the act, Zmola pulled himself up to the window, and carefully peeped out from the edge of the frame over the roofs toward the town. Only about two blocks away there was a balcony where two girls sometimes came out to sunbathe. But today it was still empty.

It was somewhat after eleven when they took Koval down into one of the offices. A man in a brown suit with a woven pinstripe was standing there leafing through a bundle of papers, which threatened at any moment to fly out of his hands and scatter in all directions.

"In you go," said the young guard who had come up to the cell to get Koval; and he stood back to let him pass through the doorway ahead of him. Every prisoner had always to have a guard as his constant companion.

"You are Václav Koval?" asked the man in the brown suit briskly, and lifted his head for a moment. The stripe on his collar changed color in the reflected light.

"Yes," said Koval. It vexed him that he was still unshaven, although there had been plenty of time since half past nine, when he had banged on the door.

"Your family requested a review of the court proceedings in the criminal case against you," went on the man, mumbling the numbers of the paragraphs concerned, and of the case, together with dates. "And you agreed with their request?"

"Yes," said Koval again. He could not prevent hope from beating in his heart afresh at this moment. The man's outward manner told him nothing—he still had the right to hope, if there was in the world a single right that still belonged to him. He could not understand why the man did not sit down at the table, and put his papers down. It appeared that he was in a hurry.

The governor of the prison came into the room, and the man with the documents stopped reading and looked up. Seeing the governor, he nodded his head by way of salutation. Then he continued: "Now see here, today at ten o'clock the District Senate met . . . yes, well, we'll skip that," and he turned several pages. "In view of the fact that you did not attend this session, and considering everything that has previously been ascertained and deposed by witnesses concerning the facts of your case. . . ." He was talking very quickly, and half his words were mangled and devoured before they ever got out of his mouth. ". . . the original verdict was confirmed . . . yes!" He raised his head, and for the second time only in all his reading and gabbling, he looked at Koval. "I presided over this court, the decision will be conveyed to you in writing this afternoon, and there is no appeal against it."

Koval stood motionless in the middle of the room.

"I couldn't attend," he said in a strangled voice. "They didn't let me out. It wasn't my fault."

The man in the brown suit stiffened for a moment, his mouth half-open in uncomprehending silence, his eyes shifting aside. He swallowed whatever he had been about to say, and it seemed that he intended to leave explanations to the governor; but finally, just as the governor was already opening his mouth, he forestalled him after all: "But nothing depended on that, Koval, that was of no consequence at all, the decision would have been exactly the same. You mustn't think that . . . well, surely. . . ." He lifted the hand that held the papers, and let it fall again. He smiled, and then was grave again. "All the circumstances were ascertained long ago. It would have turned out just the same," he repeated smoothly. "Don't let your mind dwell on that for a moment!"

Koval was silent for a little while, and it seemed that he was considering. They waited.

"Why?" he said. "Why have I been in prison eight years?"

"But, Koval!" The man tilted his head, and the governor in the background laughed, as though he simply could not believe his ears.

"Well . . . why?"

Now they were all laughing, everyone but Koval and the young guard who was standing behind the governor. The man in the brown suit ended by shaking his head broadly from shoulder to shoulder over this incredible dimwittedness. He put on the face of a father patiently explaining something to his child. Yes, all prisoners are the same. They'd all like to go home; to eat, drink, sleep. They long for women. It's necessary to repeat even the simplest thing a thousand times before they can grasp it. He wiped the corner of his eye with the knuckle of his forefinger, and said, a little reproachfully but at the same time rallyingly: "But, Koval . . . but of course you know why you're in prison, don't you?"

But his face betrayed wariness and tension.

Koval was silent.

"Or don't you know? Now don't say you don't know! Well? What have you got to say?"

"Yes," the governor joined in, "come along, answer!"

"Yes," said Koval, "I know. You mean as the class enemy, don't you?"

It seemed he had made the right answer, for the tension in the man's face immediately relaxed into a sharp smile, to which he no longer had to force his features, as when he had pronounced that final "Well?" He came a step nearer to Koval, and slapped him amiably on the shoulder. He was considerably the smaller of the two.

"There, you see!" and he repeated the pat on the shoulder.

Then he recoiled, picked up his briefcase from the chair beside the table, and began to stuff his papers into it. "When under escort, visits are not allowed . . . in any case, you know that, of course, Koval, but since you're here now. . . . Your wife came, did you know about that?"

"No." Koval shook his head. He was absorbed in his own concerns, and was no longer listening very carefully to what the judge said.

"Perhaps the governor will make an exception. . . ."

"Certainly," said the governor in the background.

"You've had no disciplinary punishments, perhaps you could be allowed to receive a parcel . . . quite exceptional, of course. . . ."

"He's a well behaved prisoner," assented the governor. "I think it could be done."

"Five pounds, shall we say?" The man cast a brief glance past Koval at the governor, who nodded.

By this time all the documents were in the briefcase, and the man seized it briskly.

"Is there anything else you want, Koval?"

He shook his head. "No."

"Then I'll run off," said the president of the court gaily, and actually did literally run out of the room. He was glad that was over. As to the rights. . . . His job was to judge, of course, but conversations like that always seemed to him painful. And this fellow . . . sentenced fully eight years ago, and he still hadn't learned anything!

"Honor to work!" the governor called after him. Then he turned to the guard, indicating Koval. "You heard that? Half an hour—and five pounds." Then he, too, left. He was responsible for the prisoners, and he dealt with them on the basis of the court's decision. Hanging in his office, of course, he had Dzerzhinský's dictum about a warm heart, a clear head, and absolutely clean hands; but his job was to maintain order, not to worry his head about motives.

The young guard coughed, and rasped his keys together behind

Koval's back. The farmer still stood motionless. The boy opened a side door, so that they could pass through into the visiting room, where Koval's wife had been waiting every since the court let out.

"Come on, then," he said at last, when Koval made no move.

Koval shrugged his shoulders.

"Well, it's only seven years now. I shall have to stick it out."

"You'll stick it out all right," said the young guard uncertainly. He was finding this very painful. He coughed again.

Koval nodded his head. He was used to being strong, to being in the right, to revering God, and changing into clean clothes every Sunday in his honor. It semed that he was content.

"All right, let's go." He jerked his head, and the guard, who was shifting impatiently from foot to foot behind him, because he was young, and there were still many things with which he didn't know how to cope, waved him toward the door, indicating that he should go, that he was permitted to go, if he was ready, and that it was for him to go first.

State Witness

The soiled, metal-plated door of the cell, painted a yellowish-brown, flew open, and the man on the folding seat attached to the wall stood up at once; but the guard remained concealed behind the door, which opened outwards, and was in no hurry to reassure himself, even with one eye, that the man inside was reacting with due respect and proper discipline. Into the cell sailed a dwarfish little man, clutching his sheet, pillow and covers in his arms. He stumbled over the threshold, let his load drop, and fell flat on the top of it. The door clanged to behind him, the key turned in the lock, and the bolt was shot home. The shutter in the spy hole opened, and closed again immediately.

"That'll be Vostárek," thought the man in the cell, meaning the guard outside. "He doesn't fool around, or go out of his way to be more poisonous than he has to." And he held out his hand to the little man, who had clambered to his feet in the meantime, and tossed his covers onto the straw mattress laid out in a corner.

"My name's Materna. Hello chum, and welcome!"

The little man offered his own hand: "Joe Kathpal from Vimpe'k. You don' know me?"

The man sat down, measured the newcomer searchingly, and shook his head.

"No, I don't."

By this time the little man had discovered some tobacco on the small shelf above the table, and even several packs of cigarettes. The discovery captivated him completely. Fascinated by this precious store of tobacco, he took a cigarette without waiting to be invited.

"Thith ith thuper, we got thumthing to thmoke. You got matcheth, too?"

The man reached under the table, which was held to the wall by two U-shapes of iron, and from the ledge provided by one of them drew out a box of matches. Carefully he took one—it was actually a quarter of the original match. He helped himself to a cigarette, too, cautiously struck the match, and lit first Joe's cigarette and then his own.

"Enjoy yourself!"

The little man took a greedy draw, and coughed.

"I haven't thmoked for thwee weekth, chum, you know that?" But immediately he reverted to the original question, from which this cigarette dropped from heaven had diverted him: "Thtwaight, though, you don' know me?"

The man shook his head again: "Sorry, pal, but really I don't."

Joe Kathpal furrowed his brow and shook himself incredulously. "Ith it pothible? You neve' hea'd of me?"

The man raised his eyebrows, and once more, this time with evident amusement and with wrinkles of laughter around his eyes and mouth, shook his head.

"Not Joe Kathpal, fwom Vimpe'k? You know whe'e Vimpe'k ith, don' you?"

Materna nodded agreement: "Vimperk, in Šumava. Yes, I know."

"Well, that'th whe'e I come fwom, man. Fwom Vimpe'k. Whe'e you fwom?"

"From Prague, Joe. I'm from Prague."

"Pwague?"

"That's right."

"And you don' know me?"

"I really don't, Joe. I'm sorry, you're a fine fellow, but I don't know you."

"That'th quee', man, that'th quee'. Can I take anothe' thigawette?"

"Sure you can, Joe, help yourself."

"Haven't thmoked for thwee weekth, you know that? Thwee weekth!" The dwarf lit his new cigarette from the man's still unfinished one, for the man had been smoking more thoughtfully and slowly.

"You've been three weeks in prison?"

"Pwithon, no! I wath in hothpital. In K'č—you know? In K'č!"

"Yes, I understand. In Krč." The man stretched out his legs and settled himself more comfortably. "And what have they got against you, Joe, to bring you here?"

Kathpal took another deep drag, and waved a hand mischievously: "Don' even athk me, man, don' even athk me! Big time, I tell you! Inte'national love buthineth and ethpionage. Fifteen to twenty yea's, that intewwogato' thaid. I tell you, man, big time!"

"Come off it, Joe." The man had finished his cigarette at last, and stubbed it out carefully on the edge of an ashtray molded from bread dough. He brushed off the ash, then tore open the paper and tipped the last pinch of its contents into a waxed carton which had once held jam, and in which he now kept his salvaged tobacco. "They don't dish out twenty-year terms any more. The highest sentence is fifteen now, did you know? Fifteen years, you can't get more. But I bet the psychiatrist has been prodding you, hasn't he?"

"I'm an offithially recognithed mental defective," declared the little man joyfully. "But that intewwogato' thaid twenty, and he thould know what he'th talking about. Fifteen to twenty yea's. Big time, eh? I tell you, weal big time!"

The man studied him attentively. Yes, he was mentally defective—that scratching at his neck and his belly—a sure case of schizophrenia, he thought, or I'm losing my grip. So at last I'm here without an informer to squeal on me—no police agent around my neck this time.

"I'm a state case, you know, Joe. A state prisoner. They moved me here to attend some new court." And in a moment he went on: "What paragraphs have you got?"

"Pawagwaphs, what pawagwaphs? Inte'national love buthineth and ethpionage, that'th what I've got."

"You must have paragraphs of some sort. Didn't they give you a paper?"

"You know," pursued Joe, refusing to be distracted, "I had one woman, I did, I thaid to he', don' pwovoke me, I thaid—thith dame wath thitting like thith, you know? I thaid, put you' legs togethe', I thaid, but no, she tempted me, tho I jumped he'. She had a degwee—technical you know? Anything I wanted I could have fwom he', anything."

"This was in Vimperk, Joe?"

"Yeah, in Vimpe'k. Thith dame had thith technical degwee— he' huthband uthed to thend he' pa'thelth, but eve'ything she gave me, chocolate, jam, evewything—man, she wath crathy fo' me."

"Is that why they put you in prison? And what about this espionage, eh?"

"No, it wathn't fo' that. But I had a gwandmothe', you know, a crathy old bag, too, and she info'med on me, you know that? In with the polithe, she wath. They uthed to thend thei' pigeonth up on my woof, to twamp my tileth to pietheth—on pu'pothe. That wath that old hag, my own gwanny, man, but a bitch, a bitch. At our plathe the polithe keep pigeonth, you know?"

"Pigeons for the post?" asked the man with interest.

"That'th wight," nodded Joe. "In a pigeon houthe. And they thent them up on my woof on pu'pothe, to twamp my tileth to pietheth. I thent a lette' about it to the Fwench ambathado', evewything I told him, about thethe polithemen, and about the tholdie'th, about them ma'ching about in the evening, thinging, on pu'pothe tho I can't thleep. That wath all that old bag'th doing. She wanted to bweak my ne've, because I'm a mental defective. I'll have anothe' thigawette, eh? Can I?"

"Help yourself," said the man, and reached for the matches.

"Go on, this is interesting. So the old woman informed on you?"

"Yeah, yeah, man, the did. Tho I thaid to mythelf, you wait, you hag, I'll pay you back, but I'll have to go about it cleve'ly. You know, you've got to be cleve'. You watch that, Mate'na, I'm telling you, you be cleve'!"

Joe's face wore the urgent gravity of a diligent teacher, and Materna nodded his agreement. He held out the match.

"You not thmoking?"

"No."

"Oh, well, me, I haven't thmoked for thwee weekth, thee?"

"So what did you do about the old woman?"

Joe dissolved into giggles: "Oh, I went about it cleve'ly, I waited, you know, I waited my chanthe till the couldn't thcream, and then I jumped he'. . . . ."

"Stopped her mouth with a fist, did you?"

"No . . . cou'the not. . . . I thee you haven't been lithening. Didn't I tell you I waited fo' my chanthe? You got to be cleve'. The wath in the mo'gue, that'th what!"

"In the morgue?"

"That'th wight, in the mo'gue!"

"Dead?"

"That'th wight!" giggled Joe delightedly. "Dead!"

And you jumped her. . . . in the morgue . . . ?"

"I fucked he'," exulted Joe, clapping his hands in glee. "I fucked the old bag . . . the mithewable bitch."

The man drew a deep breath, cast up his eyes to the ceiling, scrubbed his forehead with the palm of his hand, and then passed his hand over his entire face.

"Well, Joe. . . well! . . . I think I'll take a little walk." He rose and took a cigarette, and without regard to Joe, who was still smoking, struck a new match to light it. "Well, well, Joe! Well, well!" And he began to pace the four and a half steps between the window and the door.

"That'th thomething, eh, pal?"

"That's something!" the man agreed. "You're absolutely right, Joe, that surely is something! So it was over that, then, that they put you in jail?"

"It wath mothtly becauthe of the ethpionage, you know, that lette' to that ambathado', about thothe pigeonth and the tholdie'th, back in Vimpe'k."

The man merely nodded his head again. It had occurred to him now that he simply must share this gift. He spent a little while rapping out letters in Morse with his knuckles, first on one wall, then on the opposite one. But in the cell on the left, as he knew, the occupants had been changed, and the only tenant who could receive Morse had been taken away to court this very day. The cell on the right never answered, perhaps it was empty. So he took a rag from the corner, checked with a glance that the spy hole in the door was closed, then kneeled down, and with dexterous movements which testified to the fact that this was a daily routine and part of a program, crumpled it into a ball, and squeezed out with it the water from the siphon of the Turkish-style lavatory. The waste pipe magnified back to him the sound of falling water. Again he checked the spy hole in the door with a rapid glance, slipped off his rubber-soled shoe, and knocked three times on the floor with the heel.

Three similar knocks answered him, and a moment later he could hear through the pipe the sound of water splashing, and then the same sounds of a rag stuffed into the siphon somewhere below.

One floor below him, Materna had struck up an acquaintance with the criminal Norbert, and two floors below was the Pole, Jašek Grabowski from Wroclaw; while three below, right in the cellar, were the punishment cells, where the prostitute Monika was at present passing her days. She had poured water over one of the guards, mainly to get into the punishment cells, where she would be underneath the men's cells. She spent her time singing sentimental songs about love, such as "Vaya con Dios," into the lavatory pipes, and talking about eternal love, and sometimes she could be as choicely coarse as any trooper, when someone unknown and unseen made shameless suggestions to her via the pipes.

Materna held his toothbrush ready in one hand, and gripped the flush handle in the other. If Vostárek, outside there, should happen to take it into his head to trouble them, Materna had only to pull the chain at the first sound of the door opening, and the siphon would fill with water in an instant, and smooth away all traces of this illegal contact.

He coughed, and when a similar cough answered him, he spoke: "Norbert, are you there?"

"Hello there, boys!" That was Monika.

"Just a second, Monika. Norbert!"

"Yeah, all right now. He was just prowling down here, I couldn't speak."

"Here Jašek Grabowski, Wroclaw . . . no understand . . . please speak slow . . . I Polák, Jašek Grabowski, Wroclaw." Jašek never got beyond this formula.

"Wait a minute, Jašek!"

"No understand . . . please speak slow . . . I Polák. . . ."

"Shut up, Jašek, I don't need you."

"Shut up, you cow!" came Monika's voice.

"Please, no understand . . . I beg gentlemen speak slower . . . speak clear, speak slow . . . I Polák, Jašek Grabowski. . . ."

"Jašek, shut your trap, you idiot! Norbert!"

". . . no understand. . . ."

"What's up?" came Norbert's reply faintly. "Something new up there?" He waited a moment for Jašek's babbling to die away. "Amnesty? Revolution? Has Otto of Hapsburg arrived on a white horse? Have the Martians landed to liberate the state prison of Ruzyně?"

"I've got a new boy here, Norbert, something for you. A present from Vimperk. . . ."

At that moment Materna was grabbed by his blouse by his excited little companion, and dragged backwards from his position over the lavatory. Joe flew to take his place, face down in the opening, from which echoed one last: ". . . . no understand . . . please speak slow . . ." He began to roar eagerly: "Thith ith Joe, Joe Kathpal fwom Vimpe'k! You know me?"

A little time later — not very long — Materna, neatly trimmed by the prison barber, sat on the bench assigned to the accused. He had taken no great part in this piece of theatre, though they had allotted him a role in it along with the rest. He had not expected from it either more or less than he had known he could expect from it, the result for which he knew it had all been staged. He had known from the moment when the president of the senate read out the protocol concerning the interrogation of the witness Josef Kašpar of Vimperk, which painted a convincing picture of the obdurate animosity of the accused—and already previously convicted—Materna toward the existing regime. Signed, Joe Kathpal of Vimpe'k, in the interests of Socialist legality. At the foot of every page of the protocol was inscribed: Read and confirmed as correct, Josef Kašpar.

The presiding judge read: ". . . he often told me that the Americans would come to our country, and that we should turn Ruzyně prison into a hotel for the Central Committee of the Communist Party. He also frequently sang Nazi songs in the cell. . . ."

"Well, well, Joe," the man in the dock said to himself inwardly, "well, my little mental defective. . . . No, you weren't a police agent . . . but that interrogator of yours knew his business . . . my God, he did! Big time, my God, yes! Big time!"

The presiding judge read to the end of the convincing deposition made by the witness Josef Kašpar of Vimperk. He finished, in a full, resonant voice, the voice of a tribune of popular justice and revolutionary power, the ringing voice of a legal luminary perfectly trained—in the course of one year—to exercise sovereign and decisive sway over the fates of human beings, and faithfully fulfilling his tasks in the sector of justice. And he asked—in the interests of Socialist legality—"Accused, have you anything to say?"

Materna's eyes passed over the terrified counsel for the defense, who was fiercely studying some paper or other, over the two flanking judges who made up the bench, with the calflike expressions and puffy faces of beer drinkers. He rose, and slowly replied: "Nothing, your worship—nothing at all!"

On the Spot

I got to know Zbyněk in the prison camp. He wasn't, of course, the only person I got to know there, and either remembered or ultimately forgot, I simply mean that we've known each other since that time. He was a state-committed prisoner, a political, the élite of the camps, some old story about firearms, of no importance even when it took place, much less today. Although he came into MY particular camp at the same time as I did, they'd already been sweeping the prisons with him throughout the republic for about seven years before they enrolled me in the same university of life. He was brought into camp by the same escort as I was, and what's more, with a black eye, awarded him by one of those swine during a bladder stop in Hradec, when Zbyněk asked to have his handcuffs taken off for this act of relief after a one-hundred-twenty-mile run. From that time on we got to know each other, and in the end he even told me that old story about firearms, about the beautiful ideals of youth, and a war souvenir. An outstanding example of how things should and should not be done, a warning that you can never be too careful, and that the best of all slogans is "Hands off Korea!" Hands off, hands off! And that was all there was to this tale about carrying arms illegally against the interests of the state.

Zbyněk himself was a state ticket holder, as I've already mentioned, who took me, green, frightened novice as I was, under his wing for reasons probably known only to himself, and which for him were evidently sufficient. Most likely because he, too, had once been green, scared, and a novice, and knew what a wretched situation that can be for any man. He stretched out a finger to me, and after the finger his whole hand; a hand, by the way, which had the dimensions of a shovel. He showed me how to keep my chin above water even when I felt decidedly inclined to drown myself, when circumstances threatened that I would never reach the shore, or if I did, only to flounder into an equally disastrous landfall. It's true that he was new to MY—no, OUR—camp, but he had plenty of acquaintances there, and he knew how to manage with whatever he was given. He initiated me into camp life, and frequently saved me from all the manifold evils that must of necessity confront everyone in a prison camp. He knew his way around, and he had his dispositions made, from a very snug job at the back gate of the mine to a spare food dish, which he kept permanently polished for inspections. He could outwit every one of those gentlemen guards who wanted to coopt him for their sexual games, and he could get on well with every one of the few there who didn't make homosexuality and crude obscenities their personal program. Even guards are only people, after all, though it's true that only a certain kind of people gravitate to this particular craft. Still, even among them there are distinctions, and one idiot can create a reputation for hundreds of others.

Zbyněk knew his way around, and had his own arrangements made. Yet he was quite capable of lying for several hours in the mud waiting for an opportunity to talk to me and buck me up when, in spite of all his good advice and all precautions, I finally ran afoul of regulations, and found myself flung into the punishment block for "twenty without"—twenty days cells without a blanket. "Hands off Korea!" was no good here. Zbyněk had scooped out a hollow for himself in the mud, in the certainty that sooner or later that fuzz on guard would have to go and relieve himself; but actually it was several hours before he did. But in the end I got some food, and even a bit of tobacco, and I stuck out the rest of that sentence without damage, if it is actually possible to stick out without damage a matter of twenty days in an unheated concrete cell in eight degrees of frost, and with food once every three days. They say every generation has its own revolution, its own experience, its own war. And this was the experience and the war that had fallen to us.

Zbyněk had formerly studied at the university, after finishing high school, and like so many others, he had been pitchforked straight from the university into this disaster with the popgun, the kind of pitfall they had prepared for him and many more. But today his academic past shows only in his glasses. He knew how to turn aside attacks, and when necessary he knew how to attack, too, better than any of the professorial party in the camp. If it hadn't been for Zbyněk and a few others like him, those fellows would have been permanently in trouble, from the homosexuals as well as every other way.

Sometimes I still recall one particular roll call, we must have been just off the night shift, because for some reason I connect these memories with sleepiness and weariness, a kind of indefinite, burning pressure in my back, a numbness in my legs, and the whole sky seemingly weighing down on my eyelids. Too much sky, and too dazzlingly bright. Although in these regions where the camps were located there was very seldom a clear sky. What with the mountains, and the whole neighborhood being dotted with stinking mines and huge slag heaps, with an equally noisome chemical plant here and there, as at OUR camp, for instance, which trailed a green mist even in the middle of summer, there was not much to be seen in our countryside but desert fields and withered trees, which could barely survive in such an atmosphere.

Just at that time there was a very queer sport that seemed to crop up at roll call. It consisted of punching people in the back, and I don't even know, after all this time, who started it or where it came from; suddenly there it was. You'd get a punch in the back, best of all on the shoulder, and by the time you could turn around the culprit would be standing neatly to attention in line again, like a statue, staring indifferently into nowhere, and then guess, guess, guess if you can, who was it who got such a rise out of you?

As long as cronies and contemporaries confined themselves to playing these tricks on one another, all well and good, get on with it, boys, if it amuses you. But on this occasion, during the muster after our night shift, a group of young hoodlums, brought in only a few days previously from the youth courts, chose to pick on old Zweig, of all people, who could easily have been grandfather twice over to all of them together—not to mention the eight years he'd had ground into his poor old body here—and who in addition had ulcers on his shoulders from carrying weights in the mine. He'd been through enough; and now in his seventies, on top of everything, he was forced to haul pit props in the mine. With ulcers like that the doctors won't sign you off as sick, at the very most they'll recommend that you ask the supervisor for a change of job, if hauling pit props on your ulcerated shoulders seems to you too arduous. And of course the supervisor never has enough people, and can't accommodate you.

So old Zweig got a blow with a fist right on his ulcer, from one of these little shits who don't know the difference between Eisenhower and Adenauer, and are so well brought up by all those reform school guards, and so well repay the pedagogical example of the Ministry of the Interior, that they have swastikas tattooed on their bodies, and the bloodstained eagle of the Reich, and *"Es komm der Tag,"* though naturally they write this as "Eskom dertak," if not in some even more bizarre form. Equally naturally, thanks to this same educational process by example and by truncheon, they are antisemites to a man, due to Hitler, of whom they know just one thing, that he was opposed to Jews and Communists. Since the guards are also Communists—or so they represent themselves to be, and brandish Communism and Communist construction as Žižka brandished his flail, ready and willing to break everybody's arms and legs with it—that's reason enough for these model adolescents, these poor droppings of the epoch, these embryos fertilized by mistake and to no purpose, to be all for Hitler and "Eskom dertak." They are incurably malformed, cruel, unprincipled and malicious, in fact they are like everything they have experienced from their childhood and are still experiencing today. They are, in fact, as no human creatures can possibly be who are not young, stupid, dirty, who have not grown up without women, spending their puberty in the midst of pederasts, schooled in masturbation and homosexual indulgences, competing for the fastest ejaculation and mutually accelerating their own corruption. Degenerate faces with muddied eyes and thin, curling wisps instead of beards; and no interest in anything but a hunk of tobacco and a mess of greasy food. They have their silly fantasies of carrying out thrilling bank raids, without a hope of ever putting them into practice; without a hope of ever achieving anything more, in fact, than some wretched, drunken clash in front of a bar, or a smashed store window.

So old Zweig got a blow with a fist, right on his ulcer. He cringed like a trampled blindworm and hissed with pain. And yet it was a wonder he didn't apologize!

"Boys," he said, to those sons of bitches behind him, with their guaranteed sound Party origin, "boys, please don't play tricks. I've got ulcers here on my shoulders." And with a forefinger he traced cautious circles on his coat. "Honestly I have, they hurt me terribly." Agitatedly he turned and pleaded into the rows of ostentatiously innocent adolescent faces. "I haven't done anything, I'm just a musician, don't drag me into it, I'm not in the Party." And one of them, they called him Spotty because of the big red freckles on his eyelids—says: "Well, at least they let you know they're there, Jew!" and the others all whinnied with laughter, as if he'd made a brilliant joke. "At least you can feel lucky that the gas didn't get you."

"From the gas chambers could be heard the merry twittering of the Jews!"

"Don't push, Jews, no need to push, there's plenty of gas."

"Mauthausen!" yelped another. During the war old Zweig had

been four years in Mauthausen, and somehow managed to survive.

Zelcam, once a priest until he was defrocked, then SS man, and now foreman on the cable line at the pit, who was here precisely on account of this same Mauthausen, where he had been a supervisor, cast a crooked glance at them. He had gotten caught because he had forgotten he was on the wanted list, and made a trip to Prague, and it suited him down to the ground there, playing around at the Hotel Yalta with his Deutschemarks. He got away with it, twice, but the third time they pounced on him and reckoned up his debts at ten years; he was a Sudeten German from Kaplice. He looked at those boys, spat blood and phlegm on the ground at his feet, and emitted an equally crooked laugh. There was no way of knowing at what, whether at the successful development of National Socialist world theory in the Czechoslovak Socialist prisons, or at the stupidity of those black angels and prison wolf pups, whose only real grievance here was that they couldn't grow their hair half a yard long.

"You'd have been the first up the chimney, boys," he grated at them out of the corner of his mouth.

Old Zweig shriveled completely under this barrage, and fumbled gingerly at his misused shoulder. In front of us the posse of guards were advancing, counting our ranks, so the old man tried his best to stand at attention and at the same time keep a wary watch on his back, to be warned in time of what was going on behind him, in case somebody intended another assault on his shoulder.

He was just casting a sidelong glance to the right when Spotty hit out at him again from the left, with all the strength he'd amassed in his nineteen years. And that was plenty, for they'd kept him hard at it with pick and shovel in various prisons since he was fifteen.

While old Zweig was cringing again with tears in his eyes, Zbyněk pulled Spotty back by the sleeve, just as he was posing again with an ostentatiously innocent face, and even jerking a thumb over his shoulder.

"That's enough, chum," said Zbyněk. "I no longer find it amusing to watch you, boy. You've had your game now."

All the homo-angels around Spotty took offense. This wasn't SS man Zelcam, for whom they had some respect. Spotty felt his gang of sneak thieves all solidly behind him, and stuck out his tongue. "Or what?"

Zbyněk blinked at him over the top of his glasses: "I just don't like it, boy."

"But you know what, four eyes?—*I do* like it! It tickles me to death—even more than your glasses." This again seemed to the rest of his gang enormously witty, and they laughed aloud in Zbyněk's face at their leader's exuberant spirits.

"I've told you I don't like it, so don't try it again," said Zbyněk through his teeth, looking somewhere else instead of at Spotty's blotchy face.

"Or what? Or you'll give me a spanking, eh?" And with the knuckle of his crooked forefinger he flipped the tip of Zbyněk's nose upwards from below.

At which Zbyněk slowly took off his glasses, handed them equally deliberately to me to hold for him, and planted his fist in Spotty's solar plexus so hard and accurately that the victim swept down six people in the row behind him as he crumpled.

And with that the affair at roll call ended, if you don't include the way Spotty tried to retrieve his reputation when he came around, by lighting up a cigarette and declaring: "You fucker, if it wasn't for your gray hair I'd cut you to pieces." Which was all too obvious a retreat from glory. The black angels also prepared a mass punitive expedition against our hut, but that didn't turn out at all well for them, either. Franta Zajíc threw each one of them out as soon as he reached the doorway, and the ones that didn't fall far enough out of range got their behinds well kicked, too. A few days later they made one more try to crush Zbyněk with an ore wagon on a steep runway, but luckily that didn't succeed, either.

And now all that was behind us, runways, gates, ore wagons, roll calls and black angels, and I was coming back from swimming with Zbyněk. He worked now as a driver for the garbage department, and I as driver's assistant in the fruit and vegetable business. On Mondays and Thursdays we went to swim, and talk, and naturally to have a beer. Zbyněk's wife couldn't bear it when we talked about nothing but prison. She was a girl from the same club, but actually we only belonged because otherwise we wouldn't have been able to get into the swimming pool in the evening, while she was in such hard training she made the very water steam, and went on slaving away long after we were sitting upstairs in the bar, putting records on the juke box, or listening to the records other people put on there.

We always had something to talk about together. My father was a legionnaire, and no matter what he was talking about, it always ended up the same way, in Siberia, and mind you, that isn't taking into account what it must have been like when he sat down with one of the old comrades who had actually been there in Siberia with him. We didn't have Siberia, but we had our own domestic Siberia, the Siberia of the camps, peopled by characters like Snake's Head, Peascod, Mare's Mouth, Heart of Gold, and also by Spotty and Jarmilek. We drank our beer and exchanged assurances about how well off we were here, how easy we had it, we who could swim, listen to music, drink beer, sit in a chair with a back to it, look at women, choose our food, and wear scarfs around our necks. And even sleep with women (when it was equally agreeable to them of course!), and exchange caresses with them. Naturally that. And all the rest. Recalling by the way much ancient and now outlived bestiality.

Recalling, too, how we came to be thrown in there, what should have happened and what should not have happened. But only in silence, without words, quite without words. For we both knew that these things had been, we knew what they had been like, and we knew that every particle of this was now and always preserved somewhere within us, an insurmountable obstacle.

It was some actor, that time—except, of course, that even that wasn't true—who had wanted at all costs to buy from Zbyněk a gun which he'd had ever since the war. And this actor had seen it, somewhere in his apartment. In the end he coaxed him into parting with it, and they came to an agreement that Zbyněk would bring it to the Slavia café for him. Only there were five low-ranking police agents planted in wait for him there, and they jumped him the moment he came in the door. Zbyněk left his mark on every one of them, but in the end they got him just the same, and then began his pilgrimage through the prison camps, duly singled out with a special mark against him, so that he only traveled in irons, and at the slightest excuse he got a blow in the face, too, like that time in Hradec when we got to know each other. And that was how he came into the camp where we were both prisoners together, OUR camp, where he lay five hours in the mud just to goad me into hope again, where we were paraded at three in the morning past a group of our fellows "shot while trying to escape," though we knew that at least one of them, Vilda Kokstein, had certainly had no intention of escaping, since his term was up in a short time. Where we lived as best we might, and got our fun out of watching that same Vilda Kokstein break the windows of the guards' sleeping quarters with a sling, where Zbyněk planted a beautiful wallop in Spotty's solar plexus, and felled six other scum standing behind him, six riffraff reared and trained for prison, who afterwards tried to kill him with an ore wagon in a steep mine corridor.

This particular day Magda, that was Zbyněk's wife, was busy practicing some unconscionable number of sprints for the relay races that were in preparation, and Zbyněk and I decided that we'd go home and pass the time together there, have a nice little session with coffee and a bottle. For in our—OUR—bar above the pool there were five guards from the Prague escort services sitting, and every one of them we remembered well, only too well, and we had no appetite to linger in any bar they frequented. Especially as they seemed to be celebrating something. They're very expansive then, very hail-fellow-well-met, they drag in every-body around as they bellow out: "Now, boys, let your voices sound. Pass the beer and songs around. . . ." No, decidedly we had no appetite for it.

"What's going on here?" we asked our—OUR—waiter

Oldřich. "Such a racket, and that queer get-up . . . What is it those guys have there, some sort of eagle, or what is it? Those green uniforms. . . ."

Oldřich wiped the table with his napkin, sweeping from it the crumbs of the rolls we had eaten a few minutes ago with our sausages. He looked round in a conspiratorial manner, thought for a moment, and finally said ambiguously: "You know, gentlemen, I can't throw them out."

Which was true enough.

That bastard from our escort, that time in Hradec when Zbyněk got that black eye during the bladder stop, he was there, too. But he didn't recognize us. It wasn't even possible that he should. When a man spends his whole life ferrying convicts between Ilava and Pankrác, Liberec and Pankrác, Jáchés and Pankrác, Bory and Pankrác, he can't remember a single face, not even one he's slashed with a truncheon, because there must certainly be plenty even of those.

I could see how this was affecting my friend. But then, before we could get up and go away to find another bar, or go home for that private session to make coffee and open a bottle and listen to Radio Luxembourg, the waitress Jiřina brought our beer, without being asked, taking it for granted we would want it as always. Two brimming tankards of ten-degree Smíchov.

"We won't run away from them!" And then the muted clunk of the tankards on the table; the foam bounced aside, and a little of it ended on the tablecloth.

Then one of those son of bitches who were still roaring "Now, boys, let your voices sound, pass the beer and song around. . . ." got up and wandered away behind the curtain where a little arrow pointed, with a painting of a man's hat, to which sign somebody had also added, in pencil, a drawing of an erected penis.

Zbyněk took off his glasses, slipped them into my breast pocket, and said: "Keep an eye on these for me, pal!" And he went away there, too.

"Well, well!" I thought. *"So maybe, after all, there'll be justice in the world yet! Well, well!"* And I thought of Zbyněk's gray

hair, at thirty-three years old, the gray hair of a convict with a zest for life, of a garbage truck driver with an uncompleted university education. But for the life of me I couldn't think what all this had been good for, or was good for now. Including this eventual justice.

Coming-Out Party

I don't know why I did it. I don't know what I wanted, or what it
was all supposed to be in aid of; but when you come down to it, a
man, whether he likes it or not, is always marked by his own
nature, and also by whatever it is that has marked him as himself
and no one else, everything he has behind him, his own roots, the
shadow of the fairy stories of his childhood, and of the fables and
the wonderful adventures of the other people around him, those
among whom he was grown up, and whom, for one reason or
another, he has liked or disliked.

And this still holds good even when he's as old as I am, and has
been through what they call the school of life. Such a banal and
stupid phrase, but the worst, the most banal and stupid thing
about it is that it's absolutely accurate. The school of life. The
school of the age. In addition, of course, to the ordinary kind of
school with desks and blackboards, with a cloakroom partitioned
off into wire compartments, with gym shoes in a black linen bag
drawn up at the neck with tape, with a monogram embroidered
on it. It doesn't cease to be true even now, RETROSPEC-
TIVELY, when a man has plenty of other things in him besides
those old stories and fables; though indeed he still retains those,
only in a different sense, the histories and the fates of strangers,

entangling and fusing and disentangling again in various ways. And other things, too, which by this time have lost even the shadow of any sense they may once, originally, have possessed; so that in the midst of these streets and houses and people, we suddenly seem to be OVERWHELMINGLY ALONE, islanded in the midst of everything that functions placidly even WITHOUT US, even OVER US. So that for us, it seems, there is no sense left, no motivation, in the end not even any desires. Those quite ordinary and simple longings for something, anything, life, a woman, a car, a bentwood coat stand, a patent calendar, a gas lighter. Or maybe something rather different, to fly in a balloon, or cultivate mushrooms. Though underneath, deep underneath, it always turns out to be a woman, SHE ALONE, at the core of everything that has meaning. Always one and the same thing, which in any case we never understand, though perhaps it's for that very reason that in this alone, finally, resides for us the one, unique and lasting magic, a lost and isolated magic, which certainly we can all call up within ourselves at need, but which can also come uncalled. Out of nowhere, suddenly here it is, a feeling, a play of sense without any clarification or formulation fit for the newspapers, and nonexistent without its remainder, so that it's sort of like trying to divide prime numbers, only in place of the remainder you are left with a silence. The only reasonable and explicable thing, because explicable by whatever you please, so that it fulfills every unexpressed and inexpressible wish. A nice little calendar with an alphabetical index on the edge, and we carry it around with us as once we carried those gym shoes in the black linen bag with the embroidered monogram. A useful little calendar to give us the feeling that we have a host of cares, and a host of acquaintances who can be called up at any time; and actually it costs eleven crowns forty.

It was a long story; but every proper story is long, and yet, in spite of its length, quite ordinary and simple. And so is this one of mine. The story of a young man who has money, and who reeks of something slightly shocking. (I'm well aware of it; in this orderly world with its orderly dens of vice, disorderliness, even in the dens of vice, is inevitably shocking.) A young man to whom the staff behave either slightly disdainfully or slightly servilely. But a young man who is already known here, and who has booked the private salon where I am sitting now. The guests peer in here from the French restaurant next door, over their orderly suppers. On the tables in this salon are distributed showy little cards of black plastic, with the equally showy legend: RESERVED. The head waiter František has set them out tonight for the very first time, for this occasion. He told me so. After the two weeks I've been living here, and in the end have begun to belong here, he and I have become friends to a certain degree. The directors of the hotel acquired these cards for the sake of the foreign tourist trade, just as they did the Sabena and Air France miniature flags, and the black stylized figures of ladies and gentlemen on the rest-room doors.

The nonresidents have eaten their little suppers in the next-door restaurant, and are drinking their coffee. (They have a coffee machine here, too, an original Italian espresso.) I knew that everybody out there was fascinated by what was going on in the private salon, but it neither offended me nor gave me the plea-sure that perhaps it should have done. Their attention, avid with curiosity and wonder, was fixed there at the back of the room, where the waiters were setting out silver candlesticks and other Silvo-polished glories, such as are not used for the ordinary, cas-ual visitor. Orchards of cutlery and glasses, napkins in carved wooden rings, saltcellars tastefully placed, dishes of fruit, bowls of flowers, and a host of other things that can be had only for a considerable (and largely wasted) outlay of money. As it hap-pened I had money; not exactly a fortune, and not by any means superfluous, but it was mine, and I thought it well spent in ar-ranging a little gathering like this after so many years, and judged that a little pomp and extravagance, such as the silver candlesticks and the stylish cut-glass saltcellars, would not be out of place. There was money enough to pay for these things, for a party for ten to fifteen people; and I wasn't counting on collect-

ing more than from ten to fifteen of my former comrades and
fellow pupils—girl fellow pupils among them, too, of course. Obviously more chairs and place settings could be added if necessary;
I had an agreement with the head waiter, František, about that.
But I hadn't managed to find the addresses of all of them by a
long shot, it was impossible; many had simply disappeared, no
one knew when or where, leaving nothing behind them but frag-
mentary reports: He's doing so and so. . . . He's in Vietnam.
. . . He's left the country. . . . She married, and has children.
. . . He's married, too. . . . He bought a car. . . . He's a big
shot somewhere in the Party. . . . I haven't seen him for ten
years. . . . He went as an expert to the Congo, and was eaten
by cannibals. Yes, these were my fellow pupils. Not counting, of
course, the ones about whom I could remember nothing more
explicit than this: There was a boy who used to sit in the third
desk by the window, now what on earth was his name! There
were several of those. And: That girl who always wore her hair in
curls, her name was Jodasová, or Jonáková, or something like that.
My fellow pupils. Yes, they were mine, and we might well have the
impression that we were all much the same, and that on this occasion we were approximately as nearly the same as all those years
ago. I was filled with a very ordinary curiosity, and I calculated
that they, too, would be possessed by the same curiosity, about me
and about one another. What exactly would be changed? And
how? I didn't expect them all to come, not all of them from that
world and time which had left its mark upon us all, the age of the
gym shoes in the black bag drawn up with tape and sewn with a
monogram. To this day I still remember watching my aunt sitting
on her sewing stool—a kind of little chair without a back, that's
what we called it at home—at the sewing machine in the kitchen,
stitching out for me in red cotton on this bag the letters of my
monogram.

Now today I was standing at the same beginning which they
had faced years ago. I was curious to know how they were living,
what had happened to them in all this time. In this respect I was
at exactly the same stage today as then; it was only they who in

the meantime had been diligent or lazy, dissolute or successful—
or possibly, of course, both lazy *and* successful! In a word, alive. It
was the beginning of my personal life, only mine, which had
somehow been postponed.

I had received 48,000 crowns when I set out on my journey home,
my entire earnings over long years, and on top of that the money
left to me by my aunt, which only now began truly to belong to
me. You may consider that quite a lot of money; but I had no adequate standards as to what was and what was not money. Where I
had come from money didn't mean much, though it was a good
thing to have some. If anything at all had meaning there, it was
the actual goods a man possessed. Only gradually, and thanks
mainly to the head waiter, had I begun to appreciate what cost 100
crowns, and what was available for half that sum. There were so
many new things. All those years ago there hadn't been any television, or polyethylene bags, or Big Beat, or almost anything else.
The last big sensation had been long-playing records, and in the
field of music, for us who were just then arriving at years of dis-
cretion, Kučera's group with their Pacific island songs. No jazz.
No chewing gum. All that I had been able to find out about
chewing gum was that it was an incriminating concomitant of
high treason, which could either make things worse for a man—if
the prosecutor ruled that the culprit in question had embraced
the American way of life with malice aforethought—or allevi-
ate his offense—if it was held that he had been seduced by that
same way of life. Everything depended on the view taken. And it
was all according to instructions. Perhaps to personal reactions,
too, but I think even the personal reactions of such people pro-
ceed according to instructions. Revolutionary severity, and so on
and so on, and the opportunity of re-education.

The waiters had finished, and the head waiter František came
to tell me that everything was now in order, prepared down to the
last detail, although there was still more than half an hour to run
before the time appointed for the party to begin. All that remained to be done was to strike a match and light the candles,

clap one's hands three times, and František would give the signal, the waiters would begin to bring in the dishes, and the wine waiter, a young dandy with sideburns and a white jacket, would start to pour the aperitif.

Wouldn't I, he asked, like to look over the salon and suggest any improvements? I assured him that I had full confidence in his taste; and as I had not the least desire to wander about alone and obtrusive in that empty, polished splendor, I went and sat down meantime in my accustomed place in the restaurant, and had them bring me a vodka and some cigarettes. They drew the curtains between the private salon and the restaurant, and partially closed the folding glass doors. The people around went on eating, and didn't pay much attention. An old woman came around with flowers, and the young men began reaching for their wallets. She didn't come to me. During the past fourteen days she'd gotten accustomed to me, too. For whom should I be buying flowers, unless it was for Auntie in her grave? In all my life up to this point I had never given any woman flowers; and to the day of my death I must still be ashamed of it.

I was wondering who would be the first to come, who would come early and who late, who would JUST DROP IN FOR OLD TIME'S SAKE. But most of the time I wasn't really thinking of anything, just smoking and reaching for my glass of vodka, idly waiting inside myself and beside myself, in the middle of this event I had thought up for myself, this party I had wanted to arrange, not as some kind of standard, merely as an amalgam of memories, truths, and happenings connected with myself—things which I was only too well aware had really happened, but which, thank God, were now behind me, though that didn't necessarily mean that the whole affair was ended, or even capable of reaching an end. But at least it was in the PAST, that most secret place, and what was in THE FUTURE was only mist, and mist, and deeper mist. I knew there must be something. But where was I to go from here? And by which way? When this money of mine ran out, the money earned by all that unpleasant labor in that uncongenial life, many long years of such labor, and the money left me by my aunt.

2.

Father fell during the war, in North Africa—and that was the only moment in the trial that really affected me, the only moment when I was able to behave as I have always wanted to behave, because I was speaking up for my father, and also for the fact that it was, or should have been, a matter of complete indifference who or what anyone's father was, let alone a father already dead long ago, and dead in a better cause than the affair of this solemn court. Actually I knew him only from photographs, I'd been too young to be able to remember him from the time before he went away from home; but for that very reason the conception I had of him was all the more lofty. I got his last photograph only after the war, and my mother never got to know that Father was already dead, or how and where he died; and Father, again, never found out that she had had to go through a form of divorce from him during the occupation, otherwise the concentration camp would have been yawning for her, and God knows what for me. In this last photograph Father is standing, in a shallow helmet and open shirt, in front of some kind of dugout, all sandbags, with the barrels of antiaircraft guns jutting out from them in the background; and down underneath him and his comrades, set out in the sand in colored stones, is a big inscription in Czech and German:

> Adolf, don't let it distress you
> That a Czech should dare address you.
>
> Just a brief reply we crave:
> Where'd you like to have your grave?

This had given significance and sense once and for all to everything I had ever thought or wanted to think about war, and about the world in general: my father in a flat helmet and open shirt, with his hairy chest peering out. And afterwards, when the prosecutor at the trial blazed out at me, among other things, that my father had been an old servant of the bourgeoisie, I blazed right back and began to roar at him, too. Did he know that for that service my father had been awarded the Military Cross and a whole array of other bronze medals and colored ribbons? Would he like to tell me how many times *he* had been decorated, and what *he'd* been doing all through the war, because in my opinion his war against Hitler had most likely been waged on the black market, dealing in goose fat and canned carrots.

And it came quite easily, though it probably didn't help me much. . . . But could I ever have forgiven myself if I'd let my dead father, and all those other dead fathers, be abused with impunity by any big-bellied ox and body snatcher? So all I remember is flying out at him, and then the guards dragging me back on the bench and clapping handcuffs on me. And all I know is that it is recorded in the account I keep against that bald-headed son of a bitch and all his kind—for they *are* a kind, a party, a confederation, a conspiracy in support of the spiritual underworld—and that I will never forget it, never, never, never to the day of my death. And to the day of my death I shall will, and desire and do the direct opposite of everything willed and desired and done by him and all his confederacy of perverted fanatics.

In February of 1945 my mother was just getting over some kind of cold or influenza. I don't remember it any too clearly now, I only know that it was Saturday, she'd washed the linoleum in the kitchen and waxed it with some polish or other, given me my dinner, and then gone to lie down. She was in bed reading my homework from school; but then she stayed in bed all through Sunday, and I made tea, while through the doorway of her room, from which she could see as far as the stove, she told me which jet to light, and how much water to put on. On Monday the doctor came, and then a day or two later they took her away to the hospital. At first it was just the usual kind of winter illness, the kind we normally deal with by drinking hot tea regularly and bringing on a sweat. But in the end they moved her to Podolí, to the German SS sanatorium, where the maternity hospital is now. Later, at the trial, that also made things worse for me. It was Mr. Schlemm who got Mother in there, the German from the third floor, where he lived in an apartment which belonged to some

Jews who had run away; it must have been fairly soon after they bombarded Prague, there wasn't a bed to be had in any hospital, and obviously now, at the end of the war, Schlemm was hurrying to create an alibi for himself, because otherwise they never took in Czechs at that SS sanatorium. But it was too late, anyhow, at that time there wasn't any penicillin, or anything like that, or at least the Germans didn't have any. In a word, Mother died hardly five weeks before the end of the war. So she never knew that Father had been dead ever since May, 1943.

Mr. Schlemm, Mr. Schlemm . . . at nine years old you don't understand these things very well. He was a burly, broad-shouldered figure in black breeches. At that time no German could be seen out of uniform, so Mr. Schlemm wore a uniform, too, though otherwise he was quite an ordinary bank official. I remember him very vividly in his black breeches and slippers, lugging coal up from the cellar to the third floor, into the apartment that had once belonged to the Silbersteins. They ran away in March, 1939, almost at the last moment before the Germans came.

Later on, after the war, I got to know Thomas Silberstein and his sister Salome, for they came back, and were in Prague for about two years. But even that did me no good later on, because the Silbersteins went away again some time after the war, first to Switzerland and then to Venezuela. Thomas sent me letters and postcards from those places, and Salome married someone in Israel and sent a card with the announcement of her wedding, not to me, but to the aunt who took charge of me after Mother's death. And even this card and the announcement, and all the letters and cards from Thomas, too, made their appearance in the end, ONE DAY, on the table in front of the court, for I'd kept them all.

I used to carry coal up from the cellar, too, and that's why I remember those breeches and braces and slippers of Mr. Schlemm's. Several times he helped me when I'd filled the coal scuttle too full and then couldn't haul it up the stairs. But I got used to those journeys into the cellar in the dark, and wasn't afraid of them, or of any other eerie things, though Mother was always angry when I drudged with all my might at some work for which I wasn't yet strong enough. She didn't want to let me slave, and still less, of course, because of Father, and the people in the house, and because we were Czechs, did she want any Schlemm carrying coal for us, in his black uniform breeches, with the laces eternally unlaced and dangling around his calves, and his slippers slapping at his heels. A bank clerk in breeches. But a German without a uniform would have been a real anomaly at that time. I even know the bank where Schlemm worked, though it's been gone for a long time now, the street has a different name, and in that building there's quite a different institution. But I know it because the papers with the letterhead ANGLO-CZECH BANK were the only thing they didn't steal from Schlemm's apartment in the revolution, and I took them home, and long after the war I was still using the backs as drawing paper. The apartment and all the furniture really belonged, of course, to the Silbersteins.

Schlemm, his wife, and his two daughters, big girls with full breasts, all died during the revolution. Some German had been firing from a window, not in our house but somewhere close, so they ran in the Schlemms, too. The barber Vonásek, who used to cut my hair, split Schlemm's head with an axe, and then all the women gassed themselves. I saw them dead, covered up with blankets, laid out below in the yard. As he was a tall man, Schlemm's legs were sticking out in their black breeches with the laces unfastened, but he had no slippers on, and there was a hole in the heel of one of his socks.

That is my last recollection of Schlemm, death at close quarters. But sometimes I can still picture him crossing the yard from the street gate to the house steps, the same little yard where he afterwards lay under a blanket, when we boys were playing at how the Germans were losing the war, with prewar rubber soldiers from Bat'a. Mr. Schlemm tramped past us in his black uniform, with the spider on his sleeve, saw what we were playing, and said nothing. At this time our school had been turned into a barracks for the Wehrmacht, and we had plenty of time for play,

though actually we did go twice a week to our teacher's apartment to get some homework, when there wasn't a raid on.

Mr. Schlemm was the first dead man, but a few days later there
were mounds of them, and not only Germans, but also our own
people, for in the last days of the war the boys from the Hitler
Youth were busy gouging out eyes and hacking off genitals and
breasts; and then the Russians were shooting General Vlasov's
troops and SS men, and I had to be running everywhere to see
what was going on. It's true Auntie had forbidden it, but how is
an old aunt to keep close watch on a nine-year-old boy?

That apartment of Schlemm's was completely looted, but I
didn't have anything from it, except those papers with the head-
ing ANGLO-CZECH BANK, which everybody left there. Otherwise not a chair or a broom, nothing, just the papers, a lot of
German books, and a little album of family photographs. Even
the gas stove vanished, and that belonged to the landlord, and it
was a wonder he didn't go out of his mind when he found he'd
lost it.

Auntie was the widow of a chief engineer from a sugar refinery,
and had a pension. When Mother died, she moved into our
apartment, so that I wouldn't have to get used to new teachers
and fellow pupils. Then the war was over, and I was a war orphan, though it was some time before all that business of
Mother's divorce was cleared up; before it was cleared up offi-
cially, that is, for otherwise every reasonable person knew how
things had been and how we'd had to deal with them. I don't
know now how Mother lived without Father, but I think quite
well, I certainly don't remember any "uncle" who ever came visiting us.

After the war, for some time not even the landlord ventured to
meddle with Auntie and me, so we escaped the general search
when they were looking to see whether that gas stove from the
Silberstein-Schlemm apartment hadn't wandered into somebody
else's kitchen. The landlord was scared in any case, because almost all through the war he'd been licking Schlemm's backside;
he even had a special air-raid shelter for himself and his family,

while all the rest of us had to go down into the cellar. So after the war he was very virtuous for some time, and he and his whole family immediately joined the Communist Party. He was the first Communist I ever remember knowing; the second was Professor Pelcus at the grammar school, but they hanged him in 1951, because it leaked out that he'd been an informer for the Gestapo, and had about eleven people on his conscience. And the third Communist was Jirka, our leader in Sokol; but he was a fine boy and a decent fellow, and so he is to this day. And he didn't creep into the Party to get an apartment, or a better job, either, or because he'd been an informer for the Gestapo. To this day he still lives in the same basement apartment as in 1946, with the difference that he has to house four children there now, and he's crippled, and can only walk with crutches.

All this a man can nurse within him while he's sitting in a restaurant to which he has invited a few fellow pupils, smoking, drinking his first vodka, drinking his second vodka, ordering his third, playing with his glass and watching the bar gradually empty. But unlike those other people, he has nowhere to go. On the one hand, he really has nowhere else to go, on the other hand he has invited these fellow pupils of his, who will surely remember all these things just as he does.

After the war we began to attend both Sokol and Scouts, there were even Sea Scouts in our town, too; a boy like me could be busy all the time and in scores of different places. In addition everywhere there were weapons and ammunition; the police had to go around to all the schools explaining and issuing warnings, and all the teachers forbade us to collect such things, and naturally so did my aunt. But can anyone keep an eye on boys all the time? Just in our quarter alone we could have amassed a whole armory. One of our boys was killed by a cartridge thrown into a fire. He was one of twins, I remember that. He was raking in the ashes to see if they'd all exploded, when suddenly something went off bang, and he turned around, took a couple of steps away from the fire, and then he collapsed and died. He didn't cry out, he didn't say a word. And then there was only his twin left. For a few days this accident shocked us; we went from school to his funeral, and carried candles. But soon everything went back into its old routine, and in various hiding places there were hordes of cartridges, rockets and pistols. Every night you could hear them going off. It was that sort of period then. Once in our street two drunken Russians were firing at one another with rockets, and went on until one of their patrols took them in, and people said that they were both shot for it.

Sometimes we had arguments about which was better, Sokol or Scouts, and we who went to both usually took up the cudgels on both sides. Nobody made any pretenses, it was a golden time. On Tuesdays and Fridays we wore ourselves out on the apparatus in the gym, or outside on the sports field, on Saturdays and Sundays we fitted ourselves out from UNRRA supplies and went along the waterside, up to Kocáb, or the Berounka, or the Sázava. Best of all to the Sázava, because there the SS had had a training ground during the war, and even then, some years after the war ended, you could find plenty of weapons under every bush. We were crazy about those things. We would all carry home a pistol, an automatic rifle, a bazooka or a mine. Once even a machine gun, but our leader Jirka found that, and he took it apart and threw the pieces into the river.

That was the time when we were just beginning to know what we were, and what our companions were, and also what we should some day be, and to take care that what we said wouldn't sound stupid, and consider whether we looked at things in the same light, or differently.

I even got onto the Sokol exhibition team on the gymnastic apparatus, for schoolboys, of course, for gradually I'd begun to show what I could do on apparatus. But really it was all because of those buckets of coal hauled up from the cellar, and the cans of water from the laundry carried up to the window boxes; all that hard work had given me plenty of muscle. I was the only one to go down to the cellar now, Auntie was too old, and a coal bucket or two was no problem to me. It was a good thing for me, too, that from a little boy I'd never been afraid of the dark. "You're my gallant knight, my only knight, and you must protect me," Mother used to say. And if I was to protect her, then I couldn't possibly be afraid myself, and I took that seriously. We used to vie with one another for all those proficiency badges; I don't remember them all now, but I know there were thirteen of them, so that we shouldn't be afraid of unlucky numbers and superstitions. There were strength, silence, courage, skill, hunger and solitude, in fact everything that later stood me in good stead, very, very good stead, when it was no longer a game.

The cellar was particularly fine for one purpose; there I could store my entire arsenal entirely without risk, for Auntie never went there. The Germans had thrown a lot of arms into the Vltava, especially at the tunnel in Podolí. It's twenty-five feet deep there, of course, but all the same we used to dive there, with our ears stuffed with wax and plastered over with adhesive tape, and a waxed flashlight. After February, 1948, people began throwing arms in there again, because it was again becoming dangerous to have such things at home, it was a hanging matter; so we had a constant source of material, and I wouldn't mind betting that if I dived in there again today (we had our own special stone on the embankment from which we dived down alongside the embankment wall) and groped in the mud, with a flashlight waxed or coated in preservative, at the third or fourth attempt I would be certain to bring up a gun. And that's even after the police have been there with divers and detectors, and hunted out four truckloads of the stuff, and then brought another four trucks there, only this time for broken bottles and all sorts of scrap. At the third or fourth attempt I would still be sure of finding some sort of gun. What I liked was the big stuff, Mausers, Nagans, Parabella.

One more experience I recall from that time. In 1947, as a war orphan, I was exchanged for a month with a Yugoslav war orphan, and I spent that month by the sea at Dubrovnik. It was my father's comrades who arranged that for me, the same ones who had brought his photos from Africa, and his letters, and a few other things which every man has, just those very personal things. It was a fantastic time, seeing the sea and everything, such adventures, such pleasure. One of those same officers, a certain Kocanda, afterwards ran off back to England, where he felt safe, and who wouldn't have been drawn to do the same. He wrote to me from time to time, and sent me chewing gum, condensed milk, dress material, shirts, cowboy pants—the things came through some parcel service from Holland. Everything arrived, parcels, Darex vouchers to buy things, traitor or no traitor! And at Darex at that time you could even get chocolate and cocoa. But not newspapers, books or phonograph records. The records they always broke in front of my eyes at the Customs control, so I wrote to him that he shouldn't send any more. And letters abroad weren't accepted then unless you showed your identity papers. And later on all this was to be laid solemnly one day, ONE DAY, on the drab courtroom table, painted shit-brown.

"No," they said, "obviously we're not condemning you for this, but it does delineate your character." They made sour faces. "Typical, typical!" And the people's assessors nodded their heads very gravely, yes, it must all be taken into consideration; even to me in my isolation, by the end of it all, all this, the chewing gum, the cowboy jeans, the Darex vouchers, began to appear typical and certainly to be taken into consideration, typical and not quite in order. And silently I said over and over to myself in the spirit: FOOLS, FOOLS, FOOLS, typical that the traitorous Kocanda has sent me parcels, yes, and you are typical swine and idiots, and the best of luck! No, for that they didn't condemn me, but to be exact, they did draw conclusions from it. A half-rotten republic, and here was I getting parcels from abroad. You see, you see! Conclusions about what I was like at eighteen, and what relationship I must have to our constitution, to THEIR CONSTITUTION, for mine it never was, mine was Father, mine was Kocanda, and a whole host of other people and other things. But they couldn't understand that, they didn't want to understand it. Their souls were just exactly good enough to place them here in this dusty courtroom, behind a bench painted shit-brown; but too soiled and minor ever to send them to war somewhere in Africa.

Typical. They didn't know how to be knights. Once I knocked over Granddad Stuchlík with my bicycle in our yard. I was trying to ride down the steps at the gate, and my feet came off the pedals, and I couldn't stop before I ran into Granddad. I didn't have any hand brakes. He never told on me; but somehow it got out. And naturally the landlord told this story to the police when they were compiling their report on my reputation. It was ten years after the war by then, and he didn't have to be afraid any more, the Schlemms had been dead ten years, and people had forgotten about that special air-raid shelter. And so I suddenly heard that I'd unfeelingly knocked to the ground an old and feeble man, who had worked honestly as a laborer all his life (while I, from a child, had been receiving parcels from the traitor Kocanda without working for them), a typical incident demonstrating the deformation of my personality. In fact even the books *Our Men in the Desert* and *Three Years With Eisenhower* were hailed as symbols of the deformation of my character and my political profile. Here and there, too, there was a glimpse of that chief engineer in a sugar refinery who had been Auntie's husband, though he had been dead long before I was born, and to be exact she was a great-aunt. There was mention of some servant girl at whom he had once shouted, and who, God knows why, had been thrown out of her job, again long before I ever came into the world.

So it all went on to the end. Jirka Brabenec, who used to steal our toy soldiers when we were little, and wheedled snacks out of us and then threw them away if they weren't good enough for him, testified that we had arms and ammunition. Just like that, kept for ourselves. He said we'd declared that American cars were better and handsomer than Russian ones, that we played at American soldiers and sang "Tipperary," and that when we had meetings with our Scout leader and went out on Saturdays and Sundays toward Kocáb or Sázava, all this was really nothing but a preparation for escaping abroad.

Such things were settled in short order. Indeed, one boy from our school had tried to get across the frontier, and indeed, when they asked me whether I also would have run away if I could, I told them yes, I would, and also told them that I would gladly shoot my interrogator if I could, calmly I told them so to their faces. My God, Fučík, our example, "let us spurn the executioner's apprentices!" And the interrogator beat me over the head until my ears rang, a strong, burly man beating up a young boy in handcuffs.

In any case this Brabenec went to learn to be a miner, SOME DAY, and they put me and the other two into a reformatory, as we weren't yet eighteen. The Scout leader got nine years. Remedial education. First of all they sent us to a certain castle, but then we really did want to escape, because it was awful for us there, and the warden was a queer, and all the time I couldn't help thinking about Kocanda, and how he had always behaved well to me, just because he had known my father and been comrades with him, and how he was SOMEWHERE OVER THERE. So we really wanted to escape, and then somebody informed on us again, and they transferred us from this reformatory into a normal prison for young delinquents.

There I learned to bind books and saw and dress wood, and work on a building site, but nothing properly. I remembered the books I had at home, and how I used to read secretly under the blankets, so that Auntie wouldn't suspect, and how I once scorched my sheets with an electric bulb. I bound books, sticking various old newspapers and magazines into their spines, and in some of them there were publishers' advertisements many times older than I, for I had those very books at home. This was a part of that unapproachable world, that mysterious world where they said that we—that I!—did not belong . . . *a marked social danger.* . . .

Don't believe any of them when they try to tell you what excellent care they take of people THERE. Lies, lies, lies, . . . the guaranteed calorific value of the food, the guaranteed rights, guaranteed, everything is guaranteed, THERE, SOME DAY, IN ANOTHER WORLD. And especially in the world of those young people . . . no, really those are no ewe lambs, no contented sheep. Next to me slept a boy who had stabbed the neighbor's daughter forty-seven times, when she caught him robbing the rabbit hutches; and two beds further on was Peter, who had also killed someone, and plenty of others, a whole host of people lost to the day of their death, expecting nothing, hoping for nothing, so that in the end there was nothing left to them, if they wanted to endure being in the world at all, but to be proud of being what they were. I had somewhere else to go, I didn't want to die in this hole, and for me my SOME DAY was going to come in the end. Everything here would pass at last, the boys who didn't fight fair, the boys who in their stupidity were willing to settle accounts for the guards, who had only to egg them on, overturn a bed or two, and point a finger: HE's the one! It's HIS fault we wake you in the night, settle it among yourselves! And the enthusiastic, gullible slaves would set on, fifteen, twenty on to one, we'll show you, we'll show you! While the drunken guard laughed outside the door.

Shortly after the currency reform Auntie died. I got leave for the funeral, black uniform, the élite convict uniform, so that everybody could recognize even from a distance what I was, cap, heavy, iron-tipped boots, off you go, boy, and make the best of it, you've got four days' leave, and don't forget to report to the police every day.

While I'd been away, Auntie had taken in a tenant. As time went on she'd found it impossible to live on what she had, so she let herself be persuaded by some tramp, and now suddenly this fellow wanted me to take my things out of the apartment. When I appealed to the National Committee they threw me out, the police shrugged their shoulders, it's nothing to do with us. My leave was four days. The second day was the funeral, the third was a mad rush to get everything settled, and the last day I tried my luck. I got my ticket confirmed and reported that I was going back—but in the cellar I hunted out one more Parabellum pistol about which Brabenec hadn't known. Part of the breech was missing, and it couldn't be fired, but it was quite good enough to scare anyone, it was a pistol. Auntie was dead, and there was nothing waiting for me but that reformatory, and nothing besides. Now I really wanted to get away over the hills. But I had no luck, in fact it was impossible that I should have, for I never had a chance. All my old clothes were too small for me, I had to go in that black uniform, though I did cover it with a raincoat, and without any papers I hadn't a hope. They picked me up before I got as far as Budějovice, and took me off the train, and that was that.

And here again came all those cards from the Silbersteins and Kocanda, and even this last popgun, and Granddad Stuchlík, and my alleged praise of American cars. Where the new gun was concerned, they didn't take into account that it couldn't be fired. Here we are, you see, immediately after the funeral of his only relative, and then flight! The height of cynicism. I pretended to be stupid, and said I'd wanted to go hunting, but they ended by giving me five years just the same. They didn't take me back among the juvenile offenders this time, in a few months I was due to be eighteen, so I stayed in the prison as a corridor orderly until then, and then they shoved me off among the adults into a normal labor camp.

The only good thing was that even in this prison there was one guard with whom it was possible to talk as with a normal decent human being. I even found out in the end that he'd known my father. He took me with him after the court hearing, and I bet I would have stayed there on maintenance, only the poor guy himself was being pushed pretty hard, because he fraternized, and also because he'd once served in the army in England, and somebody threw it up at him that he took me into the kitchen to repair the sinks, and things like that. There were women there. By this time I was terribly curious about women, but most of them were lesbians. Everybody in prison is trapped in some way. And one of them had killed her husband, she hammered a nail into his head in the night, when he was sleeping. A fine anvil, and a nail, and tap, tap, tap. . . . And what's that? Just a normality. Until one day I packed up my things and they took me under escort, and off we went. I had a green stripe on my shoulder, to show I was a runaway, and handcuffs on my wrists. On the journey we passed through our street in the early morning, and in Auntie's windows—the windows of *my* apartment—the feather beds were draped to air, probably still the same feather beds Mother had had.

At the labor camp I went through all manner of experiences; that green stripe on my shoulder was good for something, after all, it made people esteem me more, and the training in fighting I'd acquired in the reformatory stood me in good stead, too. A very mixed bag of people, good and bad, I suppose pretty much what you'd inevitably expect to find in a prison camp, but most of them better and cleverer than that bunch in the juvenile prison. There wasn't so much homosexuality in that camp, either. We worked in the mines. A certain Dr. Stern took me into his group, a first-class man he was, a former partisan. In the camp library there were plenty of books in which he was written about—"this legendary figure of the Slovak national rising!"—with photographs of him, too. And for three years before he was sent to the camp he had been shut in a top security prison, for two of those years alongside a fellow from the Gestapo, who had put a price of 100,000 crowns on his head, dead or alive! He knew the Silbersteins, I found. He was an absolutely fine man; he began to teach me German to give me something to occupy my mind, naturally without any dictionary or textbooks, just out of his head. We could have got thrown into the punishment block for that, but nobody ever caught us at it. Almost the best and finest person I've ever known in my life. Anyone who really stood for anything there was most likely to be a priest, a Jehovah's Witness, or a Jew; they knew how to stick together, they had spines and culture, and thanks to Dr. Stern they gradually came to count me as one of them and to keep an eye on me so that I wouldn't blunder into trouble, although all of them had fifteen, twenty, even twenty-five years of prison around their necks, and could very well have quit bothering about anything. Fedya Rozincuk, also a former partisan, had in all fifty-six years of imprisonment before him, and about seven already served, and still he made a joke of it. He used to say:

"Those asses will have to prolong my life for me!" It was thanks to these people that I didn't get myself tattooed, so that apart from an anchor or so on my arms and a monogram on my ankle I'm absolutely clean.

Once or twice I got into fights, once with a room supervisor, while I was still a greenhorn, because of some ash in the stoves, and once because of my work in the mine, with this same supervisor, who accused me in front of the mine overseer of being responsible for not having the empty wagons ready at the loading point. It was Stern who stood by me then, that's how we got to know each other. And then when it came out that some civilian was bringing the doctor food and letters from outside, and they moved him into another camp, I stayed in his group just the same. This Fedya Rozincuk happened to know Kocanda. The room supervisor was a huge fellow, I had to use a shovel against him when he lunged at me, and the second time, when he went for me with the clasp knife at his belt, it was Fedya who flattened him. Fedya was at least twice as big as the supervisor. He was surely built to stand those fifty-six years in prison.

I learned to smoke there, and thanks to Stern there were plenty of books circulating among us even from outside, not just from the camp library. What I liked most of all was an almanac about prehistoric painting. I wrote out a request to the commander, asking him to allow me to get certain magazines, *Universe* and things like that, but he didn't grant it, according to what I heard because of that fight with the supervisor.

Every now and again the camp would be on fire with some rumor or other that lasted a few months or a few days, and then faded out. There was an amnesty expected, or at least a revolution, and everybody knew all manner of details and conjectures. In time the people who only managed to live at all thanks to such rumors came to be called the "amnesty reporters." They were always the same people, but never Dr. Stern or Fedya. In the end nothing ever came of it, of course. About a year after the fight with the supervisor they took away the green stripe from my shoulder for good work, and in the evening, when we were no longer entertained either by politics or prehistoric painting, we made great plans. The fellows drew designs for country cabins, or motor boats; everybody was obsessed with all the things he still intended to do with his life when at last they gave him the green light out of the camp gates, starting the moment he got outside. Eighteen, twenty years to serve, and plans for the next fifty. To breed nutrias, to build a house, to run a bar. As soon as life became life again, and morons were shoved out of the way, and normal time recommenced.

I suppose I grasped maybe half of all this. But there was one thing I certainly had; at our camp in Nikolaj it happened that they paid quite good money, even if the Ministry people did take most of it for themselves and leave us only a small percentage, still it was money, and I'd always been the strongest boy from our street, or among the boys at school. That was when I first got the idea of arranging something in the nature of an evening party, something like when Kocanda came back from England after the war, and they all sat down together at Šroubek's and finished off all their war reminiscences. Perhaps it was also, to some degree, because one of those people's assessors at my first trial had been a waiter, and it would have amused me to find the inn where he was employed, and make him wait on me.

But that wasn't true any longer, that childish idea of hunting out one ignoramus and getting satisfaction out of him had long ago forsaken me. It wasn't František, or any other waiter from this hotel; when it came to that point I'd forgotten the man's face long ago, and I can't imagine it ever stirring any memory in me if by any chance I should ever encounter it here and now. And actually I was in no position to point a finger at him: THIS MAN INJURED ME! There were the Silberstein letters, of course, the cards from Kocanda, the parcels from Holland, Father's photograph in a flat helmet, and: Adolf, don't let it distress you . . . but could any waiter help all that? An empty-headed waiter, out of whom they'd made a symbol of the revolution, and stuffed his skull to bursting with affairs far beyond his understanding. Could he help it if they had placed him in the seat he occupied, and left him to make decisions, all puffed up as he was with pride and inhumanity? It seems to me that he could not be held entirely responsible. But who, then? WHO? No, no one comes to mind but he, nobody else, even though I could no longer recognize his face. Is it possible that he, already an old man, failed to be clear in his mind about things which even I, a snot-nosed kid, knew and realized and felt? Is it possible? What were they all playing at? Why not just try pulling the legs off flies, if they had to get something like that out of their systems?

Once again I was in for a rough time. A mutiny broke out in camp, or it would be truer to say that a mutiny was created, on account of some dumplings which were quite uneatable, and which accordingly nobody would eat. So that made it mutiny, because when a number of people agree upon some course and carry it out together, that's mutiny, even if what they do is nothing more than refusing to eat dumplings which are not fit to eat. Again came the threat of years and years in prison, tens of years. Again a court, and those empty-headed waiters obviously think a man lives a thousand years. But at last there really was an amnesty, and nobody proved it against me that I had conspired with anyone to refuse the offending dumplings. There was an amnesty which was valid not only for thieves and perverts who prey on little children, but also for me.

I was outside. But my whole world, my WHOLE world, Fedya and all the others, remained THERE, on the other side. I had a watch, it was the first thing I bought when I got out, and whenever I looked at it I knew:

NOW IT'S ROLL CALL.
NOW IT'S DINNER FOR THE AFTERNOON SHIFT.
NOW THEY'RE DOWN IN THE MINE.
TODAY'S THURSDAY, THERE'LL BE DUMPLINGS
    FOR DINNER.

The tenant had a family by this time, had had for some time, in fact, and he lived in the apartment with Mother's and Auntie's furniture, but that didn't seem to worry anybody; and when it came to the point, I had money, so I moved into a hotel. FOR A FEW DAYS, UNTIL WE GET IT SETTLED SOMEHOW, UNTIL SOMETHING TURNS UP, as they told me at the offices. As it happened I had money. From all those years of work at Nikolaj, but mainly the money left by my aunt.

But nothing ever did turn up, nor was it ever settled SOME-HOW. The officials at the housing department and elsewhere were always just in conference when I came asking for them, and if by chance I ever did manage to catch sight of that one of mine, at the best he would put me off with something so infuriating that I had hard work not to hit him. The tenant went on living in my apartment, the furniture, they said, I could take away without hinderance, and he said yes, by all means take it away. And I went on living in the hotel and dining with the head waiter František.

But if the official of the housing department hid from me, the official from the labor office took double notice of me to make up for it. WHERE DID I WISH TO GO? HOW SHOULD I BEST FIND MY PLACE? and so on and so on, including what would happen if I didn't hurry up and get a job. Best of all, of course, in some organized recruitment field, so that the official could get a bonus out of it, eh? But in a labor camp one soon gets a shrewd grip on laws like these. I had money, they couldn't get at me for being a parasite, and I didn't want to go back into the mines again, living again in communal quarters, the only advantage being that I could go to a movie without asking anybody's leave, and choose whatever film I liked, and to a bar, naturally, too, of course to a bar. Otherwise I don't think there's much difference from a prison camp. Maybe in not having any physical searches or roll calls, and not having to wear prison clothes and take off your hat to every uniform. So I said to myself: I'm not going anywhere, my dears, nowhere that you want me to go, nowhere out of Prague, no building sites, no damned mines, I spit on your recruitment bonus, my loves, and from a great height. This is my apartment, and my right.

It was the only right now left to me. The labor official wouldn't give me a permit for any work I found for myself. I had a nice little place ready among the sewermen, found for me by a former convict, also a doctor, who was now a rat catcher in the sewers. He had plenty of practice from the camp, where rat catching was the only sport. There were more rats there than there were people.

Still in the camp canteen, but outside the wire, I'd bought a suit as well as my watch, in order to have something to go home in. As soon as I came to Prague I saw at once what rubbish it was, trash they'd stocked up with there because a man has to have something to travel home in, and they couldn't sell this stuff anywhere else. That meant buying a new one. So I could only repeat to myself what Dr. Stern and Fedya and all the others used to say: NOBODY WILL DO ANYTHING FOR YOU, DON'T DEPEND ON ANYONE, RELY ONLY ON YOURSELF, THAT'S HOW THE WORLD IS. Camp wisdom. In spite of which, of course, Fedya and Stern and those others who amounted to something NEVER took care only of themselves. And then I came back to that old notion of mine about a banquet, just as I remembered the old times, and those sunlit campsites on the Sázava, and thought of the guests I was inviting only as the boys who had shared those camps. How we had kept night watches together, cooked potatoes, and carried our UNRRA cans down to the well for drinking water.

The head waiter František said to me, after my last vodka: "Nobody's arrived for you yet, sir, and it's nearly nine o'clock now."

And suddenly I awoke from everything that surrounded me, our campsites, our night watches. I'm alone. Alone. No party. My party has remained behind in Nikolaj, it's over. Don't be a fool! And I stopped following every creak of the door and every soul who came in, in case I should find in his face something that would tell me he was hesitating, looking at the curtains of the salon. I stopped looking for the trace of an old likeness, the reflection of my sunlit campsites. Nothing, nothing, nothing, only

František the waiter, rather nervous, obviously because of all the food that had been prepared, leaning over me and pronouncing that funereal sentence which meant that it was no use waiting any longer, that what was past was past. No use waiting any longer, although life is only a kind of ceaseless waiting, and everything we do, we do to make it appear that we are not existing in a time totally without end.

There used to be endless disputation in camp: Is God the fulfillment of the world, or is the world the fulfillment of God? In all possible permutations. Man in God and God in man.

The woman whose acquaintance I had made a few days after my release, not exactly a raving beauty, a stenographer or something like that in the housing office, who was attracted to me chiefly because of that long period when I'd been without women. For I was already quite mature, and had still never slept with a woman, never kissed or caressed one. And complete stupefaction at finding how easily it went! TAKE CARE YOU DON'T GO OVERBOARD FOR SOME COW! thanks, Fedya, thanks for those words, you're still standing by me. I would like to be in love, on my honor I would; but still, thanks! I haven't gone overboard. Nothing but simple copulation in the Emperor's Meadow, and then a rush to the bus, to make sure of getting her husband's hot supper in time.

A thirty-three-year-old secretary from the housing office, the Emperor's Meadow, and later on the zoo. Thirty-three, not exactly a beauty, but a well-groomed and attractive person. I'VE BEEN UNFAITHFUL FOR YOUR SAKE, YOU'VE BEEN SO LONG ALONE, POOR DARLING!

Thanks, Fedya! All right, Dr. Stern! You gave me good advice. With all the longing I feel to kiss and embrace that beatified thirty-three-year-old body and many others like it, you gave me good advice, and I know what I'm about, at least I've got an inkling. OK, OK, OK!

WAS I THE FIRST? TELL ME, WAS I THE FIRST?

Nobody came to my party, but that was good, for what could I have had to say to any of them, and what, in fact, could any of them have had to say to me? What good would it have done to talk about my endless days and nights, here over the napkins in their artistic wooden rings, and the silver cutlery? In the light of the candles, and the crystal lusters with their rainbow glasses? People cannot talk together when they have no reason for talking, not when they are people less splendid than Fedya and Kocanda and all the others, who, in their turn, have no need at all for conjecture. What could we have found to say? Do you remember? Do you remember THAT TIME? Yes, it was wonderful, THAT TIME, and it was gone. Yes, yes. No, no.

COME HERE. WHAT'S YOUR NAME?
CONVICT VOPRŠALEK, 38092, COMMANDER.
HOW MANY DISCIPLINARY PUNISHMENTS HAVE YOU?
NONE, COMMANDER.
HOW LONG HAVE YOU BEEN HERE?
THREE YEARS, COMMANDER.
YOU MUST BE A FIRST-CLASS SCOUNDREL, THEN, IF WE'VE NEVER CAUGHT YOU ON ANYTHING.

No, nobody came to my party, but for God's sake, what could anyone have done here? What? Only hoped, perhaps, that I would want or need something from him, today, when we live without any sunlit campsites, shut up in our prison camps, in our country cottages, in our cars, in our state.

I was alone. I showed František my bundle of banknotes, so that he need have no fears for his bill, the bundle expressly prepared for this evening. I wanted to pay for the whole deal, but František talked me out of it, we'd gotten used to each other by then, he understood my situation. He was a good waiter, and evidently he'd never cherished any ambitions to become anything else, let alone a judge. The food they put into the refrigerators, the bottles were left unopened, and the preparations of the salon actually cost only a few fives.

So here I am. Single, at the age of twenty-three, free, without ties, with, as of this moment, not quite 48,000 crowns in my pocket;

and in the course of three days outside, I have managed to find not exactly a beauty, but a well-cared-for thirty-three-year-old, after whom people are glad to turn and look again in the street, and I have made love with her, and I could telephone her and know that she would come if it's at all possible, and that she enjoys making love with me.

Freedom has not accepted me, all anchors have vanished in a void. The only thing that remained was the consciousness that *every day, every hour, every minute, they are THERE, far away in oblivion, forgotten, that assembly of men compressed and oppressed, united, outlawed, enraged, reasoning, taciturn, resigned, fulfilled by their visions of motor boats, country cabins, idealized remembrances, sunlit campsites.*

We fill our lives with this effort to make secure the house in which we live. We are searching, always searching, for ideas and truths. We think up a morality for ourselves, but nothing of all this that we invent and imagine is real in the end, everything is merely a coat of plaster over the original, submerged, dark, elemental thoughts and instincts. Pure greed to gain, and not to lose. But for those exceptions! Fedya, Stern, the Jehovah's Witnesses. Somebody is manipulating us, but let's do our best to survive. Never has any part, *any part,* of this which we have had to experience and survive been to any purpose, not even to those who forced us to undergo it. In the end there is no one here but myself and the waiter František, who understand each other, because in fact we do not know each other, and have nothing to say to each other at any other time than THIS EVENING. Our lives are on the level of the cognac we are drinking, on this unsuccessful, walled-in evening party, which turned out in the end to belong to no one but us. František is easy now about his salon. On the basis of that tomorrow in which we fix our hope. How tremendous a hope!

Later on, two of the waitresses sat down with us. They were off duty, their rooms were somewhere up in the roof, and it was too warm and close for them to want to withdraw there yet. A waitress's vocation, when it comes to the point, is no bar to the vocation of a whore; even greater ladies, secretaries from the housing department for instance, can be hot in the crotch; and somehow this idea was not at all against my inclinations at this moment—less so, perhaps, than anything in the world.

"This party today didn't turn out right for you, somehow, did it?" they said, full of sympathy, full of curiosity, and something else besides, over this queer evening party for one person and the head waiter, stretched out at ease now in an armchair.

"No," I conceded. "No, I do get an impression that this evening—how shall I put it?—fell a little short of expectations. But the society of such charming ladies affords me so much consolation that I can't say I feel the slightest regret. Even my shadow has a relationship with the sun." Dr. Stern used to talk like that when he felt like it, and I caught the habit from him.

They hooted with laughter at such a polished speech, and František said, "I can see this business is still fretting you, sir. You have another cognac, and take a tip from me: Don't you let it worry you! Will you girls have another drink, too?"

"Yes," I said. "Meine. Lieber," as I filled the girls' glasses. And it came into my mind then that there were foreigners in this hotel, the kind of foreigners who have passports, with the right to cross over frontiers actually written into them. "Ja, meine lieber . . . " and I played with the cognac in my mouth as Fedya had taught me. "Couldn't one get a place here with you in the hotel?" I saw how the ladies laughed at that. "No, I don't mean only for one night, and an inch and a half wide and eight deep."

And slowly I began to tell my story.

The king's rage is as the roaring of a young lion; he who provokes it, sins against his own life.

Show great anger by remitting punishment; for by this act of remission you punish all the more thereafter.

A Rainy Night

We were making our way slowly back from a casual job. None of us was particularly eager either to go somewhere or not go somewhere, but it was raining, and Emil suggested we go to Dicky's. We three were colleagues and comrades; and Dicky kept a nightspot, and was also a comrade, and in a small, a very small, way a colleague. We simply needed somewhere to be together and talk, and since it was raining, we couldn't do that somewhere in the street, or in the park.

"We're still closed!" The doorkeeper ran out at us from the cloakroom opposite, obviously more concerned that the door was open and we had been able to get inside, than over the fact that we had come there at all. He never recognized us. Actually he was a kind of amateur at the doorkeeping business. Most likely a police spy or half-spy.

"It's us, Mr. Vach," said Bedřich, and I added quickly: "We've come to see Dicky."

Emil said nothing; today he'd gotten hold of some gloves in washable deerskin from somewhere, and he had them on for the first time. He was proud of them, and they took up all his attention.

The doorkeeper didn't answer; he always received us as a nec-

essary evil. He crossed quickly behind us, and hurriedly turned
the key in the door. Then he tried the latch again to make sure it
was really locked. Then at last he growled: "We don't open till
nine!"

"Don't be annoyed, Mr. Vach," I told him, and reached into
the pocket of my raincoat. On the bus I'd paid with a ten-crown
bill, and the conductor had given me back a pocketful of small
change. I watched the doorkeeper gradually give up hope. Emil
and Bedřich had already vanished down the stairs into the inn.

Outside somebody rattled at the door. Behind the glass stood a
couple, the man curtaining the glass with his hand and peering
uncomprehendingly inside.

"We're still closed!" Vach yelled at them, and pointed at his
wrist. "Until nine!"

I saw the man outside also look at his wrist, and then make
some remark to his companion. He offered her his arm, and they
turned and walked away. As they reached the rim of the light
from above the doorway, their shoulders glistened in the rain.

"They'll soon be coming here looking for lunch," grumbled the
doorman.

We'd come to see Dicky, and therefore in a small way we belonged to the establishment, though only as a necessary evil. But
for Vach all the people in the world, practically, were necessary
evils, and those who came patronizing the "Submarine" most of
all, of course. So much so that it was as though they were not
really people, but only THAT BUNCH. Just like the guards,
when they counted the convicts, and bellowed up to the guard on
the next floor above: "Twenty-three of THIS BUNCH passed to
you. . . ."

I gathered the change in my pocket into my fist, and handed it
to him: "All right, don't be annoyed, granddad!"

"This is a nightspot," he answered, as though I'd asserted the
contrary, and dropped the money into his pocket without so
much as looking at it. Thanks to our acquaintance with Dicky we
never paid any entrance fee here, and it seemed to me fitting to
give the doorman a few crowns every now and then. It was our

nightspot, with Dicky, who was a comrade and in a small way a colleague, and the waitress Helena, who was willing to sleep with one of us for two hundred crowns, when, that is, she was in the mood to sleep with somebody at all. The occasional *pourboire* to the doorkeeper was an absolutely essential investment. Maybe he really was a police spy, or semispy, and to pay an additional fee to your own police spy is quite amusing, like in the short stories of Chekhov.

I went down. Dicky was loafing behind the bar counter, and the apprentice waiters were throwing cloths over the tables and laying out the cutlery. In front of the bar Emil and Bedřich stood with their coats unbuttoned, with wet shoulders and drops of rain in their hair. They were drinking something golden-brown.

"Hi, Dicky!" I said. Usually the barman Olda was at the bar, I didn't know why Dicky should be doing this job himself today.

He was just lifting out two bottles from inside the counter. He raised his eyes to me, placed both bottles on the shelves behind him, their labels turned toward us, and only when this was done did he answer: "Servus! You're welcome!" and reached in for another pair of bottles.

"You getting yourself adopted by the old man?" asked Emil, jerking a thumb over his shoulder in the direction from which I'd just come.

"Sure," I said, nodding, "on account of the inheritance." I unbuttoned my coat and clambered onto a stool. "Anyhow, I would have broken his heart otherwise, he says I'm the image of his first love."

Behind us the bass player in the orchestra crossed toward the main hall with his instrument.

"Evening, gentlemen."

"Cheers!" we answered, and Emil and Bedřich lifted their glasses a few inches from the counter. The bass player laughed, tossed his head back, and replied: "Praise God, long live Slavonic Prague, good health, my best respects, and down with imperialism!"

The paths by which all of us had arrived at this bar, I, Emil,

Dicky, Bedřich, and this bass player, had begun in the none too distant and daily renewed past, avid of memories. After a raid some years ago in quite a different nightspot, long since closed and forgotten, they had put all of us, until then quite unknown to one another, to loading coal, turnips and potatoes at the railway station. The railways were having difficulties, and someone had hit on the genial idea of supplying them with a labor force by means of a statewide raid on the bars. They even published an article about it in a weekly paper: "The workers on night shifts are making their contribution to the well-being of all of us . . ." and so on. Thus we all met. Except in Dicky's case, of course. Dicky was an exception, and quite a special case. Dicky was a Jew, and his actual name was Lentz. His brother had formerly been a big shot, even a minister, and some time after the war they hanged him. It's true that Dicky himself had never been anything but a waiter and barman, but he suffered from it, too, even though he hadn't any political ambitions. Since they'd hanged his brother, probably they felt it to be their duty to hand out a long term of years in prison to Dicky, as well. But he only served four of them. And at our railway station where we met he was voluntarily repairing his cadre profile, so that he could regain his reputation and become a waiter again, for there was nothing else he knew how to do. Now he worked as manager of the "Submarine," and was secretly buying up apartment houses. He already had two, and just at this period he was busy working on Emil to buy a third one for him.

"What'll you have?" he asked. He was all this time pulling out bottles from the counter and standing them on the shelves behind him. I sniffed at Emil's glass. It was sherry.

"Sherry," I said. Dicky wiped his hands, drew out a bottle from the cooler, and placed a glass before me on the counter.

In the mirror behind him I saw the saxophonist pass by behind our backs with his instrument flashing. In the oblique mirror at the side Helena stood, leaning against the wall by the kitchen door with her arms folded behind her back.

"How is it you're at the bar today?" I asked. "Olda isn't here?"

"He took a day off," answered Dicky. He pushed the glass close to me, corked the bottle, sighed, and reached inside the counter for another one.

"He pretends he isn't well," Bedřich shook his head. "Is this what the best sons and daughters of our nation bled for?"

Dicky flapped a hand. "Thirty-three years now I've been working as a barman, boys, and always at night. It doesn't amuse me any more."

"Thirty-three years?" Emil spoke up indignantly, or at least with pretended indignation. "And what about those four years of recreation?"

I drank my sherry. It tasted good. Drinks like sherry usually do taste good to me, and being friends with Dicky had this advantage among others, that he didn't pour out any crude slop for us, whom he knew. What Emil had said didn't seem to me a joke in too good taste, not as entertainment for a man whose brother had been hanged, but I knew it didn't worry Dicky. Indeed the majority of things in this world didn't worry Dicky. And today, in addition, he had other things to think about, what with the ten-day return of stock and profits to do, and Olda away. He was straightening his papers, and not really listening to Emil at all. He muttered some calculations in an undertone, and then reached in for two more bottles. He shook his head.

"What a way to work! He's got it in such a mess, I don't know where anything is . . ." and he revolved to demonstrate his help-lessness. On his waistcoat at the back the belt dangled unstitched. He took a pencil from a drawer and struck out something in his lists. "Boys, boys. . . ."

Upstairs somebody rattled the door violently, and we heard the doorkeeper abusing them. Then Helena came over to us.

"Hi!" she said, as though she hadn't noticed us until that moment.

We raised our glasses, and Bedřich stretched out his toward her with a gesture that meant: Like a drink?

She shook her head and smiled. For an instant we glimpsed the gold crown on an upper tooth, well back in her mouth.

Two sets of footsteps thumped heavily down the stairs.

"I knew they'd be coming. Catch them forgetting!" Dicky raised his eyes. He stopped writing, and set out two more glasses on the bar counter.

Helena pulled out her handkerchief from her apron pocket and blew her nose. "I've got a cold."

Emil folded his hands under one cheek, leaned sideways and closed his eyes. An international gesture—a lullaby. Then he pointed at Helena and at himself: "Tonight?—eh?"

She stuck out her tongue at him. But she stuck it out in quite a nice way, and in any case it was quite a nice tongue. She shook a hand at him with her fingers spread wide: "Nothing doing!"

Bedřich took note of this and indicated himself: "And me?"

She repeated the trick with her tongue, the motion of her hand, and her smile: "No!"

"And me?" I turned a thumb toward myself.

She laughed again: "No, not a chance!"

"Boys, boys!" sighed Dicky again. "When will you get some sense?" He shook his head over us in a fatherly way, and we all laughed again, even he. The gold crown flashed in Helena's upper teeth. In any case we knew that what Helena said at nine o'clock need not still hold good when closing time came. And it wasn't even nine o'clock yet. And she knew it, too. When she hesitated most, it was usually enough to say: "But, Helena, you'd be disappointing me so terribly," and suddenly everything would be OK. She said we were bastards, but she never wanted to disappoint us.

The footsteps on the stairs had finally thumped to the bottom of the flight, and in upon us rolled the uniformed patrol, swathed in straps and hung with the usual service trash the police drape around themselves. Top sergeant Zajíc, who had served through all the regimes that had rolled over us, and a sergeant who, some years previously, when we still had the former woman secretary of the Party in this town, made his name by arresting her by mistake. He was new, and he didn't know her. It so happened that the whole local committee, including her, went swimming in the fountain in the square, after some party or other. The sergeant impounded their clothes, and ran them in naked to the station.

It's quite true that this endeared him to the town at one stroke, but although the secretary was finally deposed on account of this contretemps, still the sergeant had remained a sergeant for many years afterwards. And probably would all his life.

"Good evening," they greeted us.

We nodded our heads vaguely, and Dicky answered: "Good evening, gentlemen."

Zajíc took off his cap, and laid it on the edge of the bar counter. Plainly he found it unpleasant that he had caught us here so early, and even more so that we had caught him on his sponging round. He was torn between the temptation to refuse the rum Dicky had poured out for them, and the longing to pin something on us. But the rum was fragrant, and he couldn't think quickly enough of anything he could charge us with.

"These are friends of mine," Dicky explained quickly. "Drink up, officer, nobody here will see anything."

"I shouldn't, on duty . . ." said Zajíc, but in the next instant he tossed the rum into himself so quickly that we couldn't even follow how it happened. One moment there was a full glass standing on the counter, and a moment later there was an empty one in exactly the same place.

"Friends . . . from a wet quarter, eh?" he said, chuckling, and twisting his face into what was evidently meant to be a friendly grin. Then the sergeant drank, too.

"Well, did you see anything, boys?" asked Dicky.

"Did we see anything?" repeated Bedřich. "Did we see anything, Emil?"

"If we're supposed to have seen something, you've only to say, officer," said Emil.

Zajíc repeated his grimace. He didn't much like the tone of these speeches. In addition he'd never liked us much, if one can put it as mildly as that. But the rum in its time had smoothed over greater gaps between people, and he had it inside him now. He picked up his cap from the counter, took a step back, and belched.

"I'll look in again," he said uncertainly, and raised two fingers to his forehead. They turned and went. Helena was standing, again with her arms folded behind her, by the door into the kitchen. She looked them over with indifferent eyes, and I knew that they were doing as much for her, but of course without the indifference. They turned to have another look at her from the stairs, and began to mount them resoundingly.

"Fuck you!" Bedřich said after them.

"May you rot in hell!" Emil elaborated, and made a threatening jab of his finger toward the staircase. In 'fifty-seven he had gotten swept up in some cleaning-up operation against hooligans, and Zajíc had locked him up because, after coming back from military service, he didn't go straight to work again, but made off somewhere to a cabin in the country with a girl. That was according to Zajíc. Zajíc was acting on somebody's orders, but Emil didn't know who had issued the orders, so he had it in for Zajíc himself. They ran in about fifty people in the town, that time. It was a nationwide operation, and they had to pick up somebody just to prove that they were on the job. All the prisoners—strictly in accordance with orders received FROM ABOVE—were shaved completely bald, and taken out under guard for four months to sweep the streets. Ever since that time Emil preferred to break an arm when he didn't feel like working; never again did he simply shirk it and go off with a girl.

"You take it too hard," said Dicky. "It's their job, what can the poor devils do?" He set down in the middle of the counter a great tea caddy of thick glass, filled with drinking straws, and a sugar bowl. "If he hadn't run you in, others would have, and shaved you, too." Then he looked round to see that everything was in order on the counter.

"Are you staying for supper?"

We looked at one another. Not one of us wanted to go home. Nobody was waiting for us anywhere. In the morning we had to go to work, and this was really the most wretched part of the day. Not that it was in any way more wretched than usual; but sitting at the bar like this, with Emil and Bedřich, and with a glass of sherry in front of us, it did seem possible to hope that what was coming afterwards might be less wretched than usual.

"Well—for a while," said Bedřich.

It was always the same. Either Bedřich would declare that he had nothing against the idea, or else I was the one who had nothing against it. Or of course it could just as well have been Emil. In the end we always took root there until morning.

"I'm in no hurry, either," I said.

Curious how people can sometimes come to an understanding without words.

At that moment they opened the doors upstairs. I imagined a stream of wet people hurrying inside, to the cloakroom, and then down through the checkpoint at the top of the stairs. From the rumpus they were making up there it wasn't at all difficult to picture them.

"Frank," called Dicky to one of the apprentices, who was just scurrying past, "take the gentlemen's coats upstairs for them, would you?"

Frank checked his rush and came to a halt.

"Yes, Mr. Lentz." Politely he helped Emil out of his coat first, and with that one over his arm he waited while Bedřich and I stripped off ours, too.

"Do you know what a hard life a National Security guy like that has?" said Dicky, returning to his original subject. "Take that sergeant—he mistakes the Party secretary for a whore, and he's out of luck for life. . . . Boys, boys . . ." and he shook his head again, and was sad. "It isn't any gravy being an ordinary cop on the beat, especially now!" And he sighed anxiously, and shook his head until the jowls of old, withered skin under his chin quivered.

"Go on!" Emil waved a hand. "The best thing would be to trample the guts out of the lot of them." Emil liked to wave his hand over things. Only gradually did the sense of what Dicky had said strike him, and he demanded: "What do you mean— NOW?" Now could obviously just as well mean the last fifteen years as the last two hours. A relative impression, this NOW, at least in our part of Europe. And Dicky sometimes liked to be portentous, when it was a matter of the international situation, or cars, or the management of restaurants and dining rooms, among which the "Submarine" was listed.

"What do you mean—NOW?" repeated Emil. He had on a new checked jacket, and he pulled down the sleeves to his cuffs; they had been pulled up when he took off his overcoat.

Frank, buried under the mound of our coats, vanished up the stairs.

"Helena, I shall demand a seal of virginity—guaranteed . . ." Bedřich called to the waitress. I could feel that my hair was still damp and limp, and I hunted through my pockets for a comb.

"Well . . . what?" Dicky raised his head with an air of bewilderment. He buttoned the top button at his collar, and over his arm he carried a made-up bow tie on an elastic band.

I had no idea what. Certainly these was always SOMETHING, but Dicky now began to look so secretive that today's SOMETHING must be something extraspecial.

"You really don't know of ANYTHING?"

"What are we supposed to know?" asked Emil. "Have they dropped the price of vodka?"

"No, but HONESTLY, you DON'T KNOW?"

We shook our heads. Ever since morning we'd been on this moonlighting job, and then we'd come straight to Dicky's. Plenty of things could have happened in that time.

"Khrushchev's finished," said Dicky. "Lost his footing and came down with a crash. Janošík on peas, and this one on maize."

"You're raving!" Emil jutted his jaw at him, but then he regretted flying out like that, and added more placatingly: "I can't swallow that! Now, now, now, little Jew! It's the devil who maintains you here!"

"Nuts!" Dicky interrupted him briskly. "Don't shove your oar in when your elders are speaking, wise guy!"

"He's dead?"

"I said FINISHED, didn't I?" Dicky shook his head patiently. He fixed his bow tie, and turned the collar of his shirt down. "He's handed in his resignation!"

"RESIGNATION?"

"That's right." He passed a hand down over his vest, and triumphed over us in silence. "That's something, eh?" Slowly he looked us over one by one. "I must go and dress." And he took himself off by the passage alongside the bar counter, and went to put on his evening coat. The belt that was coming unstitched swung from the back of his vest, and down the stairs came the first couple of guests.

"Better go and sit at our table," said Emil, and I got up.

In an hour it was full. We were sitting in the first box on the right, beside the orchestra. We sat there regularly, when we stayed for a meal. The parquet was well trodden by dancing couples. Right in front of us revolved an unknown major in a well-worn tunic with sagging pockets, with a Cyrano nose in a pallid face. We had just finished the second bottle of sherry. It was good wine, genuine Spanish, but it was beginning to be clear to me that it wasn't the right liquor for all-night drinking. I knew that after sherry one usually has a headache in the morning; but right now I was beginning to be aware of a growing pressure in the nape of my neck, although for a long, long time yet it wouldn't be morning. Indeed it had better not be!

In the box next to ours sat a terribly ugly and badly painted tart with an undershot jaw, who was singing "La Paloma" into the ear of her companion, a man of whom nothing was visible except the hairy back of his neck and his sagging shoulders, since she had dragged him into the "Submarine" already in that advanced state of drunkenness that droops a fellow's head into his chest. It's true that the orchestra was playing "Tipiti Twist," but the tart didn't let that bother her much; she wouldn't be put off, but went on squeezing out "La Paloma." At the table across the dance floor sat a party of drunken idiots from the local National Committee, haggling about who was going to pay. They were washing down Khrushchev.

While there were people dancing we couldn't see much of them, but we could hear them all too well, clean through the twist. Above and behind them, standing by the wall, and naturally with her arms folded behind her again, stood Helena, smiling and rolling her eyes toward the singing tart. We nodded back at her and pointed delicately at the gorged bigwigs from the Committee. We knew them all, and they knew us. They belonged

to the group which allotted among themselves (like that children's game where on the word 'Go!' everybody has to change
places), the posts of cadre chiefs, political vice-chairmen, security
heads and specially accredited directors of everything whatsoever
in the entire district. Dr. Muňanský and Karpíšek, who originally
had sat on the social commission, and now ran the Labor office;
the partisan Douda—though as a matter of fact he started being a
partisan two days after the Germans had capitulated, but for all
that he got plenty of medals for it, and the partisan star, which he
wore even on his civilian jacket: he warmed the chair at the department for Internal Affairs. They didn't like us. They couldn't
help that, but neither did we like them. That roundup of hooligans, all the head shaving and street sweeping and all the other
similar stupidities, all stemmed from them, or from their cronies
in the appropriate offices. Their mouths were always full of things
of which we, again, were always fed up to the teeth. And they were
well aware that nobody liked them, that Helena regularly served
them slops and charged them top prices. This did give us mild
pleasure, that even if they'd been ten times as prosperous and
powerful, or the contrary, it wouldn't have made the slightest
difference to the fact that they were authentic, grade-A fools. The
teachers from the local school told incredible stories about their
stupidity. When some order was made about the qualifications
required of cadre leaders, all of them—with the exception of Muňanský, who because of his doctorate had ranked as an agrarian
father as early as the first republic—took their maturity examination extramurally; and obviously they all passed. Could such a
local teacher let his own boss get ploughed?

They'd decided that they'd have another bottle. They were
embracing one another, slapping one another on the shoulders
and bellowing: "Cheers!" and "Hurrah!" They always carried on
like that when they got a bit elevated. Now it was particularly
noticeable, because the orchestra had just finished a number, and
the dancers were slowly dispersing. You could hear that whore
singing "La Paloma" more plainly, too, but the girl at once lowered her voice as soon as she realized it. The trombonist tipped

spittle out of his instrument, and the bass player, the one who'd been with us at the railway wagons, stepped down from the dais with an empty pint tankard in his hand and went off to the bar.

Muňanský, who hadn't registered our presence until then, was looking at us. He jabbed his elbow into Douda, and Douda passed it on to Karpíšek. They spoke a few words together. I knew they were talking about us. For perhaps a minute we measured each other, and then Muňanský shouted: "Don't stare, clown!"

I turned the other way. I knew it would soon be high time to get out of there, and maybe I would have done it, for the thick feeling at the back of my skull was growing, it was quite positive now, and occasionally shot into my neck and temples. Sherry really is no liquor for all-night drinking.

Helena came back.

"Helena, love!" I said.

"Coming in a minute!"

She raised her eyebrows and smiled. In her hands she held a bottle with a napkin wound around its neck, and the corkscrew stuck out of the pocket of her apron as she walked. I watched her legs and her back as though I might discover there something I'd never yet known. Then I saw Muňanský and his party, who had all turned toward us, not even watching as Helena opened their wine on the table and poured it for them.

Bedřich, Emil and I had had trouble with them every so often; with the offices they represented, perhaps, rather than with them, but then again, the offices actually were the men themselves, that was the trouble. Especially Emil. He was well above six feet tall, and a boxer in the bargain. Once one of his opponents, in a clinch, jerked up a knee between Emil's legs, and this so incensed Emil that he threw him over the ropes and out of the ring by his hair. It was the biggest coup I know of, maybe the biggest in the world, but after that affair they never let him into the ring again. Nobody'd noticed that knee. But I knew that Emil would never have done that to an opponent without good reason. The jerks from the Committee knew all this, too; even sport they supervised from their office chairs. Especially football, they talked very wisely about football sometimes. When they were sober they managed to control themselves now and again, but as soon as they got tight they always began to waltz back into their revolutionary past. Douda even wrote an article once in a newspaper, about how the local partisan division captured a bridge from the German army. The trouble was, they'd only built that bridge there about three years after the war. They were crazy bastards altogether. And we were offensive to them because we despised them. We didn't have to tell them. They knew. Above all it offended them that they'd done us dirt a hundred times over, shoved us out of their way and had us carted off to some hard labor or other, and written all the sick malice they felt toward us into the cadre records they kept on us, and we still despised those records as heartily as we did them. We lived by working. And let them do their worst, still and always we were younger, and had younger and prettier girls than they had. So they took offense at everything, Emil's jacket, Bedřich's golden waistcoat, my red trousers. Everything outraged them. That Helena cheated them on the prices, and that they could never prove it. When there was nothing left to outrage them, they would have to find something. And today they had us.

The tart beside us bit her guest on the ear. Muňanský was hotly discussing something with his gang. The musicians, those who had stayed on their dais, and not walked off to the bar like the bass player, watched the group attentively from their vantage point. If they had judged that they were now ripe, one of them would have gone across to beg a bottle for the band. But maybe they weren't, yet, for none of the players went to try his luck.

"Comrade Chairman is as tight as a tick." Bedřich passed a hand over his mouth, and drank. Suddenly we realized that for rather a long time we had not spoken, but had simply been watching those on the other side, in a kind of mounting tension, as they watched us. Emil raised his glass.

"Forward to a further successful alcoholization of the people's administration!" Toasts were his speciality. He played it like Erich von Stroheim. "Cheers, gentlemen, cheers!"

"I, too, have studied, dear colleague!" Bedřich had studied medicine, until they threw him out as an insufficiently reliable political type.

At that moment Karpíšek threw his glass on the floor, and absolute silence fell, into which he babbled for a little while, until they seized him by the back of his jacket and shoved him back into his chair.

". . . I won't give up Nikita, I won't, you understand, comrade, I'm a man of action, mark that, I'll take a rifle . . . ta . . . ta . . . ta. . . ." When they jammed a glass into his hand—he was already sitting down then—and filled it, he jerked out once more: ". . . I won't give him up!" and drank. By the speeches they made in bars, those warlike activities of theirs had been worth at least thirty divisions and three ballistic missiles. When they were back in the past, it emerged again quite clearly that it was actually they who had conquered the Germans, and it was only by some carelessness that they left the taking of Berlin to the Russians.

Muňanský saw us laughing, and came staggering across the dance floor toward us. We leaned our elbows on the table and waited. For perhaps a minute he did nothing but stand over us. Then he wagged his head: "So you're drinking, eh?"

We raised our eyes to him.

"We're drinking at our own expense, and putting it in our own stomachs," said Emil. He looked at the table as he said it, and sipped a little sherry. He didn't say it to Muňanský. He merely said it.

Across the empty parquet we could be seen by everyone in the hall, and we felt that the whole hall was looking at us. It was not pleasant.

"Is that so!" said Muňanský with a short bark of laughter. Then he turned and shouted: "Waiter!"

Helena, who was standing by the door (with her arms folded behind her, of course), took two paces toward us, then turned back again and vanished in search of Dicky.

Muňanský took the bottle on our table by the neck and turned the label toward him. I took it from his hand and replaced it in the middle of the table.

Dicky surged into the doorway, calling out even at a distance: "Gentlemen, gentlemen, please!"

"The gentlemen will pay and leave!" Muňanský described a circle over our heads. "They've had enough."

Douda and Karpíšek had shoved back their chairs and were wavering over toward us. Now all the faces in the room were definitely turned toward us. The bass player, who had come back in the meantime, stood with a full pint of beer on the edge of the dais, and tugged the corners of his mouth down in a grimace which I understood.

"But these are good boys," Dicky said soothingly.

"They're drunk," said Muňanský.

"Well, if they were, they're old enough for it, Doctor . . . here everybody drinks well, he wouldn't be any guest for us if he didn't."

"Do you know who I am?" swelled Muňanský.

"A lush and a swine," said Bedřich.

"Now, boys, boys!" Dicky put on his reproving face. "The doctor means well."

By this time Douda had arrived, at an unsteady reel.

"You'll stop serving these men, you understand!" he said. "They've got the devil in them already."

You know the formula: OUR MANNER OF ADDRESS: COMRADE! OUR GREETING: HONOR TO WORK! The question was, whose was this Party in which all were comrades? Certainly not ours, and not for the majority of the people in the town, either. As for work, who had last seen them soil their hands with it?

Dicky flapped his napkin and winked at us: "Comrade Chairman, I'm responsible for running this enterprise."

"That's just the point!" Douda interrupted him. "Just the point! It's prohibited to serve drink to people who're drunk already, you can be fined for it, do you know that?" Then he turned directly to us: "You've had enough, boys. Haven't you? Well, what do you say?"

We said nothing. Muňanský and Karpíšek still had something to say, but we weren't taking any notice of them. All we heard was Dicky blurting: "The guests would like to dance, gentlemen, the guests want to go on dancing!" But we were better entertainment than any dancing. All around us there were crowds of people who had not the least desire to dance.

Douda shook his head over us. He even made as if to lay his hand on my shoulder, but at the last moment he thought better of it.

"I see you'll have to go along to the police station, eh, boys? You've already gotten used to the drink, eh?" The mechanism of summary arrest belonged under Douda.

The tired, pale major jutted, nose and all, half a head above all the others at the edge of the crowd: "Let these boys alone and go to the devil!" he cried. A few people growled agreement. The major could afford to roar at Douda. He was a major and he was a stranger. He didn't come from our town. Douda didn't know him, or any of his family. He didn't have him in his register.

But at least the shout confused him. He turned to face the crowd, Karpíšek revolving with him. At that moment two heads appeared in the doorway, Zajíc and the permanent sergeant. Douda caught sight of them.

"Comrades!"

It shook them; they drew back quickly, but then they realized WHO it was calling them, and that they couldn't simply make themselves scarce and pretend they hadn't heard anything.

It was clear to me that we'd had it. In the end we always have had it. The fact that only a few hours ago Zajíc had swigged down a cadged drink with us and in front of us couldn't change anything. To be run in and charged would cost us a few hundred bucks, once they got us there. If you've got the money, it might be worth it for every such mishap, but to let them charge you a fine which you've first got to earn somehow, that's far worse. It wasn't just; all right, of course it wasn't. But there was nothing to be done about it.

"Good evening," said Zajíc, saluting at our table. "Honor!"

"Honor!" they responded in chorus.

"What's going on?" He smiled at everybody, including us. "What is it? It's raining outside. . . ."

The tired major thrust his way forward. Now he was standing behind Zajíc, smoking. More and more people kept crowding in toward us, and the sergeant turned to them.

"Go and sit down, folks." I think it was the only complete sentence I'd ever heard from him, apart from a simple greeting. "Sit down!"

"A disturbance," said Douda.

"A disturbance?" echoed Zajíc.

"These boys need to be escorted to the station," and Muňanský pointed at us.

"At least I might as well knock this guy's teeth out before we go, shall I?" suggested Emil philosophically. "If anybody here needs running in for a drunk, then it's you. Get that!" And we waited to see if he would add some term of abuse—ox, bastard, swine. . . . They would have fitted, all right. But he didn't say any of them.

"Don't argue, where's the sense!" Bedřich stubbed out his cigarette in the ashtray and got up. "All right, we're going. Come on, boys." He smiled at the major, and even at Zajíc. "That's the best thing, isn't it? We won't disturb you any longer."

Dicky stood in the background, pointing with a thumb and rolling his eyes over his shoulder at the door. Next door there was a smaller private room for weddings. There we could drink in peace; and in the end it's better not to let oneself be put out by fools. One isn't always in the right humor for it.

The major was ashamed. Maybe even Zajíc was ashamed. But he was STUCK WITH IT, just as we were STUCK WITH IT. Bedřich picked up our things from the table. Cigarettes, lighter, some photographs of an actress that we'd been looking at. I was a little bit sorry for the major. He didn't know his way around here, and he'd meant well, poor guy.

"First, you'll pay!" barked Douda. He had a boy in the reception school where they try to decide whether the backward kids are educable at all. He had to take it out on somebody. He watched with dismay as we got up. I was tempted to coo at him something like: MAMA LOVES BABA, or THE CAT SAT ON THE MAT, but it would have been pointless malice.

"I'll take care of that," said Dicky, waving his hands good-naturedly, and led us out. "You did well, boys," he said, as soon as we were a few steps out of earshot. "Come on!"

The apprentice Frank spread a cloth over the bare table. Dicky put out the main light, and left on only the imitation candles on the wall above us.

"All right, eh, boys?"

We didn't say anything. It wasn't a moment when there seems much to say.

"Another bottle?"

"Yes," I said, "vodka."

Dicky went away, and we sat down. Now all that was wanting was a woman, and then home to bed, but our only chance was Helena. In the entire nightspot called the "Submarine" there wasn't a single available lay that day, not even a little one. Nothing.

"All washed up, what do you say?" Bedřich spoke up. "Absolutely washed up and gone off the rails." He rattled emptily in his pockets. "In any case we haven't got any money. We owe Dicky something from last time, don't we?"

"About fifteen crowns," I answered.

Emil hunted a bill out from his jacket, certainly the only one there, and his last; but this was not the moment to be pondering whether the money we had was our last or not, or whether we actually needed it more urgently for something else. He calculated silently.

"How much do you reckon we've made today?"

Now Bedřich was also inwardly calculating, and helping himself with his fingers: "About 200 crowns."

Emil turned his free bill between his fingers: "No good for Helena." The corners of his mouth turned down. "We'll haul down the flag, guards!"

We were like white mice at the wall of an acquarium. Money was the wall; but it could be used to push the affair with Douda a little way behind us.

Dicky trotted in with a waiter's forward-leaning gait, and ro-
tated the bottle in front of us: "Don't give a thought to this,
boys!" He sighed and flapped his hands as if he wanted to tell us
some extremely important thing. "You did the right thing, believe me. . . ." But at that moment there echoed from the hall,
divided from us only by glazed folding doors and a curtain, the
sound of shivering glass, and a crash that drowned out the band
and the rustle of the dancing. It sounded as though a table had
gone over.

A second later Helena flew into the room: "Mr. Lentz! Muňanský's tipped the table over in there!"

Dicky didn't fly into a rage, he only shoved the napkin deeper
into his pocket and said to nobody in particular: "My God, and
this stock return on top of everything, it's a joy to have such
guests!" Once again he flapped his hands, and rolled out of the
room.

In the meantime we had all pulled out what bills we had, and
stuck them in the middle of the table, under an ashtray.

"Helena!" called Bedřich. She stopped and turned. She saw the
money on our table, smiled and shook her head: "Not a chance!"

"You don't know yet what I want," cried Bedřich, pretending
annoyance.

"Oh, yes, I do know." She smiled again, and again said: "But
no!" Then she added more kindly: "Not today."

"We just wanted to drink with you."

For a moment she was embarrassed. She didn't know whether
this was the truth, or some kind of trap for her; but even though
she was quite certainly avidly interested in everything that was
going on at this moment in the next room, she came back to our
table. I took my glass of sherry, emptied it into a flowerpot in the
corner—they were paper flowers, anyway!—and poured her a
glass of vodka.

"Cheers, love!"

"And the same to you," I said, and we all drank.

"I have to go now." Helena set the glass back on the table. "I'll
come back, shall I?"

That was our life. Neither existing nor being free of existence. Vegetating in the "Submarine" with Helena. Neither love nor pure business, neither a proper debauch nor its opposite. (I don't know what the opposite of a proper debauch can be, perhaps simply work that gives a man pleasure of itself alone, but that was something we'd never experienced.) We could have been everything, if . . . only the IF hung upon the fact that there existed always some sort of hindrance OUTSIDE US, with which we could not come to terms, which could not come to terms with us. And thus we never had been and never could be more than whatever we were able to be at any given moment. And we had learned not to believe in any change, in any other possibility. Somehow we managed to make a living, and not to let anyone get the better of us, so far as that was possible. The majority of people were not so clever.

Emil had had a love, and a life's misfortune; a cage that collapsed. And Bedřich, and I, too. We sat drinking vodka, and we had these things behind us and within us. They held us by the guts. Karpíšek, who during the war had cut our hair, and then had grown from a barber into the district cadre officer. . . .

As Helena came back for the second time, suddenly Dicky came rushing in. First he shouted at her rather crossly that there was plenty of work waiting for her next door, and took his stand with his back to us until she had gone away. Then he leaned down in a conspiratorial manner, as though we were not alone in the small salon.

"Come and see how the Czech man in the street always comes into his own in the end!" He beckoned with a crooked forefinger. "Just come and have a look!"

We left the table, the vodka, the money, and the remains of the sherry, and followed him. When Dicky invited us somewhere in that tone, it was usually worth taking notice.

We passed through the main hall and the bar. Past the kitchen. Dicky vanished under the stairs, through a door marked with the silhouette of a man.

Beyond the tiled anteroom with the two wash basins and the

out-of-order electric hand dryer we came to the inner sanctum. With his head and body in the ceramic gutter, all wet and stinking of urine, Douda lay in his own vomit, and slept the impervious sleep of the dead drunk. Pretty plainly a considerable number of gentlemen had already taken turns over him.

I observed that Emil was slowly and thoughtfully unbuttoning his trousers, and Bedřich was slowly and thoughtfully unbuttoning his . . . and slowly and thoughtfully I followed their example.

When we went back, Dicky was again in his place for the day, behind the bar, just placing some glasses of soda water and cognac on Helena's tray. Emil and Bedřich went on past him into the small salon. Several exhilarated gentlemen were hurrying from the big hall toward the lavatory.

I halted with a hand on the bar counter.

"Can I wait?"

Helena looked at me searchingly, and put out the tip of her tongue between her lips: "All right!" she said.

She smiled, and Dicky smiled, too, although he was really completely occupied with his brandies and sodas; and Emil and Bedřich would certainly have smiled, too, if they could have been present, but if they'd been present Helena would not have said all right!

The world seemed good; everything could be tossed out of my head. I preened myself that Helena must like me best of our party, and I gazed after her as she swept like a ballerina into the hall, the tray balanced on one hand.

"A good joke, eh?" laughed Dicky, jerking his chin toward the lavatory; and he wiped the bar down with a cloth.

"Yes, good," I said. "Quite good. God send us a hundred more of them!"

The Generation of Leaves
A Concluding Note

. . . for everything passes, the trees grow green and put forth
leaves, the leaves turn yellow and fall, one thing leads to another,
yet nothing happens, we are hurrying toward the society of the
future, which will be Communism, a pittance of grain and a few
rags, so that a man has to go with his buttocks bare, and one
thing leads to another, somewhere there's a horizon, and somewhere God alone knows what, and somewhere again something
utterly different, but we, we are here, calming our nerves, or
something, clipping our wings, or something, anything you
please. . . . Nine months after loving a child is born, a little
miracle, an endless age, nine months, that's nothing, nine
months, that's 270 days, do you know how a convict feels who has
270 days still to serve . . . ? You know nothing, he's waiting to be
born, 270 days needed for the bearing of a child, my God, that's a
secret, a biological secret the technical parameters of which are
known to us, but can anyone explain to us the technical parameters of those nine months of nerve-calming routine, that's what I
should like to know, that's what I should like to know, such a
joke, 270 days, what's that to fine fellows like us, imagine 2,700
days and then what about 3,650 days, or 7,305 days, imagine how
many people will have been born in the meantime, and learned

to walk and live and talk, and also to steal and all the rest of it, and everything that will have happened, for everything passes, the trees grow green, if we're lucky we can even watch them, the trees put forth leaves, and the leaves turn yellow and fall, while we cultivate bronchitis, our chief concern that there shall be something to smoke, something to acquire that's more or less forbidden, that we won't have to slave too hard, that they won't find anything for which they can punish us, for everything passes, only time once halted does not pass, only the bronchitis gets worse, and nothing has any lasting direction, everything shifts, movement, movement, movement without any aim, movement for its own sake, movement enclosed in a narrow space under lock and key, while the trees grow green, and the rats scuttle out of the latrines, and we kill them, and the rats kill one another, rats are like people, rats are omnipresent, and the trees still grow green, once, twice, ten times over, the trees never fail to grow green again, and we shall see them, when the time comes, if we're lucky, once, twice. . . .

This book has been set on the linotype in Baskerville.
The display type is Torino.
The composition, printing, and binding is by
H. Wolff Book Manufacturing Co., New York.
The design is by Jacqueline Schuman.